# FLURY

## JOURNEY OF A SNOWMAN

## TONY BERTAUSKI

# THE ARCTIC

Malcolm Toye fell.

He had seen nothing but ice for days, wandering the Arctic in search of the men that brought him this far north. Their ship crushed by the ice, they had struck out on foot, dragging boats over frozen snow and through open leads of water until landing upon Bennett Island. Ravaged by frostbite and scurvy, no one should've lived. But they continued south, and that's when Malcolm had become separated.

With rifle in hand, he had given chase to what he thought was a wounded seal, but had slipped into the icy water. Soaked and numb, he returned to camp to find that the men had already moved on. Shortly after, snow began to fall, and he was eternally alone.

And now he had fallen for the last time.

He couldn't feel his legs. He was certain that if a miracle occurred and the men found him, he would lose his feet to frostbite. At the very least, his toes.

It was a foolish journey, but men like Malcom Toye had always pursued such folly. The North Pole called to him, dared him to conquer it. He was eager to join the expedition, see parts of the world very few had witnessed with their own eyes. Only the dubious tales of explorers existed about the endless sheet of ice that topped the world. He wanted to be one of the first men to ever see it.

He had come close.

When he fell backwards, landing in the soft embrace of fresh snow, he didn't feel the impact. He was certain, as he gazed into the sky where, somewhere past his feet, the sun was just below the horizon, that he would not only lose his feet to frostbite, but his nose as well. That didn't bother him.

*I will die alone.*

He labored to breathe as he tore at the buttons of his U.S. Navy-issued coat, his fingers plastic things that refused to bend or grasp. Violent shivers made it difficult, but he managed to slip his hand inside his coat to find an inner pocket. Despite the numbness, he felt the cold metal fall into his palm.

A gold locket.

The latch was too tight for his stiff and senseless fingers. Instead, he clutched it tightly before the shivers tossed it from his hand. The attached chain pooled on the fabric of his frozen coat. He yearned to see, one last time, the photo of his bride, hope that she would be the last image he took with him in this unforgiving wasteland of ice. He imagined her green eyes and brown hair falling over her shoulders, the way she smiled when she woke.

As his breaths grew shallow, he let go of the pain squeezing his chest and melted into the snowy embrace. A warm sensation filled him. He drifted into sleep, where a sweet dream was promised and, perhaps, his wife would be waiting.

It was in these last moments that the wind began to swirl.

Malcolm didn't notice the ice shudder or the shadow pass over him. He had given himself to leaving the world. He opened his eyes one last time to look at the dark sky. Instead, he saw two massive legs straddling him.

A giant blotted out the stars.

# GRANDMOTHER

*Every once in a while, Santa skips a house.*

# 1

O liver feels weird.

He drops his iPad. He'd been reading a zombie apocalypse where the guy lets his infected wife bite him so she's not alone. He got to the part where someone sees two zombies holding hands when his blood sugar crashed. He should test his blood. Instead, he sucks on a glucose tablet while leaning his forehead on the passenger window.

The curvy roads aren't helping. The hills and trees, endless.

Mom is strangling the steering wheel while grinding her teeth. A partially plowed road would turn most drivers' knuckles white, but that's not it. When they left Austin, it was sunny and warm, but that wasn't it, either.

Colorado is home.

*Home doesn't welcome everyone.*

She puts on the right-turn blinker and begins to slow.

The snow has been cleared from a nondescript opening in the trees. Mom pulls beneath the weeping branches. The wrought-iron gate is already open. She stops the car, lips silently moving, a private pep talk.

The black road beyond is plowed better than the main road, with swirling sweeper patterns on the asphalt. Mom eases down the private drive, the sunlight blotted out by overgrown trees. Oliver looks over the luggage in the backseat to watch the gates close behind them. The last time he was here he was five years old.

That was ten years ago.

His blood sugar is coming up, but the weird feeling remains as Mom steers down the curving road, her lips still moving. Her knuckles still white. The three-story house appears around the last turn. Several trees reach out like Nature is coming for the house.

*Like zombies.*

Mom stops in the patch of sunlight just short of the circle drive-way. The steering wheel squeaks in her sweaty palms. She adjusts the wide headband that holds her thick hair off her face and takes in the three-story monstrosity. A round window looks down from the attic, snow frosting the lower half.

No sign of Christmas anywhere.

"This is just temporary," Mom says. "Okay?"

Oliver nods, but the last time she said that, the cable never came back on. Maybe this time she was telling herself this was temporary.

He takes her hands off the steering wheel before she tears it out of the dashboard. Her slender fingers squeeze his hand like a bear trap. She nods, compulsively, before letting her foot off the brake. The house's shadow falls over them. Mom adjusts the wide, paisley head-band again and rubs her face before opening the door.

Oliver rubs his bristly short crop of brown hair. He can feel the heat leaking from his scalp. Snow-capped mountains rise above the trees. If they're going to live here, he'll have to grow some hair.

*Even if it's temporary.*

The weird thing about *the property*, as Mom calls it, isn't the gut-punching cold—it's the silence. Colorado is a mountain man's paradise, a place to hike and fish and sleep under the stars—commune with nature, that sort of thing. Not here.

Here, it's dead silent.

The attic window watches them approach. The entry walk has been brushed with a coarse broom. Mom stops on the top step, playing with one of the many hoop earrings piercing her cartilage. A small sign is embedded just above the doorbell.

*Toye Residence.*

She pushes the button.

A faint melody of bells echoes inside the house. Oliver can see distorted patterns of light and dark through a panel of ornamental glass set alongside the door. Long after the bells have gone quiet, a dark figure moves.

"Take off your shoes," Mom whispers.

She already has her shoes in one hand.

Oliver slides his shoes off. His toes are as stiff as the wooden porch. He's imagining the hot sands of South Padre Island when an eye—green with blue around the perimeter of the iris—appears in a diamond-cut section of the window.

The doorknob begins to turn.

The seal around the doorway breaks open to reveal an old woman plucked straight from the crypt of an ancient library. Her kinky gray hair is pulled back in a tight bun. Her posture, perfect. Vertical grooves dig around her joyless mouth.

"Debra," she says.

"Mother."

Oliver's mom steps over the threshold and hugs his grand-mother. The old woman pats her on the shoulder and lets Debra hug her.

"Quickly now." Grandmother waves Oliver inside.

The foyer is expansive.

Sounds echo off the high ceiling. An immense stairwell is to the left of a dark hallway that leads deeper into the house. Photos of stodgy old men are hung in ornate frames. It doesn't feel cold inside —he can't see his breath, after all—but somehow it's no warmer. No sign of a Christmas tree, stocking or greeting card.

It's as if Christmas died at the wrought-iron gate.

"Oliver." Only she says *Olivah*.

"Grandmother."

He takes half a step toward her when she sticks out her hand. The knuckles are knobby, and the fingers slightly curled. He shakes it, careful not to crush it. It feels like paper, smells like medicine.

"You have grown."

She doesn't let go while looking him over: his hair, the stray whiskers on his chin, the insufficient winter clothing. She stares at the floor. His socks are loose at the ends of his frozen toes, specks of snow clinging to the fabric. Small puddles begin to bead on the polished floor.

"And how old are you?"

"Fifteen."

She purses her lips like he just lied. "And your health?"

"Good." That time he did. His blood sugar still isn't right. "I'll get the luggage."

"Nonsense. It's not going anywhere. You will come in and eat. Diabetics need a balanced meal."

If his memory is correct, she's called him "diabetic" more than she's called him "grandson."

She holds her hand out. Mom offers her elbow, and Grandmother takes it. They walk down the dim hallway. She's wearing big, puffy boots but doesn't slide them over the floor. Instead, her steps are carefully measured and silent. Dead silent.

*Like outside.*

Oliver quickly knocks the snow crystals off his feet and mops the water with his socks before following. The dim hallway feels like the house is swallowing him. Just past the stairway on the left is a doorway leading to the family room. A large picture window offers a panoramic view of the property. On the right side of the hallway, there's a long table with three table settings, including a teapot.

Grandmother opens a drawer in a small table against the wall and takes out a towel. "You may join us once your mess is cleaned up, Olivah."

His mom makes a silent apology as she guides Grandmother toward the dining table. He takes the towel to the front door and wipes up the little streaks of water. A gust of wind pushes against the door. A draft sneaks through the bottom. Oliver looks through the decorative pane of glass and sees the last wisps of snow swirling on the sidewalk.

A mess of twigs are scattered over the pavement.

He opens the door. The trees are still, and the silence is perfect. Not even the icicles hanging from the gutters are dripping.

"Close the door, Olivah. Come along."

With damp towel in hand, he returns to the dining room for bitter tea and dry muffins in the place he'll call home.

*Temporary home.*

## 2

Oliver hauls the last bit of luggage up the stairs.

The worn steps are slick beneath his socks. They're shallow for easy climbing. He holds the railing to keep from tumbling down three stories' worth.

The photos watch him trudge up the flights. Not photos, paintings—the kind you'd find in the back of a resale shop. It's mostly grizzled old men with sharp eyes and mirthless mouths. There are a few women in the mix, just as joyless. The last painting, just before the third floor, is of a ship. A small crowd of people are gathered at a ramp. With its bare rigging and leaning bow, it's as haunted as the old men.

All the doors are closed on the third floor, except the one to the far left. The floor creaks along the way. His breath puffs out in thin clouds, quickly dissipating. His room is in the front-left section of the house with windows looking east and south. There's a dresser and a nightstand with a lamp, along with a waist-high bed covered with a thick, white comforter.

Everything is dusted and wrinkle-free.

He drops the luggage and finds his kit. Rubbing his fingers together, he does a quick blood test to measure his blood sugar. It's too high. He should've done the test before tea. He quickly measures a dose of insulin and, pinching a fold of skin over his stomach, injects himself.

He checks his phone. No bars, no wifi.

All of his books are in cloud storage. It's doubtful Grandmother has Internet. Doubtful she's ever seen a computer.

Oliver drops his bag below the frosted window offering the same view as the picture window in the family room. There's a break in the forest and a view of the mountains. The sun has fallen behind the peaks, and the waning daylight casts a long shadow from a rustic windmill. The blades turn even though it seems calm. When a gust of wind hits it, the windwheel turns faster.

Lets loose an earsplitting squeal.

Something has crossed the clearing. The tracks are too far away to distinguish what kind of footsteps. He looks for binoculars—his dad used to sit around with binoculars when he lived on the beach—but the dresser drawers are empty and clean. But there's something in the bottom drawer of the nightstand.

*A journal.*

The cover is hardback, faded and worn at the corners. The yellowish pages, however, are blank. The binding cracks as he turns the stiff pages, finding not a spot of ink. He runs his fingers over the smooth cover, imagining a quill and a pot of ink that might've been used to record thoughts in something this old.

"Hey, kiddo."

"Ho!" The journal flips out of his grip, smacks the wall, and bounces on the floor.

Oliver's heart hammers his chest.

His mom is in the doorway with a black hoodie pulled over her head. She apologizes for scaring him.

"What'd you got there?" she asks.

Oliver retrieves the journal and assesses the damage to the corner, hoping Grandmother doesn't see it. He might have to hide it. His mom flips through the pages, but her mind is somewhere else.

"Sorry about freezing up on you when we got here," she says, twisting one of her earrings. "I thought I was ready for this. I didn't expect to...change."

She hasn't said much since they arrived. They ate a bland lunch mostly in silence. Grandmother cut her tuna salad sandwich with a knife and ate it with a fork.

"I felt like a kid when I walked through the doorway. I could feel my insides, like, churning and morphing back into a little girl...I'm sorry, you don't need to hear this."

"It's all right, I get it. You can't go home, right?"

He read that somewhere.

You can't go home because expectations get in the way. But his mom was sent to boarding school when she was ten. Strange she feels like this is home. Oliver would never have that problem. He's lived too many places. There'll never come a time he steps over a threshold and breathes the familiar essence of childhood.

"You test your sugar?"

He nods. She knows when he's being a bad diabetic.

"You get all your stuff?"

"Yeah." He kicks the duffel bag.

"You've got the third floor all to yourself. It's an old house your great-grandfather built. It's going to sound a little haunted. I'll be in the room below you, so if you need anything, you know where to find me. We'll make the best of it."

She pulls her headband around her neck and scratches her scalp. She notices him watching her.

"What's wrong?" she asks.

"I don't like seeing you this way."

"Change is hard." She sits on the bed and puts her hand on his. "We just need to be thankful we have a place to stay." She looks around the sterile room, then whispers, "Even if this is where Christmas came to die."

They lean into each other and laugh. His mom wipes tears from her eyes.

"I don't think Santa can find this place," he says.

"Trust me, he'll find it."

She scrubs his bristly hair, then pulls a stocking cap from the pouch on her hoodie. It's a North Face cap. She pulls it over his head and kisses his forehead.

"An early present," she says. Even her lips are cold.

He thanks her. "You think tomorrow we could go somewhere with service?" He holds up his phone. "I need to download books."

"There's a library in town. Maybe we can pick up a few Christmas ornaments and smuggle them into the house. I still have a few presents to get."

"Look, Mom, you don't need to buy me anything. I mean, this is plenty."

"Let me worry about that."

She kisses his forehead again and leaves. Her footsteps slide over the creaking floor like a kid with footy pajamas. The stairs groan with each descending thump.

Oliver plugs his ears with headphones and unpacks. He thumbs through the journal again. When he looks out the window, a full moon casts a glow over the property. Oliver cups his hands on the window and holds his breath to keep from fogging it.

There are more tracks.

# 3

"Good morning, Olivah," Grandmother announces.

Oliver is startled.

He knew someone was awake, he could smell coffee, but didn't expect his grandmother to be standing in the kitchen waiting for him.

The floors broadcast every movement through the house—except for his stealthy grandmother with the padded Ugg boots. Her hair is tightly pulled back, as if attempting to stretch the wrinkles from her cheeks. Mom sits at the breakfast table, hovering over a steaming mug.

"You will find breakfast on the stove," Grandmother says. "Help yourself."

His hunger drags him around the island bar beneath a dangling rack of pots. A wisp of steam escapes a white teapot on the back burner. On the front, a cast-iron pan still sizzles with eggs and bacon. He can feel his grandmother's blue-green eyes on him like department store security as he fills a plate with bacon, eggs and a warm slice of toast.

When he turns around, she's gone.

He sits down to check his blood sugar. The plastic snap of the needle draws a tiny bead from his pinky. His mom watches him eat while sipping her coffee and smiling. A brown headband holds her hair back this morning. She doesn't look so frail. Maybe she just needed a good night's sleep. It had been months since she had one.

Oliver mentally calculates the carbs sitting on his plate and injects a dosage of insulin, this time in his leg. He thumbs through his phone while eating. The battery is almost drained.

"Did you hear the rumbling last night?"

Mom shakes her head. "I told you the house makes noise."

"This was out in the woods." He woke up to use the bathroom. It sounded like trees were falling in the distance, but when he looked out, nothing had fallen. The tracks were gone, even though it hadn't snowed.

"You slept well?" Grandmother asks.

The half-eaten toast leaves Oliver's hand and hits the floor. She looks down. Oliver finds a paper towel to wipe up the mess.

Grandmother doesn't move.

"I'm sorry." He looks for the trash.

"Pantry," Mom says.

He finds the pantry door opposite the oven. The trash can is beneath a shelf of canned goods. A small chalkboard is attached to the inside of the door, the green surface clean. The vertical wrinkles deepen around Grandmother's mouth. Oliver sits back down, and his mom winks, patting his hand, whispering, "It's all right."

"So, I trust you slept well?" Grandmother fills a teacup from the kettle.

"Yes."

"And you found the breakfast suitable?"

"Yes."

She brings her tea and saucer to the table and places a napkin next to Oliver's plate. Methodically, she spreads another napkin across her own lap and pauses. When he does the same, she resumes. Her posture is rigid as she stirs cream into the tea, as if she hasn't slouched since the day she was born. ,

Oliver takes small bites, but mostly pushes his food around.

"We're going into town, Mother. I was thinking of bringing back a Christmas tree."

"Absolutely not."

"Come now. This house could use some spirit."

"First thing's first."

She reaches into the sleeve of her white sweater and retrieves a crisply folded sheet of paper. Smoothing it open on the table, she slides it toward Oliver. The script is delicately handwritten.

"There are a few rules," Grandmother begins. "While at my house, you will tidy up after yourself. Whenever you leave a room, you will leave no trace that you were ever there."

He left clothes strewn on the bedroom floor and the bed unmade.

"Do you agree?" she asks. "Good. Next, a list will be posted inside the pantry door each morning. You are expected to complete your chores at the start of the day. When school begins, you will need to complete them before leaving in the morning. These chores will include repairs, cleaning, kitchen duty, etc."

"Mother, we'll be homeschooling while we're here. It's just easier. And Oliver is already a good student."

Grandmother's lips pinch together. Mom sips her coffee, waiting for the storm brewing on Grandmother's tongue.

Grandmother clears her throat, instead.

"Do you agree? Good. Given your condition, you will also be required to exercise outside for two hours every day."

*"Your condition" must be diabetes.*

"Dress appropriately, of course. When your chores consist of chopping wood or other such duties that will count toward your exercise quota. Otherwise, you are expected to be active on your own. You may explore the property as you wish, but you will be expected to be inside before the sun falls behind the mountains. Do you agree?"

"Why?"

"Do you agree, Olivah?"

"Yes. I'm just wondering...why can't I stay out later?"

Grandmother lets a few moments of silence be his answer. "We will eat our meals together. You are expected to have proper manners. Also, there will be no electronic devices in the house."

"At all?"

"Correct. I expect you to honor that rule while you are outside."

"Mother, he reads books with his iPad. They're called ebooks."

"There is a library in town. I believe they have books you can borrow. Do you agree to this, Olivah?"

He desperately wanted to say no. More than that, he wanted her to stop saying his name like it was something fancy to eat. Instead, he nodded. Anything else would make it harder on his mom. If he needed to work as an indentured servant to make this work, then he'd wax the car and paint the fence.

"You will also start referring to your mom as 'mother'."

"Now, wait a second, Mother."

"I see nothing wrong with cultivating manners into this impressionable young man."

"I've always called you 'mother', but to Oliver, I'm 'mom'. Don't interfere with our relationship."

"Your relationship is living under my roof. What you do outside this house is your business."

Mom pushes away from the table and stands, replacing the chair beneath the table before rinsing her cup in the sink. This is the person Oliver knows, the one that showed up at his school to argue, or refused to leave dealerships when they wouldn't agree to her offer. Not the one that drove up to the front door.

She offers a smile but doesn't agree.

"You may go wherever you wish," Grandmother continues. "However, if you find a door is locked, it is locked for a purpose."

Grandmother goes to the sink to rinse her cup, wipes the counter, and carefully folds the dishtowel. She stops at the doorway and says, before exiting, "Lunch will be served at noon. Have a pleasant morning."

Oliver pushes his plate away. His appetite has been murdered. He holds the list in both hands, the paper quivering. It has nothing to do with blood sugar.

His mom rubs his shoulders. "Let your *mother* take you shopping."

Despite covering their mouths, their laughter echoes down the hall. They clean the kitchen. When they leave, it satisfies rule number five. The wording, like the others, is odd. As if it's saying more than the obvious.

*Rule #5: Leave rooms as if no human had ever passed through it.*

# 4

Two nights later, it snows.

Six inches of fluff covers the land, including the sidewalk and driveway. Oliver clears it with a brand-new shovel.

They still hadn't made it to the library. Mom told him to sneak his phone into the bathroom or read the iPad beneath the covers. He just couldn't do it. It felt like Grandmother could read the guilt on his face.

They ate at the absurdly long table. At lunch, Grandmother instructed him on proper tea etiquette. It didn't help that the tea tasted like boiled cabbage water.

At dinner, they lit the massive candelabra and ate in silence while shadows danced on the walls. His mom made small talk, but Grandmother refused to open her mouth except for small, appropriately gauged spoonfuls of food. She chewed her food twenty times before swallowing, staring ahead as if she was counting.

His back aches from shoveling.

This will count for exercise. He's halfway around the circle drive in forty-five minutes when his mom calls from the front porch.

"Watch your sugar!"

Oliver waves. She's wearing an apron. He'd rather shovel out to the main road than help in the kitchen. A strand of white lights twinkles above the doorway, Mom's attempt to summon the Christmas spirit. When Grandmother saw them flashing, she set her jaw and narrowed her eyes like a bear had dropped a load on the porch. But she said nothing.

*Christmas still has a pulse.*

It takes almost an hour and a half to finish shoveling. He's sweating beneath new winter clothes. He could go inside and warm up, but that would require ten minutes of knocking snow off his pants, and then he'd just have to turn around for the remaining half hour of outside exercise.

*Rule #22: Fulfill your duty to the second.* He adds a thought. *Fulfill your duty before you take a doody.*

He chuckles, but then stops. Having those thoughts is dangerous. If she turns those blue-green x-ray eyes on him, she's sure to know what he's thinking.

He can warm up when he takes his mandatory five-minute tepid shower that fulfills the rule on personal hygiene.

He walks through the virgin snow to the decrepit windmill. The windwheel turns at a slow mechanic pace even though there's no wind. The artifact is as old as the house and just as solid, but something has to be done about the squeal. He can hear it in his sleep. He'd already gotten used to the thundering ruckus in the far-off trees. There must be construction somewhere, but at night?

He doesn't want to overanalyze.

The windmill, though—something has to be done. Maybe if he had some oil, he could lubricate the bearings. The struts are close enough to climb. And even if he falls, the snow will soften his landing. It may knock him out. Given the state of things, that doesn't sound so bad.

He grabs one of the four legs, thinking maybe he can gauge the sturdiness with a swift shake, when the world turns into a photo negative—black turns white, white turns black.

He lets go.

A strange tingle lingers in his arm, and his teeth feel numb. Suddenly, he feels weird. But his sugar isn't low.

*The thing is wired.*

Cattle ranches are hot-wired, he knows. He had gone to a friend's ranch and was told to watch out for the bare wire running along the top rail, but he got confused at the gate and grabbed the wrong one. The world turned inside-out.

So climbing the windmill is out.

Maybe Grandmother should know that it's electrified, but then he'd have to explain what he was doing touching it, and then she'd turn her x-ray eyes on him.

*Rule #441: Don't climb rusty windmills full of electricity, dummy.*

Oliver walks around the trees where the clearing opens up. The land slopes down. On the far side, the forest is dense. That's where the rumbling happens. The tracks he'd seen the last couple of nights have vanished. He looks back at the house and identifies his bedroom window on the third floor. Even with the fresh snow, it seems like there should be slight depressions.

But there are none.

He starts for the house and notices the orange snow shovel by the driveway. He's not sure where it goes, but it's definitely not the front yard. A detached garage is tucked into the trees. Oliver retrieves the shovel and takes it around the back.

The large garage door is locked. He finds a door on the back, out of view from the house. The doorknob turns easily. A wave of hot, dry air breathes out. A creepy sensation crawls under his skin.

*If you find a door is locked, it is locked for a purpose.*

This isn't locked, so he steps inside the dark confines of the heated garage, but not before stomping the snow off his boots.

It's so much warmer than the house.

A black Cadillac Eldorado is parked inside. Its trunk is massive, and the convertible top is down. Panels shine like it just came from the factory, but the red leather seats are worn like they'd seen a thousand road trips. He steps around the back end, careful not to touch the flared taillights.

Another oversized car could fit into the other half of the garage. The open floor is slightly darker than the concrete below the car, but both halves are clean—not a spot of oil, grain of sawdust or fleck of dirt anywhere. Large triangular blocks are wedged under the wheels as if it's on a slope, but the garage floor is level.

A workbench is attached to the wall with a pegboard above it. Hammers, screwdrivers, clamps, hoses, and things he's never seen are hung on hooks with their outlines painted behind them.

A single window faces the house, letting in diffuse light. A pair of binoculars hangs next to it. The view to the house is at an angle. No one can see him here. He pulls them off the nail and admires the cracked leather strap and well-oiled hinge. He brings the windmill into focus, the blades still turning.

He slings the strap over his shoulder.

A filing cabinet is to the right, nestled between larger shelves. Ducking below the window, he puts his hand on the top drawer.

His heart is pounding.

He looks at the window one last time and gives it a tug.

The drawer slides on lubricated rails. *It's not locked*. Manila folders are stuffed inside with bent tabs and scribbled notes. Oliver nervously swallows. His hand quivers as he pries them open, revealing endless pages of handwritten notes and sketches and schematics.

There's more of the same in the other drawers, each one so full that, it seems, another sheet of paper couldn't fit. Oliver's palms are sweaty. He tugs out a handful, carefully noting where their location is before placing them on the workbench.

In the dim light, the thrill of rebellion courses through him. Once he snooped through his dad's dresser drawers and found a pistol and a plastic baggie with white pills. That was nothing compared to now. His head fills with helium and threatens to lift him into the rafters.

He can't decipher any of the notes. It's all higher mathematics and engineered plans. One folder contains a folded map that appears to be a nautical chart with notes scribbled in the margins and lines drawn throughout the Arctic Ocean.

THUMP.

The snow shovel clatters on the concrete.

Oliver jumps back; his heart seizes for a full beat. His legs turn to jelly as he tries to catch his breath. He hurries to put the folders back together, shoving them into their correct slots, easing the drawers closed and then wiping his fingerprints from the handles.

He grabs the shovel and starts for the door...but notices something under the workbench. It's where the sound came from, like something hit the outside wall.

A large chest is hiding in the shadows.

His heart is still thumping. He should just take the shovel and go. Besides, the excitement is working on his blood sugar. He doesn't have his pack with him.

*But maybe, next time, the door will be locked.*

He squeezes the snow shovel with both hands until his knuckles ache. He lays it on the floor—if it fell again, he'd have a heart attack —and squats to get a better look. It's a green footlocker with a leather handle and brass rivets. He takes a deep breath before crawling underneath.

The buckles unlock with a sturdy tug. The lid cracks open, releasing stale air. Oliver scoots closer. It looks like blankets. He digs his phone out and uses the flashlight app.

It's an old coat with a row of buttons. The material is coarse. Beneath it, though, are stacks of leather-bound books. Six of them. Oliver gently lifts the jacket out. The books are similar to the one in his bedroom, although, he discovers after prying one open, these are filled with words and not the kind written with a ballpoint pen. These appear to be quilled with a bottle of ink.

The binding cracks as he carefully opens the one on top. There's a date scribbled on the first page. He briefly flips through the pages, all dated and filled with notes and hand-drawn illustrations.

Next to the journals are miscellaneous items—a tattered long-sleeved undershirt, a sextant, a collapsible telescope, a jewelry box, and a weird key with a blue cube instead of teeth. There's also a small wooden sphere about the size of a golf ball.

Oliver picks up the sphere.

It hums in his hand. The vibrations drive up his arm and spread across his chest, but not like the windmill. This current, if that's what it is, feels warm and mild. It feels good.

*Safe.*

There are numerous lines carved into the surface—intricate shapes and designs that vary in width and depth, as if carefully crafted with fine instruments. It's heavier than he expected, too; perhaps the center is weighted.

He holds the phone closer, rubbing the smooth surface with this thumb, digging his thumbnail into the grooves. It reminds him of one of those drawings in the filing cabinet.

"Oliver!"

He bumps his head on the bottom of the workbench and scrambles to slam the footlocker. Mom shouts his name from the house again. The latches won't catch. He opens and closes the lid, and they snap this time. Oliver sweeps the shovel off the floor and slowly peeks out the window. She's on the back porch.

It's getting dark.

He rushes around the car, careful not to touch it, and sneaks out the back door, shutting it without a sound. He takes several breaths, afraid to let her see him coming from the garage. Instead, he flees into the forest and heads for the windmill, staying just inside the tree line and out of sight of the house.

To his right, the forest is dark and deep. He holds the shovel like a battle staff, breaking small, dead twigs. His heart bangs inside his head.

The squeal of the windmill calls from his left.

Just a little further and he can exit into the clearing. More twigs snap when he sees the dim light of the sunset ahead. He slows down, but the sound of breaking branches continues.

He spins around.

Something's back there, in the dark. Oliver stumbles into the open, tumbling into the snow with both hands on the shovel. The sun is behind the mountains. He scrambles around the trees until the house comes into view and stops with a stitch in his side and his breath burning in his throat, expecting a wolf or bear to come flying out, claws extended.

Nothing does.

He wouldn't have the strength to swing the shovel if it did.

The binoculars press against his ribs. When he shoves his hand into his coat pocket, he finds a small orb at the bottom.

*The wooden sphere.*

He doesn't remember taking it.

## 5

There's a small Christmas tree on the dresser.

Oliver stays beneath the thick comforter, watching the miniature lights glowing on the tips of plastic branches, splashing colors across the walls.

It's the smallest tree he's ever seen.

A black kit containing the blood test, injections and glucose tablets is next to the tree. It's too far to reach and too cold to get out of bed. He's sluggish and moody. His sugar is always low in the morning, but just a few more minutes.

He reaches under the bed. His phone is charging on the floor. He feels the binoculars wedged beneath the mattress. The wooden orb is next to them. He grabs the orb and holds it on his fingertips. He assumes it had been hand-carved, but the spherical shape is so perfect and the lines so precise that something had to fabricate it and certainly not those tools on the pegboard. Yet the footlocker looked a hundred years old.

The bedroom door begins to open.

If the hinges didn't creak, he never would've gotten the orb under the blankets before the gray-haired, tight-lipped old woman stepped inside. Oliver slides down until his nose perches on the comforter's edge.

Grandmother is momentarily distracted by the tiny tree. She tilts her head curiously.

"What are you doing?"

"You should knock."

"This is my house."

She takes a step into the room, glancing at the window. If she gets to it, she'll see the phone.

"I'm naked." He slinks lower. "I sleep that way."

"Well, I...Olivah, that is not appropriate." Color seeps into her ashy cheeks.

"I learned it camping. It's better for body heat."

"Well, then, you will have to wash the sheets."

Unexpectedly, she leaves the room, forgetting whatever she had come to do. Even her footsteps are loud, creaking all the way to the stairwell, where they stop. Mom must've been waiting. They begin muttering in low tones, but the words carry through the house.

"You didn't need to wake him."

"He cannot sleep all morning."

"Mother, he's been working ever since we got here. Let him rest."

"He's a diabetic, Debra."

"Yes, and let him manage it."

It had been three days since Oliver discovered the garage.

Every night, a few inches of snow would fall, and he would take the shovel out for another workout. Strangely, the road leading to the roundabout was always cleared, as if Grandmother paid someone to leave the roundabout for Oliver.

"Olivah should be on a schedule."

"He's not an infant." Mom's voice echoes.

"Don't raise your voice to me, Debra."

"Don't raise my son."

"He needs structure to shape his life."

"Structure worked wonders on me."

Footsteps come heavily toward the bedroom. Oliver doesn't hear his Grandmother's descent. His mom looks into the room. Her headband is around her neck, her brown locks falling over her eyes and ears, hiding her golden line of earrings.

"Sorry," she says. "Take your time."

"I need to shovel?"

She grimaces. "Yes, sorry. Your cousins are coming in a few days."

"Henry and Helen?"

"Remember them?"

Barely. They came down to Texas when he was seven. He doesn't remember that being fun.

"Grandmother wants to get the house ready. Once you get your chores done, you can do whatever you've been doing outside." She squeezes the lump at the end of the bed that happens to be his foot. "What have you been doing?"

"Exploring, that's all." He yawns to cover his lie. Grandmother and Mom have been around the backyard or calling for him too often to make another trip to the garage. "I've been, you know, just walking to the trees and stuff."

"Don't go too far. I don't want you stuck out there or lost."

"What happens when the sun goes down?"

"You know, the usual—monsters and trolls, things with teeth." She laughs, but not in the way she does when she's hiding something. It's not trolls she's worried about. It's her diabetic kid lost in the forest on a cold night.

"It's not so bad here, Mom."

She rolls her eyes.

"No, seriously. I mean, not the chores so much. Or the tea. But I don't mind having the third floor to myself and thousands of acres to explore."

"You're a good kid." She squeezes his foot again.

"What if I was bad?"

"I'd still love you, just not as much." She winks. "Now get your naked butt out of bed and get dressed."

"I'm not...you heard that?"

She swats his knee. "That was good thinking."

Oliver stays beneath the warm comforter, listening to his mom's large steps grow more confident. She's hardly the little girl that drove up to the house.

And they have a Christmas tree.

"Thanks for the tree!"

"You're welcome!" Mom's voice echoes throughout the house.

HE SHOVELS AFTER LUNCH.

The afternoon is sunny. The icicles drip from the gutters, and despite the ache in his back, Oliver hikes past the slow-churning windmill and out to the clearing. His kit is in one pocket, the orb in the other. Once out of sight, he enters the trees.

There's no path, but soon he finds the broken branches from his panicked escape. It's still dark in the deepest part of the forest, but nothing moves or snaps—it's just the calm, wintry silence that follows him to the garage.

Despite layers of sweaters and thermals, he's shivering. He's not made for the cold. "You're a skinny lad," a teacher once told him, "with not an ounce of meat."

The snow around the garage is undisturbed. He stops short, wondering where his footprints are from the other day. He pulls off his glove and wraps his fingers around the metal knob. It feels like a block of ice. He's afraid to turn it, to feel it refuse to open. He closes his eyes...

Pop.

Warm air heaves out.

Oliver jumps inside. He kicks the snow off his boots and opens his coat. The garage feels like the beach in July. If only the sun were over-head and the sand between his toes.

His distorted reflection follows him around the car, stretching his long face even thinner, turning his arms into noodles. The triangular blocks are still wedged under the wheels, although they seem to be slightly askew this time.

The afternoon sunlight beams through the only window, making the chrome gleam and black side panels shine. The seats are still worn. He always pictured Grandmother driving something more sensible.

Like a tank.

The wooden orb feels warm in his pocket. He places it on one of the little shelves above the workbench, next to a metal oil dispenser, and then turns his attention to the filing cabinet, careful to stay clear of the window.

He starts with the top drawer.

Most of the contents are handwritten. Portions have a large X over failures or wrong equations. Many of the folders are loaded with statistical calculations and circuit schematics. Occasionally, there are illustrations of gadgets that look more like large animals or flying wagons than anything practical: the daydreams of a fantasy world. None of it seems to jibe with his grandfather.

He was a mechanic.

It takes an hour to finish the top drawer. He starts on the next one and, after plowing halfway through it, finds himself bored with the tedium of details and indecipherable equations.

But then he strikes gold.

It's a folder with sketches, mostly; nothing out of the ordinary but this time he recognizes the object. Oliver rolls the wooden orb over the notes.

The designs match.

It's a schematic of weights and dimensions. The details of the lines illustrate exactly where they should be cut and how deep. There's also a cutaway of the internal mechanisms that shows circuits and finely manufactured components.

Oliver holds the orb up, examining the rough-hewn lines that don't exactly match the plan's precision. It's close, though. The plans, however, call for the shell to be constructed of aluminum, copper and an iron-nickel alloy. Maybe those metals are inside, but the outer portion is definitely wood.

Also, the sphere in the plans is thirty centimeters in circumference, about the size of a softball. The wooden one must be a proto-type, but what are they for? Some kind of a game?

*It doesn't feel like a game.*

Oliver checks the time.

He puts the plans away before crawling under the workbench. He found the wooden orb in the footlocker; maybe there's a quick answer inside it. He leans deep into the dark recess beneath the bench and powers up his phone's flashlight.

He pulls the jacket out and places it across his lap. It delivers a one-two punch of mold and old and brings about a violent sneeze. Next, he takes out all six journals. He puts them in chronological order based on the date found on each of the first pages, ranging from 1881 to 1883.

With his phone perched near his chin, he opens the first one. The script is shaky and faded, as if penned with the opposite hand.


SEPTEMBER 10, 1881.

*My name is Malcolm Toye. And I am a dead man.*


OLIVER FUMBLES HIS LIGHT.

The garage, once warm and empty, feels crowded with ghosts. Malcolm Toye was his great-grandfather. His mom once mentioned there were relatives in the navy, but there were no pictures to prove it. And rarely did they visit family.

When his heart rate nears normal, he turns on the light.


*I HAVE SOMEHOW FOUND myself separated from my party. We reached a chain of Siberian islands. This, we suspect, being Bennett Island. The men are weak and frostbitten. Soon, we plan to take the boats in search of the mainland, in hopes of finding a native settlement.*

*And, somehow, I find myself alone.*

*There is no feeling in my toes and most of my legs after having fallen into an open lead. If I survive, which is doubtful, frostbite has already claimed these parts of my body. My nose, as well.*

*I write only with the hope that my love will know that, in these final hours, I am thinking of her. I was a fool to attempt this journey into the Arctic. No man will see the North Pole without perishing, this I am certain. Why would I think this expedition would be any different?*

*As I lay here, it is your love, my bride, which offers me the warmth and knowledge that I will pass through the gates of heaven with a smile.*

THERE ARE several unintelligible passages that follow as his fingers appeared to stiffen on the water-stained pages. It ends with scribbles, like a man attempting to record his dreams long after he's fallen asleep.

There are several blank pages.

But then the entries resume, this time with sharp lines and fluent script, not the handwriting of frozen fingers. And oddly similar to the plans in the filing cabinets.

DECEMBER 10, 1881

*Is heaven a warm room? Is it a full belly and the comfort of a bed? If it is, my love, then I rest peacefully in the afterlife.*

*I can only guess the date at the time of this entry. It feels like months have passed since I last wrote, but I cannot be sure. I can only report what I see before me.*

*I write to you with not a quill and ink but an instrument much smoother. My belongings are heaped into the corner of this very small room, whose walls appear to be fashioned from blue ice, yet when I touch them, they feel no more frigid than a ship's deck. The floor, too, is ice, yet when I step on it, I do not slip.*

*What is more remarkable, if that is even possible, is that my fingers and toes are fully functioning. There is a slight discoloration on the smallest of my digits, but it appears that I have made a full recovery.*

*How is this possible?*

*My memories are scattered. I recall, with the help of this journal, wandering the frozen tundra and becoming separated from the party. I remember lying in wait of death, yet here I am, writing to you.*

*I have slept much. When I wake, there is little energy in my body, but I find food next to the bed. When I slumber, I hear voices that are never here when, once again, I wake. It is strange and impossible that I am still in the Arctic, but I have no other explanation.*

*I hesitate to record what is next, but feel certain you will understand if somehow you find these journals. I recall, in my final moments before waking in this room, there was someone with me. Or, perhaps I should say, something. When I was dying in the snow, I felt its shadow fall over me as my breath leaked from me. It was a large thing, an angel of sorts, that whisked me out of Death's clutches. Its body was massive, and its arms thick. My love, there is no other way to say it.*

*It was made of snow.*

*I am very aware of how this sounds, that these ramblings are the sort from a madman, that perhaps I damaged some part of the brain and tell you my dreams instead of reality. Perhaps I am still on the ice and dying after all, and these ramblings are a dream.*

*But I think not.*

Tap, tap, tap.

The phone tumbles into Oliver's lap.

He finds it in the coat and scurries away from the noise. It wasn't a mouse or a branch. That was someone knocking. Something weird is about to happen. This is a different weird than low blood sugar weird. This is out there. He starts to climb out when the doorknob rattles.

Oliver slams into the footlocker and hides beneath the old, musty coat, fumbling to turn off the light.

A key slides into the lock.

The door opens, and someone kicks their boots on the doorjamb before coming inside. Oliver is as solid as granite. He squeezes his eyes shut, breathing as slowly as possible. Footsteps quietly cross the garage. Oliver dares a peek through the fuzzy slots of his eyelids.

Grandmother's padded boots stand at the storage rack next to the filing cabinet.

She's humming.

It could be Mom wearing Grandmother's boots, but Mom shuffles. And she doesn't have an old, spotted left hand. Grandmother's right hand is clad in a strange metallic glove, something made of metal links and silver plates.

What's weirder is that she's humming.

He assumed she disapproved of all things fun and expressive, like music and dancing and laughing.

*Rule #534: No joy.*

She's tearing plastic wrapping, maybe opening paper towels. If she turns around and leaves, she'll never see him from that angle. But whatever she's got, she brings to the workbench.

Close enough he could grab her knee.

Oliver's fingernails dig into his palms. His head is getting light. He forces himself to breathe, trying to remember if he left anything open. Did he leave any papers out? Did he close the filing cabinet?

*The wooden orb!*

He stops breathing.

Hiding in the garage with great-grandfather's belongings on his lap, he's pretty sure will be breaking a rule, written or not.

Grandmother goes back to the shelves, humming a little louder, and then heads for the door, but not before unloading a three-step fart.

A moment later, she closes the door.

He takes a long breath just before things dim. He holds completely still, though, muffling his breathing with the coat. He stays that way for several minutes, just in case Sing-along Grandmother comes back with another dose of walking farts.

When he finally moves, it's in full-blown panic mode.

His legs are weak, but there's no time to check sugar. He shoves the items back in the footlocker. The wooden orb had rolled against the wall and wedged, luckily, behind a tin can of rusty nails. He grabs it and heads for the door.

He stops.

He might not come back for a while. He might not come back ever. He checks the window and sees Grandmother's tracks heading back to the house. Quickly, he digs into the footlocker and tucks three journals inside his coat.

He runs through the forest, sprinting out to the clearing as the long shadows begin to fade. He takes a moment to rub snow on his cheeks and forehead, pulling his gloves off to chill his fingers so that, when he returns, he's sure to look and feel like he's been exploring the property.

Just as he climbs onto the front porch, he realizes two things.

One, Grandmother had to unlock the door to get inside the garage, but he never locked it. But it's the second realization that sends chills down his neck.

Grandmother didn't notice his tracks leading into the garage.

*Because they had been erased.*

# 6

O liver stands at the pantry door, stunned. Maybe he's asleep or Grandmother's alarm didn't go off. Like she has an alarm.

*Like she sleeps.*

But two weeks until Christmas and there it is, a blank chore list. Christmas came early.

Oliver grabs a quick breakfast and returns to his bedroom. He listens at the door for a few minutes. When silence remains, he creeps to the dresser and leans into it, tilting it towards the wall and reaching underneath, where three leather-bound books are stashed. They barely fit. He's not going back to the garage anytime soon.

He should've grabbed all six of them.

He flops his backpack on the bed and shoves the journals inside, covering them with *Snowboarder Magazine*, something Mom picked up at a gas station. He'll need more magazines and books, just to make it look good. But what if Grandmother inspects the backpack?

*Grandmother? What if Mom looks inside? How am I going to explain that?*

This horrible plan worsens when footsteps come toward his

room. He slams into the dresser like a linebacker. It thumps the wall just as a light knocking raps the door.

"Just a sec."

He can't fuss with the journals; it'll sound like he's up to something. Instead, he throws the backpack on the other side of the bed and takes several deep breaths before opening the door.

"Where've you been?" Mom's in a robe with a towel on her head.

"There are no chores. I was just, you know, relaxing."

A look crosses her face. She knows he's hiding something. He's as transparent as a glass of water. Then again, his lies are generally about how many bowls of cereal he ate or whether he checked his sugar, not hiding antiquated journals.

"Sorry, kiddo, no relaxing today. Your Aunt Rhonnie and cousins are coming today."

She slings a suit bag on the bed and pulls the zipper down the center, exposing a dark blue jacket and striped tie. A little handkerchief tufts out of the breast pocket.

"No, Mom. Please, no."

"It's not going to kill you."

"Yes, it will."

"I went to boarding school when I was ten and wore a uniform every day. It didn't kill me."

*Yes, it did.*

She holds the suit to his shoulders. He's heard her talk about boarding school, heard her say it did kill a part of her. She laughs when she says it, but it's only half a joke. Oliver feels like a part of her died before that.

"You've got two hours," she says. "Get a shower, get dressed, and you'll have time to sneak a few games on your phone."

"I don't know how to do the tie."

"Lucky you." She holds up a clip-on.

His friends back in Texas had dads that wore suits. Oliver was convinced it sucked out their souls. Oliver's dad never wore a tie. He made money with investments, but he was pretty sure his dad already sold his soul.

Oliver didn't want his soul sucked out by a suit or boarding school.

"Your chores for today are entertaining your cousins. Grandmother lives for this stuff, darling." She lathers the last word with stuffy English entitlement. "Be on your best behavior."

She turns at the door and, in bare feet, curtsies as if her robe were a ballroom gown.

HIS SHINY SHOES are stark against the dull grain of the staircase.

Each step sends a hard-soled clack through the house, biting into his heels as he descends to the first floor, where Grandmother, dressed in pearls and dead animal fur, is waiting.

"Why good day, sir," Mom says.

"Debra, don't be foolish."

Mom curtsies, this time in a blue dress that hugs her neck. Her brown hair is off her face, except for a looping curl she pulls aside. She straightens his tie and fusses with his hair that's still too short to brush.

"Mom." Grandmother turns her steely stare on him. "I mean, Mother."

She doesn't stop fussing. She looks beautiful; he looks handsome. But, honestly, they look absurd. She must be thinking what Oliver is thinking. They try not to giggle and fail.

"Debra, behave yourself." Grandmother folds her hands beneath the draping fur. "What kind of example are you setting? Honestly, I expect more out of you. This is not how I taught you. If you had listened to me, Olivah would have a father to teach him these things."

That's when the light vanishes from Mom's eyes.

She rests her hand on Oliver's shoulder. The joy that a few moments earlier was bubbling out drains from her. She turns to Grandmother and lifts a finger.

"Don't," is all she can say.

Grandmother defiantly lifts her chin.

Beneath the rosy strokes of blush, her skin is the color of sun-bleached wood. Mom's complexion is a growing flame, and shallow creases form around her pursed lips, something he'd never noticed before. Oliver could swear that, despite the emotionless gaze, a tiny, infinitesimal twitch crinkles the corner of Grandmother's mouth.

A micro-smile.

*Rule #575: Grind children under heel.*

A silver car can be seen through the fractured panel of decorative glass. It eases up to the sidewalk. The tinted windows reflect the looming house.

"Olivah. Be so kind as to greet our guests."

He opens the large door, and a bitter breeze hits him.

Grandmother goes out to the porch.

Mom continues staring, as if the ghost of her mother is still in front of her. In a few words, Grandmother kicked the legs out from Mom's life, spilling her emotions all over the floor. She picks them up, though, and gives Oliver a half-empty smile before going to the porch.

A slender woman gets out of the driver's side, with a low-cut blouse. Round sunglasses, lenses the size of coasters, are perched on Aunt Rhonnie's pointy nose. She waves, fingers only, but her bright red lips don't move as she strides around the front of the car, her heels spiking the sidewalk, with a furry coat over her arm.

"Mother," she says.

They don't hug, but rather loosely take each other's arms and air-kiss each cheek. She's a stretched and younger version of Grandmother with a wrinkle-free complexion that's smooth, yet plump and expressionless—courtesy of her plastic surgeon.

Mom's twin sister—fraternal twin sister—approaches her.

"Welcome home, sister," she says. They embrace like normal people, without the fake kisses. Aunt Rhonnie holds her at arm's length. "Look at you with all your earrings and inner beauty. You look wonderful, you really do."

"And you, with your Michael Kors sunglasses and perfect skin."

"And who's your date?" She lowers her sunglasses. "Don't tell me...oh my Lord! This handsome young man can't be! It just can't be!"

Her lined lips form a circle that swoop in to plant a sticky kiss on Oliver's cheek. She wraps her bony arms around him, pulling him against her engorged chest until he smells like a cosmetics sampler.

"You look wonderful, Oliver," she says. "You really do. You remind me of your handsome father, all dressed up like a grown-up. Let's go inside before I catch pneumonia. I'm not made for this weather; I don't know why I live here."

She rushes into the foyer.

Grandmother and Mom follow. Oliver is last, wondering how long she's staying with the car still running.

"Where are the twins?" Mom asks.

"They're finishing their games. They'll be inside as soon as they're done. Oh my Lord, I am so happy to see you. It's so nice to have the family together. When's the last time we had tea?"

"A while," Mom says.

"Actually, never," Aunt Rhonnie says. "Oliver was too young. This is going to be so much fun, I can hardly stand it. Let me powder my nose. I must look dreadful after being in the car. Really, Mother, you need to move into the city. There's no point staying on the property."

Aunt Rhonnie, still wearing her sunglasses, sways down the hall-way. Oliver waits for one of the pointy heels to hammer into the floor.

Grandmother goes to the kitchen.

Mom licks her finger to wipe the lipstick off Oliver's cheek.

"You wait here," she says, as if there's a war zone down the hall-way. She rubs his hair, kisses his head, and goes headlong into the battle.

Oliver stays put as a draft creeps under the door and up the pant legs crumpled around his shiny shoes. A door slams outside, followed by another.

Henry adjusts his tie as he waits for Helen to come around the car. The twins open the front door without knocking. They stand across from Oliver, shoulder to shoulder like a pair of aliens. A few years older and just as many inches taller than Oliver, they have blond hair that, if he's not mistaken, is too blond. Almost gold.

Their features are angular, like Aunt Rhonnie's. Helen's hair is pulled back in a tight ponytail that, seventy years from now, will be gray and wrapped in a bun. She's sort of sucking in her cheeks.

They look like a commercial.

"Where's Mother?" Henry slicks his hair to the side without disturbing the part.

"They went that way."

And then the two, side by side, walk down the dim hallway. Oliver stays at the front door until his legs turn cold.

MOM IS IN THE KITCHEN.

She's hyper-focused on arranging silver pots and bowls and miniature spoons on an oval silver tray with intricate etchings. Muscles are bunched on her shoulders. She doesn't notice him standing behind her as she fills one of the bowls with sugar cubes.

"Are you all right?" Oliver asks.

She drops the last sugar cube and curses. She covers her mouth and giggles, letting the tension fall away as she rubs her face and curses quietly again.

"Oooh." She sighs. "It feels like we've been in this house forever."

Strangely, this still feels like an adventure to Oliver. Parts of Mom, though, have never left this house.

"Can I help?" he asks.

She directs him to fill the other tray with scones and condiments from the refrigerator. He puts it together, but Mom starts methodically changing the placement of the little pitchers and plates.

"Grandmother's thing is tea," she says. "When I was little, I'd focus on the details to make it go faster. If I didn't think about it, just engaged in the action one hundred percent, no matter how I felt about it, then it was over before I knew it."

She tweaks the orientation of a small knife.

"We did this every time we had company. It's her ice breaker."

"More like ice maker."

Mom snorts.

She pinches her nose, but it doesn't help. Oliver smothers his laughter. She turns away, twice, before getting herself under control. Straightening the wrinkles in her dress, she says, "Let's get serious."

Once the trays are ready, they exit the kitchen and stop at the dining room, where company sits properly in their high-backed chairs. Grandmother is at the head of the table. Aunt Rhonnie and the twins are to the left.

"Tea," Mom announces, "is served."

The sarcasm is skillfully camouflaged, yet highlights the absurdity of bizarro world. Oliver waits for Mom to place her tray before putting his down.

"Very strong boy," Aunt Rhonnie says. Her sunglasses are hooked on the neckline of her blouse, exposing more of her very bony, very tan chest. Her eyes are intensely blue, like they've been Photoshopped.

Once they're seated to the right of Grandmother, tea begins.

They pass around the sterling silver decanter and pour the stringent, hot tea through a screen to filter the loose leaves. The small boats of lemon wedges and pitchers of milk are passed around. The twins, sitting ramrod straight with eyes cast down, drop three cubes of sugar with silver tongs into their cups and stir with miniature spoons without making a sound.

"You two, stop it," Aunt Rhonnie says. "Oliver can't have sugar."

She says it as if he's an alcoholic and they're guzzling booze. He pours creamer into his cup and remains unnoticed until his spoon clinks the porcelain.

Grandmother's lips tighten.

Rule #954: Don't clink your cup.

Everyone samples the tea with pinkies properly curled inward and not, as Grandmother explained, extended. That sort of nonsense is for the movies. They sip silently, staring down so as not to spill a drop. There's a long pause before the scones are passed around.

"So, Mother," Aunt Rhonnie says, "how do you like your new roommates?"

"There have been no surprises."

Oliver doesn't know what that means, but Mom flinches.

"Sometimes predictability is nice," Aunt Rhonnie says. "Lord knows, my life could use some. I was just saying that the other day."

She plies a scone with strawberry jam and talks about her divorce lawyer's counterproposal to her soon-to-be ex-husband's ridiculous offer. They'll just end up paying the lawyers more money, and, Lord knows, lawyers already make enough.

"I mean, what I offered the first time was more than fair. It could've ended right there. But if he wants to play games, then okay, let's play."

She tears a piece off the scone with her long, red fingernails.

"How's school?" Mom asks.

The twins look up, but Aunt Rhonnie answers. Helen had the lead in the school play and received a standing ovation. She posted pictures on Facebook, didn't they see them? Mom really needs to move into the twenty-first century and get an account. If she did, she'd also know that Helen just got her first modeling job. There's a chance that she'll end up in J. Crew's fall catalog.

Wouldn't that be wonderful?

Mom watches the twins dress their scones with jam and clotted cream and dab their mouths while Aunt Rhonnie describes Henry's violin concert.

"He received a standing ovation, and, believe me, he deserved it."

"School play, huh?" Mom says to Helen. "Was it hard memorizing your lines?"

"We practiced every night," Aunt Rhonnie says.

"Were you nervous?"

"Nervous?" Aunt Rhonnie says. "This girl has ice running through her veins."

Helen takes a carefully measured sip of the sugared tea while Aunt Rhonnie describes how much the costumes cost. Helen focuses on placing the cup back on the saucer without a clink. Is she doing the same as Mom, keeping her mind empty to get this over with?

"Henry." Mom pauses until he makes eye contact. "Did you bring your violin?"

"No, ma'am."

He hides behind his teacup, and Aunt Rhonnie describes the magical concert. They just have to come to the next; it has to be seen to be believed.

Mom exhales very slowly.

In the meantime, Grandmother cuts her scone into bite-sized pieces and chews twenty times apiece. She may as well be having tea alone.

Oliver's scone tastes like a clod of flour.

Against his will, he swallows a gulp of tea to wash it down and receives a glance from Grandmother. You don't wash down scones with tea.

"What do you do, Oliver?" Aunt Rhonnie asks.

All attention turns to him. He's slouching. This time, he pretends to sip from the cup.

"What do I do?" he replies.

"In your spare time."

"Mostly read, I guess."

"Smarty pants, huh? You hear that, Henry? Oliver likes to read. Henry read all of the Hunger Games books in a day and the Harry Potter books, all seven of them, in a week and, let me tell you, those last two were ridiculously thick. I mean, there's like 200,000 words or more in each one. Can you believe that?"

Oliver fakes another sip. He likes Aunt Rhonnie. No one looks at you when she's in the room.

"What else?" she asks.

"Ma'am?"

"What else besides reading? Surely, you've been doing something else in this house besides reading. What else do you like to do?"

"Oh, um." He thinks about the journals in his room and feels his face warm. "Chores."

Mom snorts. She quickly lifts her cup.

Aunt Rhonnie's perma-grin falters. "Chores? You like chores?"

"Yes, ma'am."

The funny thing is, he sort of meant it. He didn't mind the shoveling and making his bed and all the ritual that went with preparing meals and cleaning. Before they moved, he was glued to his phone. Maybe he wouldn't feel the same if he hadn't discovered the garage and the mystery in this bizarro world.

"How is our chore master, Mother?" Aunt Rhonnie asks.

Grandmother dabs her mouth. "Olivah has done a fine job."

And that's all she says. It's all she needs to say. It's as close to a compliment he's ever heard. It makes him feel warm and fuzzy.

"Chores and reading, then," Aunt Rhonnie says. "Good...that's good."

"Don't forget handsome," Mom adds.

They finish tea and learn more about Rhonnie's new career opportunity as a model consultant. Oliver doesn't have to talk. And that's just fine. Instead, he imitates the twins' mechanical tea performance, lifting and sipping, eyes cast down. He even finishes the scone by chopping uniform slices and chewing twenty times. Before he knows it, tea is over.

Later, he goes outside for exercise.

That's when he meets the real twins.

# 7

Henry's on the back porch, dressed in a wool coat buttoned just past his waist. He tucks a black scarf around his neck and, looking up at the clear sky, slides on a dark pair of sunglasses. With his hands in his front pockets, he passes Oliver and peeks through the garage window.

"Wish we could go in there, right?" he says. "That's the one door the old lady never forgets to lock."

Oliver doesn't comment. *Maybe I got lucky.*

"You see that car?" Henry spits a hole in the snow. "We ever get the keys to that, Ollie, we're going on a road trip and never coming back."

The back door closes again. This time, Helen comes down the steps, pulling on gloves. Her sunglasses came off the same rack as her mom's.

Henry starts towards the windmill.

"Are we taking Ollie?"

"We can't leave him."

"We're not taking him with us, Henry." Helen still hasn't looked at Oliver. "I don't trust him."

"He's family."

"You're hilarious."

Henry looks back at the house, then at the windmill. "You a rat, Ollie?"

"What?"

"Can you keep a secret?"

"Yeah."

"Come on, walk with us."

Helen leads them toward the windmill that, mercifully, continues its silent mechanical churn. Despite the sunny day, the cold air pinches Oliver's nose and cheeks. Henry hooks his arm around Oliver's shoulders.

"We've been coming out here since we were born, Ollie. We've done more chores than indentured servants. You seem like a smart kid, doing your work without complaining. That's how you work the old lady, just do what she says and shut your mouth. But how long have you been out here? Two weeks?"

Oliver nods.

"That means you don't know squat. Am I right, Helen?"

She's ten steps ahead. Henry stops at the foot of the windmill and, with lips forming a circle, exhales a column of steam.

"I like your cap," he says. "Where'd you get it?"

"My mom."

"Yeah? Like an early Christmas present?"

"Something like that."

"Nice. Let me try it, see if it fits."

Oliver's legs get colder.

"Come on," Henry says. "I'm thinking about getting one. That's all. Don't be a selfish turd."

Oliver hesitates before pulling the cap off. He can feel the heat seep from his scalp. Henry pulls it over his product-stiff hair. He checks his reflection in his sunglasses.

"Helen, what'd you think?"

Now thirty steps away, she turns around, hugging herself. "You look like a douche."

Henry chuckles before scooping up a handful of snow and heaves a snowball at her. She starts for the open field again.

"Come on." Henry whacks Oliver in the chest. "You going to let her get away with insulting your hat? Nail her one, why don't you."

Oliver keeps his hands in his pockets. The cold fear seeps into his stomach. Henry smacks him again and points in his face.

"Don't leave me hanging, Ollie. You throw a snowball."

Oliver bends over slowly, giving Helen enough time to get well out of range before throwing one short.

Henry snatches two fistfuls of his coat.

"What are you doing, throwing a snowball at my sister?" His eyebrows furrow behind his sunglasses, his teeth clenched between tightly drawn lips. Oliver stares at his black reflection in the lenses, the cold fear creeping into his arms. They're still in view of the house.

Henry lightly slaps his cheek. "I'm just playing."

He drags Oliver with his arm hooked around his neck. They follow Helen's tracks around the trees. She's yelling at them to hurry up.

When the house is out of sight, Henry straightens Oliver's collar.

"You're a good kid. You're smart, you read and all that good stuff. I trust you can get lost for an hour. Don't let the old lady see you wandering around on your own."

"What if she comes outside?"

"Grandmother? You joking? Have you ever seen the old lady outside? Besides going to the garage, I've never seen her come off the front porch. And I mean *never*. Don't let any of them see you, for that matter."

Helen has already started across the open field, her shoulders hunched.

"We're going that way, Ollie. Don't follow us."

Oliver nods.

"I mean, don't follow us ever."

Pause. And nod.

"Good." Another playful slap. This time it stings. "This is your test. Don't disappoint me."

"Where are you going?"

"Don't worry about that."

Oliver stands near the trees, watching Henry catch up to his sister. The cold is feasting on his ears, but he doesn't move until they reach the other side and slip between the trees.

He has one hour to kill.

Oliver had no intention of coming to the garage.

It would've been safer to wait. But Henry took his stocking cap, and his head feels like a block of ice. Oliver goes to the house and, after knocking off the snow, goes inside. He announces that he's just come to use the bathroom and do a quick blood test. Henry and Helen are waiting for him in the field.

He sneaks up to his room and, listening for footsteps, stuffs one of the journals down his pants.

Aunt Rhonnie is in the kitchen, pouring liqueur into a cup of coffee. Oliver rushes out before she starts talking, and finds himself, after wandering through the trees, going to the garage door.

Once again the doorknob turns easily.

Oliver opens his coat. He's got an hour before he needs to be at the field, pretending to wait for the twins to return. He sets the alarm on his phone and crawls under the bench.

The footlocker is just like he left it. Oliver takes the journal from under his belt and, with his phone illuminating the yellowed pages, looks for where he left off. There's not much time.

He turns the brittle page.

DATE? *I don't know the date. I don't know how many days have passed, don't know if I'm still dreaming or awake.*

*Sleep feels like eternity.*

*I awake, or so I believe, with lotion on my hands and feet. My flesh still has an odd color, something closer to ash, and I've lost some sensation. But* my toes wiggle and my fingers write, and someone seems to be making sure they do so.

Some mornings (I'm calling them mornings, but there is no way to know) there are fresh clothes stacked on the floor, clothes that I've never seen. They are newly tailored and warm, fitting perfectly over my pudgy frame. I can no longer see my ribs. And if I stand up straight, I can hardly see my toes.

I call out, but no one answers.

I feel buried, but awake with a full belly and salt on my lips. Someone is fattening me up. Perhaps I have fallen prey to a sea monster. I will wake, one morning, to find myself not walking the confines of a square cubicle but swimming in boiling soup!

Time has become my enemy. I am thankful for life, but what life is this? It is survival, I tell myself.

Survival until I see you, my love.

I pace the room and count my steps. And I do push-ups and sit-ups, fifty at a time. And then I start over.

Judging by the curly whiskers hiding my chin, I can guess that I have been here a month or so. Still, the unending silence, broken only by my own breath, pushes me toward madness.

Why am I alive? Why me?

And what of the crew? When I think of my mates, the room becomes smaller and the silence heavier. I can't think of them. Their fate has surely been cast. They either made it home or died on the ice.

Either of those fates tortures me with envy.

THERE ARE pages torn from the journal and mad scribbles on the ones that follow—sketches of ships and desolation, of wistful clouds and sunrises in full array. Some of the entries are difficult to read, as if written on the brink of sleep or despair.

WHY?

I shout after waking. I shout it to no avail.

*My captors tease me with compassion, but leave me only with the company of my thoughts. Dreams of you are all that I cling to. You reach for me in a field of green, and we walk the water's edge. We lie down in the summer and watch the clouds pass. I hold this locket to my heart, open it to see your loving face. I am tempted to touch your photo but too afraid it will blot the image.*

*It is all I have.*

*And just when I think I cannot wake another day without you, my savior appeared. With grizzled bush upon my face, I pushed curly locks from my eyes to see him enter the room*

*And he is nothing what I expected.*

AN ALARM GOES OFF.

Oliver drops the journal, accidentally prying the cover until the spine cracks. He touches the phone's screen, turning off the alarm. The time passed too fast.

It's the last entry in that journal.

There's no time to find the next one. He makes sure he's not leaving anything behind, squeezing the orb in his pocket and feeling the surge of confidence before closing the door behind him.

He makes it to the clearing, the sun hanging above the mountains.

A sharp whistle echoes off the trees.

Henry and Helen exit the far side from about the same spot they entered. One of them is waving. Oliver waits at the edge of the forest, rubbing his ears, watching them trek through the snow. Henry, with the black stocking cap pulled down to his eyes, starts running. He scoops up a ball of snow and throws it. It falls short of Oliver.

Oliver's head is already cold.

He starts to ask for his cap back, but Henry puts him in a head-lock, thumping his scalp with his knuckle.

"Good doggie."

His coat smells like smoke.

Oliver pulls his frozen ears out of the arm-vise. He falls on his hands and knees. Just like a dog.

"Hey, come on." Henry yanks him up. "You did good, waited for us just like I said. Maybe you can come next time."

"Can I have my cap?"

"Not until we get back."

Oliver's ears are burning.

He can't stop frowning, but it doesn't bother Henry. It only makes the smile widen. Oliver can't wait until they're gone. He starts for the house, forcing himself not to run.

Helen is still behind them. Oliver isn't waiting for them. He's stomping a path back to the house, where he can get a shower and rinse the cold from his bones.

Maybe they'll be gone by the time he's out.

Henry shouts at his sister to hurry. Oliver buries his hands, now colder than his ears, deep into his pockets and hunches his shoulders when something moves in the trees near him.

The snow falls from branches just inside the tree line.

Something is lurking.

FOOP.

It shoots between the branches.

It arches high and hard.

A snowball, something the size of a basketball, rotates as it peaks. Oliver watches it fly over his head and descend.

All the way to Henry's face.

The stocking cap flies off, landing twenty feet behind him. He falls backwards, arms and legs out, landing flat in the snow. Oliver, with his hands in his pockets, watches his cousin rise up, his face as red as a flame. He shakes the dizziness away and looks around.

And finds Oliver.

His face turns a shade darker as he crawls to his feet and begins running. Oliver looks back at the trees, wondering if Henry saw it, too. Although Oliver didn't see what threw it, maybe Henry did. *Why didn't he dodge it?*

Henry buries his shoulder into Oliver's chest.

Oliver goes down, eating snow all the way to the soil.

Henry lands on his back with all his weight, driving him into the frozen ground. Oliver can't draw a breath, struggles to find air as Henry rolls him like a log and drops his knees into Oliver's stomach.

Oliver gasps like a speared fish.

The side of Henry's face is starting to swell. Spittle bubbles in the corners of his mouth. He grabs handfuls of Oliver's coat.

"Stop!" Helen closes in on them. "Get off him!"

Henry slams Oliver's head off the ground.

The world is washed in light, but pain is overridden by the desperation to breathe. Snow falls over them as Helen slides into Henry, wrapping her arms around him. Oliver rolls onto his hands and knees and, finally, finds his first breath.

Drool dangles from his lower lip.

"He didn't throw it," Helen pleads. "Ollie didn't do it."

"What?"

"It came from the trees. I saw it, Henry. I swear, Ollie didn't throw it."

"Who did?"

"I think...I don't know."

Henry is huffing through clamped teeth, looking at the trees and back to Oliver. His gelled hair has been sculpted into a rogue wave. He starts toward Oliver, but Helen gets between them.

"Don't." She pushes him. "You drag him inside with a bloody nose and Grandmother will tie you to a stump."

He wipes his nose and checks the back of his hand. It's swiped with blood. He spits red, staining the snow.

"Who's over there?" he shouts.

He takes a step and stops, looking back at Helen. If someone is in there, he's not too eager.

"It came from the trees," she says.

"What's that mean, it came from the trees? Did you see him or not?"

*See him?*

"I don't know! I just saw it, that's all."

He spits again.

There's a long pause between them, unspoken words not meant for Oliver. They know what's out there but don't want to admit it, not in front of Oliver. Or to themselves. Hands on his hips, he wanders over to the trees, but doesn't enter the forest. He points at the spot, and Helen nods. A few more steps. And that's it.

He doesn't say another thing, doesn't come to shake Oliver like a broken toy or kick snow in his face. He heads back to the house.

Helen helps Oliver stand, wiping the snow off his coat. He sees his reflection in her glasses, his cheeks pink and scuffed.

"Wipe your nose."

He rakes his hand across his upper lip. A faint red blur remains on his hand. She pinches his nose, then straightens his coat. Without saying a word, she follows her brother's footsteps leading to the house.

A headache begins to blossom while Oliver catches his breath. He feels shaky, too. It'd be good to get inside and check his sugar. First, he waits until both twins are in the house. Oliver trundles out to the clearing, his legs cold and nervous. He finds the buried stocking cap and knocks the snow off before pulling it over his ears.

Something looms in the tree's shadows, right where Henry's tracks stopped short. Snow falls from the branches.

And then it's gone.

# 8

———

Oliver finishes shoveling the circle drive.

The night of the mystery snowball brought a light dusting. He leans on the handle, looking down the spotless entry drive, contemplating where the snowball had come from. Someone had to throw it.

Once Aunt Rhonnie and the twins left, he realized the obvious hadn't freaked him out. *Someone had to throw it.* A snowball doesn't just spontaneously launch from the trees with the precision of a rifle. The thing that didn't occur to him until he was lying in bed was the obvious:

*Henry and Helen weren't freaking out.*

They were scared, but not freaked. Strangers don't come out to the property; they don't hang out in the woods and toss random snowballs. Henry and Helen weren't shocked at all. They were scared. They knew who was out there.

Or what.

Whatever threw the snowball meant to hit Henry, to knock the stocking cap off his head.

Holding the straps of his backpack around his shoulders, Oliver jogs to the side of the house and leans against the wall, just below the family room window. He'd like to hide in the garage and read another journal.

*Who threw the snowball?*

The thought causes his heart to work harder. He swallows the fear and clenches his fists, mumbling, "You can do it, Oliver. You can do it, you can do it, you can do it—"

He leaps before his thoughts change to *go to your room and hide.*

Eyes fixed on the trees, arms stiff at his sides, he marches across the backyard. His heart swells into his throat as he nears the darkness between the tree trunks. He ducks beneath the heavy branches, can hardly feel his legs as he forces his way into the shade.

Turning left, he forges toward the clearing like a nutcracker soldier, stepping quickly and stiffly. Nothing moves deep in the forest; snow doesn't fall from the branches. Nothing jumps out to greet him.

He reaches the forest's edge.

*Nothing at all.*

Oliver leans against a tree, staring into the shadows. There are no hulking figures, no snapping branches or mystery footsteps—just his raspy breath. He could go deeper, but he doubts his heart could take it. Besides, there's one more thing to find.

He looks across the wide field.

Their tracks have vanished as all tracks do on the property. It doesn't matter. Oliver starts across the open field, keeping his eyes on the sparse trees near the twins' exit point.

When he reaches the other side, he checks the compass app on his phone. He'd been camping enough to know that trees can all look alike. He gets his bearings, thinking north seemed a little more to the left the last time he checked the compass.

Maybe he didn't calibrate it.

The trees are long and stringy between hulking trunks of mammoth conifers. He makes a mental note of the bark chewed off a large poplar, maybe a woodchuck or a beaver. Still no tracks to follow. He moves side to side, searching for a trail or broken branches. The snow isn't as deep, but he grows weary and bored. This feels too far. The twins aren't nature lovers.

There's another poplar missing bark.

It looks just like the other one.

He gets closer and notices footprints. *It is the same one!*

He didn't turn around, he's sure of it. The compass is reading north slightly to the right this time. The app is broke. *That's great. Get lost in the woods looking for the twins' secret. If the weather doesn't kill me, Henry will.*

He takes a moment to consider which way leads back home when he hears something splash. In between the blood pumping in his ears, he hears it again.

He follows the sound instead of the compass, where the land begins to slope downward. He climbs over a fallen tree. Then another. Ahead, branches litter the ground, some the size of telephone poles. The tops of trees are broken in various locations, some dead, bent and hanging.

*This is where the forest rumbles.*

He'd been sleeping through the nightly ruckus lately, even wondering if he'd been imagining its odd nature. Maybe that's just how it was supposed to sound near the mountains.

The rushing water is beyond an uprooted cedar.

Oliver hikes around a tangle of vines and nearly steps in an oversized hole.

Heart leaping, he looks down the gullet of a ten-foot-wide sinkhole—the smooth sides funneling deep into the ground.

Pebbles splash into a dark pool at the bottom.

*No coming out of that.*

He walks around, watching the ground for another potential death pit. The rushing water grows louder. Ahead, a deep trench is carved from the ground, snaking along the base of a steep slope like a scar. Oliver approaches warily, grabbing a sapling sprouted near the edge. An innocent stream runs across the bottom; debris caught in the rocky sides suggests stronger currents when snowmelt comes off the mountains. He leans forward, feeling the cool, humid updraft from the frigid waters.

Ice breaks under his boot.

Oliver's balance spills forward. He grabs the sapling with both hands and spins around as the backpack sways. His foot finds the sharp edge of a stone.

The young tree bends and cracks, but holds his weight. He hugs the tree and pulls himself onto solid footing, falling into the soft bed of needles.

His heart is full throttle.

That's a sign. As soon as the feeling returns to his legs, he's heading back to the house. Whatever the twins were doing can remain a secret.

He follows the stream, keeping a safe distance from the edge while watching for sinkholes until he's ready to turn south for the house. Tree debris increases. Up ahead, the gorge turns north where a fallen cottonwood spans the shores, its roots upturned on the opposite bank.

Oliver pauses.

He should go back to the house and warm up, that's the smart thing to do. It wouldn't hurt to look, though. He'd come all this way, braved two brushes with one-way trips into hypothermic water.

*Just a look.*

He makes his way to the broken tree.

The bark is smooth, and the leaves long fallen away. Rot has hollowed out several openings where branches once grew. He climbs through the debris and finds a clearing on the opposite side, a narrow trail that weaves to the foot of the shore, where flat stones lead up to the massive trunk.

He tests his footing.

The trunk is plenty wide and, strangely enough, somewhat flat. He wouldn't even have to step like a tight-rope walker, rather walk as if this were a sidewalk. The surface looks dry and tacky.

Oliver looks back. He knows he should turn around, play it safe. Let the twins do whatever it is they do. That would be the smart move.

*Not this time.*

He keeps his eyes on the radial roots fanning the opposite bank.

Oliver always follows directions. He's never had detention, never received a demerit or failed to apologize for a conflict regardless of who's at fault. If a sign says "Keep Off Lawn," he walks in the opposite direction.

Today, Oliver takes his first step on the forbidden lawn.

His legs become colder when he's over the water.

Refusing to look down, he feels the icy updraft. The water echoes from below, warning all warm-blooded animals to stay out.

Halfway across, with his arms out to the sides, he notices a stack of boulders on the rising slope. Across the river, the ground looks like jagged outcroppings over granite, but this pile is out of place—a pyramid of rounded stones.

There's another set of stone steps at the end of the natural footbridge. Oliver climbs down while holding onto stray roots until he's firmly on the ground.

*Footprints.*

The tracks lead around the array of root flares.

Oliver follows the skinny trail with convenient roots to grab. It goes up the hill, and then, without warning, the tracks vanish. He finds a snowless hollow beneath a rocky ledge where the base of the great tree was uprooted.

The pyramid of rocks is to the right of the opening.

His phone does little to illuminate the depths. He pauses after each step, looking behind him before taking another. The hollow is deeper and darker than expected, more than what the roots would've excavated.

*Two more steps*, he promises. *I'm not going to wake up a grizzly.*

The earthen cave continues beyond the light's reach. He's about to turn around when he sees the L-shaped root.

Maybe he wouldn't have noticed if there were other sticks or roots this far inside, but it's the only thing attached to the wall.

A light dizziness fills his head.

He lays his hand on the dry, gnarly root.

*Click.*

An earthen door swings on soundless hinges. Inside is a dark stone hearth with hand-carved chairs. The smell of soot lingers.

Oliver slams the door and runs to the foot of the upturned tree.

*There's a room inside this hill.*

*A room!*

He should leave. That's the smart thing.

He should go back to the house and hide in his room, check his blood sugar, take it easy, and no one gets hurt. That's what he always does.

Plays it safe.

This time there's something in his belly besides icy fear.

Excitement.

He squeezes the wooden orb.

Against every instinct he's accumulated his entire life, he turns around. He goes back to the door. Standing on the threshold, he stares into the warm confines, blinking rapidly as if, any moment, the illusion will vanish and he'll be staring at a mud hole instead of a furnished room.

Oliver steps inside.

It's a simple room with an arching ceiling that's just within reach.

Although the coarse walls and hand-carved furniture befits a hobbit, the space is almost full-sized but not quite. There's a small table with candles against the wall and a rug on the cedar floor.

A small window is to his right, a circular port that one would expect to see on a ship. He peers through the dusky glass. Mirrors are positioned to reflect the light through a short tunnel draped with cobwebs. He sees the fallen tree bridging the stream.

Henry and Helen couldn't have possibly built this place.

It's been carved from granite. And there's a fireplace that funnels up to the pyramid of stones that, individually, are too large for a grown man to lift.

His phone sounds off. A message has arrived.

A shiver slithers down his spine.

He hasn't heard that sound since they arrived on the property. Oliver pulls the phone out and slides his thumb across the glass.

*151 unread messages.*

He's getting five bars of reception.

The instinct to bolt out of this place overrides all other thoughts. Only the numbness in his knees keeps him from running.

And the excitement. The curiosity.

*How is it that I'm getting reception in a place more remote than the house?*

He falls into one of the chairs and scrolls through his messages.

He begins downloading his books.

He updates his apps and checks social media.

Occasionally, he gets up to look through the window and open the door. He's warm and alone with no chores to do or tea to drink. And now he knows why Henry and Helen trek out here.

And why they're keeping it secret.

OLIVER EMERGES from his phone trance. It takes a moment to realize his mistake.

*The sun has set.*

He fumbles toward the door but returns to put everything in order, just like he found it. In the dark alcove, he stops. The roots look like knobby claws in the dusky light, but that's not what sends a shiver up his throat.

Leaves are stirring, twigs snapping.

*The forest is waking up.*

He creeps to the edge, squeezing the wooden orb in his pocket for strength and confidence. For luck. Something quakes above him. Rocks trickle down the hill. His knees almost quit. Oliver pulls the backpack straps tight against his shoulders and eyes the stone steps leading around the tree. The next disturbance is closer.

Oliver shoots for the exit.

An avalanche of stems and leaves slide down the slope.

Oliver swiftly climbs the stones and swings onto the tree, speed-walking across the river with his arms held out to the sides.

His eyes fill with water.

He keeps focused on his steps. The water, cloaked in dying light, calls from below. He's almost across, only three steps to go, when the tree vibrates.

Something stepped onto the bridge.

Oliver takes one giant leap off the tree, stumbling down the stones and into a thicket of vines and branches. The wooden orb flies from his hand, disappearing into the snow.

The fallen tree groans behind him.

Oliver scrambles to his feet, blindly sprinting through a world blurred with tears and panic, pulling at ropey vines and tangled branches, tripping on stones. Ignoring where he's going or what's in front of him, he pushes ahead—

And slams into a wall.

If it was a tree or a boulder, he'd be unconscious. Oliver bounces on his backpack, flails to his knees, wiping the tears to see what's in front of him: two enormous stumps of snow.

*Legs.*

He grinds the heels of his hands into his eyes.

Ten feet tall.

Thick body and long arms.

Head like a turret.

*It can't be.*

A snowman looks down.

Branches are breaking. The ground trembles. Before Oliver sees what's coming, the snowman sweeps him off the ground. The wind shrieks in his ears, ripping the stocking cap from his head. A wintry blast hardens his cheeks and fills his head. Tree trunks fly past and disappear. Then the open field is all around.

The world is spinning.

It happens so fast that he's unaware of when the spinning stops or how he ends up lying in the snow, the screech of the windmill nearby.

The acrid taste of vomit stings his throat.

Oliver looks up at the massive form. Again, he wipes his eyes.

Twilight highlights the hulking figure, snow like sparkling skin. It remains still, and, for a moment, sanity returns, and the thing looks like an intricately carved figure of snow, not something that picked him up and flew him across the forest.

*I am not an "it."*

Just like that, reality tilts back into fantasy.

The snowman is not an "it." Oliver thought that. No, he heard it. He thinks he heard it..."him"...think it...and Oliver heard him think it.

The weird fills his head.

It's the blood sugar weird feeling, a weird-weird feeling combined. It's falling off a cliff of reality and waiting to land.

The snowman's chest inflates.

Something's inside him, a source of light beaming through the snow, illuminating his body as he bends over, reaches out and wraps his hands around Oliver's arms and pulls him up.

The snowman opens Oliver's hand and drops the wooden orb into it. It vibrates through his arm.

"Oliver!" Mom calls.

The snowman straightens up and turns toward the windmill. It steps back and, just before dissolving into a shimmering flurry, tosses the stocking cap on Oliver's lap. The once massive form swirls into the forest like a sparkling cloud of diamonds, no footsteps left to follow. In the midst of the snowy dust, something glimmers.

*A metallic sphere.*

"Oliver!" Mom runs into the open field.

She sees him. Snow has filled her open-laced boots, and her coat is unbuttoned. "We've been looking for you. Where have you been?"

"I'm sorry. I got...turned around."

He keeps looking at the trees. There's a light, a shimmering light that lingers.

"Are you all right?"

"What?"

Mom looks where he's staring. "What is it?"

"I don't know."

She walks closer to the trees. The light goes out.

Grandmother is behind them. Her arm is tucked inside a long black coat. Mom takes Oliver's arm. Her fingers are cold and quivering. Grandmother waits for them to approach, silently scolding. He apologizes again.

She turns her back and leads the way home.

As she slides her arm out of her coat, he catches a glint of a metal glove.

---

## 9

Grandmother watches Oliver descend the staircase.

He slides his hand over the ornate post marking the end of the bannister. Arms crossed and lips chiseled, she nods.

Oliver turns around and begins his third ascent.

His legs are beginning to burn, but he's okay with that because none of this makes sense. The world has rules; existence has limits. The sun rises in the east, diabetes is incurable, *and snowmen aren't alive!*

The universe has laws. A snowman that can fly him across a field is not part of those laws. A snowman putting thoughts in his head, either. The world doesn't make sense anymore.

*He's not an "it."*

"What are you doing?" Mom is outside the second floor bathroom, toothbrush in mouth.

"Grandmother told me to walk the steps."

"Why?"

"Exercise." *Punishment. I'm not going outside anymore.*

"Ridiculous," she mutters. "Get your things. We're going to the library."

Oliver looks back. Grandmother can't see them, but Mom's voice carries through the house.

"Go on, get your backpack. I'll meet you at the car."

He picks up the pace, pushing through the muscle burn. The stairs squeal with glee. He packs books and magazines into his backpack. Checking the door, he grabs the journals from hiding and slides them between the magazines. He needs to get out of the house.

*Off the property.*

He returns to the staircase.

"What about lunch?" Grandmother says.

"We'll grab something," Mom says. "Do you need anything while we're out?"

Oliver pauses on the bottom step while Mom pulls on her coat, keys rattling in her hand.

"Do you need anything?" she repeats.

Grandmother shakes her head. Lips pursed.

"All right, then. We'll be back for supper. Come on, Oliver."

Oliver goes around his grandmother, turning so the backpack faces away, fearing her x-ray vision will see the journals.

"Bye, Grandmother."

He pulls the door behind him, but she follows him out. Oliver runs to the car. Mom drives around the turnabout, lines scraped across the icy windshield. Grandmother watches them leave from the front porch.

Mom twists one of her earrings. "You all right, kiddo?"

He nods. She sounds confident, but she's playing with her earrings. She'd be terrible at poker.

He looks out his window, feeling the rules of the universe come into balance the farther they get from the property. Maybe if he closes his eyes, he'll wake up in Texas and discover they never moved to Grandmother's, that he imagined secret journals and a hobbit house in the woods.

A snowman.

He feels the wooden orb in his coat pocket.

"Anything weird ever happen to you?" Oliver asks.

"What?"

"Have you ever seen anything, you know...weird?"

She's coming out of her driving trance, twisting her earring.

"Growing up on the property, I mean." He can't tell her the truth. She'd send him to therapy and blame Grandmother. "Did you ever, like, see anything in the woods? Anything strange."

"Strange."

Oliver stares through the windshield. She's frowning—confused not angry. "No," she says. "Have you?"

"No."

"Did something happen last night?"

"No, no. I just mean...it gets weird at night, you know? Funny noises and things, that's all." He glances at her. "You know what I mean?"

"You having bad dreams again? We can move you to the second floor. There's a room next to mine."

"No. I just wondered if, you know, you've seen anything weird. That's all."

"I have." She twists the steering wheel. "Your grandmother and Aunt Rhonnie."

Oliver chuckles.

Mom begins to laugh.

Before long, she's in a fit of laughter that's spilling pent-up emotions. She wipes away tears and, just when it seems like she's done, lets go of another round.

"Family is weird." She sighs.

THE LIBRARY IS OLD.

It's the kind with water-stained ceiling tiles and faded carpet. The air is thick with aging books.

Oliver checks his phone. His ebooks have already been down-loaded, emails and texts received, reminding him that the hobbit

house was not a dream. The memories of rushing water and wood-
land pursuit bring a wave of nausea.

"You look lost." A girl pushes a squeaking cart past him.

He holds up his phone. "Password?"

"You need an account to use the wifi."

"Oh, yeah. Sure. How do I...?"

"Come on."

The name tag on her *Doctor Who* T-shirt says Molly.

He follows her to the circulation desk. She abandons the squeaky
cart and leans over one of the counters. Her braided brunette ponytail has a streak of candy-apple red weaved into it.

She slides a form at him.

"Bring it to me if Ms. Chatty Pants is still busy." She nods at the
heavyset librarian. Before Oliver can say thanks, she's back at her
cart.

He fills out the form and waits for Ms. Chatty Pants, who, without
breaking away from her conversation about her gifted grandchildren,
takes it to process.

Instead of waiting, Oliver scouts the library.

He goes through the nonfiction section and snags an oversized
book on his way to a dark corner behind a rack of magazines. Settling
in, he opens his backpack and, not without looking up and down the
aisles, hides one of the journals in the oversized hardback.

Cracking the journal open, he's reminded of what really old
paper smells like. He looks around before slumping deep into the
chair.

The weird sensation he left on the property finds him.

NOG IS HIS NAME.

*But I'm getting ahead of myself. My head is a storm of thoughts that
blow like dust. The Arctic is not what we thought, my love.*

*People live here. Well, not people.*

*Nog is half my height and as round as the moon. His cherub cheeks are
buried in his bushy beard, and his green eyes glitter beneath thick brows.*

*He is more than short, my love, barely up to my waist. He slid into the room on bare feet as wide as paddles. He appeared to be a man.*

*An elven, he said he is. An elven.*

THERE'S a crude sketch of a cubicle with two men and a bed. One of them is twice as tall as the other. Several more sketches take up the next couple of pages. Some are abstract scribbles with resemblances to faces and bodies lost in a mess of static.

The last of the sketches is a very round man with a thick beard lying over his belly. His sausage fingers extend from fuzzy sleeves, and his wide feet have tufts of hair on the toes.

HE ASKED ME TO SIT.

*A great peace fell over me. It was like an angel had spoken, his words filling me with love. He said to me, "Welcome to the North Pole, Malcolm Toye."*

*I was startled. "How do you know my name?"*

*"That is not for now," he said. But he told me, in great detail, of the Jeanette Arctic expedition with Lt. Cdr. DeLong. He knew of the ship becoming lodged in the ice and our hellish escape.*

*"You were dying of malnutrition," he told me. "And hypothermia."*

*"Where am I?" I demanded.*

*"Inside the Arctic ice."*

*I did not have the clarity to ask how that was possible. How could there be a perfectly square room cut from the ice floating on the Arctic Ocean? Where would this bed come from? Food and clothing?*

*Yet I stared at a person built more like a snowshoe hare than a man. "What are you?" I blurted in the most unapologetic way.*

*My manners did not harm his disposition. Perhaps he expected it. He folded his hands atop his plump belly and drew a deep breath before answering. He explained that he and others like him were an ancient race that evolved during the Ice Age. That is when I first heard him say elven.*

*I must admit, I felt a small sense of vertigo at that moment, yet I observed this short, fat, and hairy man that appeared to be built for the cold.*

THERE ARE MORE RANDOM SKETCHES, as if he had been trying to clear his mind or make sense of his words. Much of the illustrations are, once again, lost in scribbles, but there's one of a very large foot. It's bent to reveal a sole covered with V-shaped lines. An arrow points at the sharp texture and is labeled "scales."

This would explain the ability to slide over the ice. The sharp ends of the scales, pointing at the heel, would grab the ice to shove forward. Lying flat, they would glide.

*"WHERE ARE THE OTHERS?" I demanded.*

*"It is best that you talk with me," he said. "For now."*

*He took my hands and turned them over. I appeared to be a giant in his company, yet felt like a child. His pudgy fingers were smothered with wrinkles. Next, he inspected my feet. I let him examine the slightly numb and off-colored flesh.*

*"Frostbite," he said. My core temperature had dropped to fifty-seven degrees Fahrenheit. I never should have lived.*

*How did I?*

*I was rescued, was all he said.*

*And the others? The men on the journey? I had vague recollections of them suffering as I did. He confirmed the worst of my memories, that many had succumbed to the dire conditions. But not all of them, he claimed. Some had made it home. I know not if that filled me with hope or dread. I think, when I lie in bed, that his tone suggested I have lived, but am I going home?*

*He told me that human expeditions were venturing closer to the North Pole, that soon our race will traverse the ice with ease. I felt mild surprise that he referred to my "race" as if he was not human. Strange as he may be, I still considered him to be human.*

*This was my first mistake.*

*"Why?" I muttered. "Why save me?"*

*He stood to his fullest height. We were eye to eye, for I was sitting on the bed, when he reached for me, retrieving the locket from around my neck. It looked so large in his hand. He lifted it, as if to say this was the reason.*

*That you, my love, are the reason.*

"DID YOU FIND THE DIRTY MAGAZINES?"

Oliver launches the book against the wall. The journal bounces on the carpet. For a moment, it feels like the entire library sees the open journal. Before he can sweep it into his backpack, Molly picks it up.

"This is really old. Did you get it here?"

"No. I mean, yes. I mean, I was just reading..." He takes it from her. One of the corners is dog-eared from the fall. "It's mine, I brought it. I swear."

"Don't forget your book on succulents in the Southwest." She holds out the oversized hardback he was using to hide the journal. "And you're pretending to read it? Cute."

Oliver accepts the botanical textbook and, despite being the property of the library, stuffs it into his book bag with the journal. When the bag is zipped, he sits back and stares, waiting for her to leave. A steady beat bleeds from the earbuds slung over her shoulders.

"You really live at the Toye property?"

"How did you..."

She holds a plastic card between her fingers. The library card is crisp and warm.

"I thought it was just the widow living there."

"That's my grandmother. It's just temporary."

"Temporary how?" she asks. "Days? Weeks?"

"So far."

Her funny look shifts to confusion. "You going to school?"

"Homeschool."

"So you stay there all the time?"

"So far."

Molly looks around, but no one's in sight. Still, she leans in. "What's it like out there? No one's seen the property in, like, thirty years, not even Google Maps. Check it out; there's like a distortion field blurring the details of that place."

"What?"

"I'm just saying, your grandmother keeps to herself. What's it like out there?"

*What's it like?*

How does he answer that? His tyrannical, choremaster grandmother is a shut-in. His lunatic aunt is a narcissist, and his cousin is most likely to be indicted on a future felony. There's no wireless service in the haunted house, but there's service in a hobbit hovel stashed in the woods surrounded by monster-things.

And there's the snowman.

"It's cool," he says. "So, you know."

Molly waits for more. Instead, she takes the hint. "Well, get back to your old dirty book."

"It's not a...dirty..."

But she's already plugged her ears with music buds. A few minutes later, a wheel squeaks across the library.

Oliver checks the time.

His mom won't be back for another hour. He sits quietly for a few minutes. He shouldn't let what just happened bother him. Besides, this is his chance to read the journals. Once he's back on the property, reality will blend with fantasy.

He might never find his way back.

He searches his coat pockets and finds the wooden orb, runs his thumbnail through the intricate grooves. The snowman saved him from whatever's across the river that comes out at night. *Is that why Grandmother won't let me stay out after dark? Of course it is. And that means she knows what's out there. But does she know about the snowman?*

He carried Oliver across the field and fled just before Mom got there, but not before revealing a glint of metal. And that reminds him of the plans from the filing cabinet, the ones that called for a metal sphere the size of a softball. It looked like the one in his hand.

*It's all a dream.*

But no matter how many times he thinks it, he just can't believe it's a dream.

Because this is happening.

Molly's crossing the library. The squeaky cart stops somewhere in the fiction section. Oliver swaps the orb for his phone and pulls up Google Earth. It takes a few minutes to find the location and load the graphics. He goes to Street View and scrolls down the main road until he finds the gates leading toward the property. From there, he zooms up to a satellite view and swipes toward the house.

It's a green blur of trees. The house is a nondescript blob centered in a patch of fuzzy snow.

*Not even Google Earth knows.*

Oliver packs up and begins looking down the aisles. He finds her filing novels in the K-L section. With her back turned and head bouncing to music, he waits for her to turn around. When she does, the books fly out of her hands.

She shouts in surprise, quickly covering her mouth.

"I'm sorry," Oliver says.

"Don't sneak up on me like that." She pulls out an earbud and playfully shoves him.

"Sorry, sorry." He squats down to pick up the books. "How did you know about Google Earth?"

"What?"

"My grandmother's property. You said it wasn't on Google Earth."

"Everyone knows." She begins shelving books and, like before, looks around before whispering, "No offense, but the place is haunted. I mean, ever since your grandfather disappeared, Ms. Toye hardly ever leaves the place."

"What do you mean 'disappeared'?"

"No one has seen him in decades. All I know is that people around here are a little weirded out about the Toye property. No one goes near it; no one knows what goes on out there. When she calls for groceries to be delivered, people say it's creepy. You know, like that feeling you get when you just know something's hiding around the corner."

Oliver's stomach drops.

"And then you can't see it on Google Earth. I mean, North Korea hasn't even figured out how to block satellite images. You all right?"

"Yeah. Low blood sugar. What else?"

"You need to sit?"

He waves her off even though the shelves are beginning to swish. "I'm fine, really. What else do you know?"

She studies him for a moment. Oliver watches her sway. She knows something about the property. Everybody does. Why didn't he think of that before? There must be stories about the Toye property. The house has been there for over a century. There have to be urban legends, too.

*Every urban legend has a grain of truth.*

"Come on." Molly abandons the cart. "You're turning into a ghost."

Not until he falls into a chair does he realize how wobbly his knees have become. She pulls a bottle of water from the fishnet pocket on his backpack.

"Are you diabetic?"

He nods while taking a sip.

"The shot kind?"

"Is there another kind?"

"My grandma controlled hers by diet, that's all I'm saying."

"Type 2."

"I guess." She watches him drink. He's thirstier than he thought. "Do they hurt?"

That's usually the first question. He shakes his head and returns the bottle. "So what else do you—"

"Molly?" Ms. Chatty Pants librarian approaches. "Is everything all right?"

Molly explains that Oliver needed help finding a book. Good call. People can get weird when they meet their first real diabetic. *The shot kind.*

The gold chains around her neck are wedged beneath her second chin. She suggests Molly finish shelving her cart.

"Can I help you find something?"

"No, thanks." Oliver holds up the succulents textbook. "I got it."

Ms. Chatty Pants raises an eyebrow. There's a long moment of uncomfortable silence before Molly says, "Okay, good. I'll see you later."

"Wait." Oliver grabs her arm. "Can I...I mean, I might need more help about...you know, what you were saying."

Molly pulls out her phone. A few seconds later, his phone buzzes. She goes back to her squeaky cart. Ms. Chatty Pants pauses long enough to make sure Molly doesn't return before going to the circulation desk.

He reads the text. *Smile Café. Tomorrow morning at 9.*

He punches the phone number into his address book, types "Molly." He still feels a little dizzy when he stands. He stays in Ms. Chatty Pants's line of sight while walking toward the fiction section. At the K-L aisle, he snaps a photo.

Molly bobbing her head.

# 10

M om drops Oliver off at the town square in the morning.

He walks past storefronts, his reflection passing large plate glass windows with painted letters. Inside are dance studios and law offices, a bookstore and hairstylists. The Smile Café is on the far corner. Molly is in the front window, sunk into a low sofa chair.

A bell rings when he opens the door.

The smell of ground coffee beans and toasted bagels rides on a thick wave of Bob Dylan. Molly is wearing a Ramones T-shirt with black leggings and fuzzy wristbands. She looks up from her iPad and smiles. He hadn't noticed the gap between her front teeth in the library. Maybe she hadn't smiled quite like that.

"Get the chocolate pecan." She raises her cup.

Oliver goes to the counter and orders what she said. "You want room for cream?" the barista asks.

He doesn't know what that means, so he nods. She comes back with a tall, hot cup of coffee. Oliver passes a small platform, a miniature stage for poetry slams and acoustic guitarists, and places it on a small table. It smells better than Mom's coffee.

"I got you a present." Molly slides a gift bag across the table. She dumps out the contents. A book hits the table.

*The Wonderful World of Succulents.*

It takes a moment to make the connection with the book he was using in the library. "I saw it at The Little Professor. It was just sitting in the window, isn't that weird? I just had to buy it."

"Thanks."

He leafs through the glossy pages while Molly hums along to Dylan's "Like a Rolling Stone." She loves Dylan, she says, but doesn't think he really knows how to play the harmonica. Now Neil Young, she says, he can play. Oliver agrees without conviction. He streams radio for background noise, not deeper meaning.

Molly sinks into her low chair, duct tape hiding cracks in the vinyl armrests, and begins a countdown of her favorite folk singers.

"Things are weird," Oliver blurts.

The words exploded from his chest, shot off his tongue like lead weights. The admission lifts the suffocating feeling. His shoulders wilt, and, for a moment, he's afraid he'll tear up.

His whole life he's wanted to tell someone that.

He's always felt like an outcast. A weirdo. He didn't quite realize it until he blurted it out. He could never tell his mom, and he's only known this gap-toothed hipster for less than a day. But he said it, just like that.

"What kind of weird?"

He stutters as his filters engage. He can't tell her everything. People have their limits for weird, even Molly. But how to start? And where? He feels himself backtracking into panic.

"The journal," he spits out. "The book I was reading in the library, it's my great-grandfather's journal."

He pulls the leather-bound book from his backpack. He only brought the first one—the one that's mostly normal. Molly's eyes get big. She pulls her other earbud out and opens it, running her fingers over the worn cover and yellowed pages while Oliver tells her about the historic journey that ended in tragedy.

The words thaw his tongue, so he keeps going. He tells her about his grandmother's old mansion and the chores and exercise; how he's required to be in the house before dark and if you touch the frozen windmill, you get zapped.

She flips the pages, one at a time.

"Very cool," she says. "That's worth, like, a fortune."

"There's more."

He tells her about the garage and the car, the footlocker below, but not what's in the other journals. Despite what he's read, he's still not convinced these aren't simply diaries of a madman.

"I wish I had something like that. I didn't even know my grandparents." She sits back, twirling her candy-red swatch of hair. "I'm sorry about yesterday. I shouldn't have come up and asked all those questions. We're not supposed to be looking through people's personal information."

He fidgets. "I want to know about the property."

"Where you from?"

"All over. Florida, Georgia, Louisiana...just about every Southern state, really. Moved here from Texas."

"Why?"

"Mom lost her job."

"Sorry." She shakes her head. "I need to shut up now."

"No, please don't. I just...I want you to tell me everything you know. It's just...I'd like to find out what others think."

He can't tell her he doesn't trust anyone on the property to tell him the truth. His mom doesn't know it, and his grandmother is hiding it.

"Well, I don't know everything, but here's what most people think. In case you haven't noticed, it snows here a lot. Your grandmother orders out for supplies, and every deliveryperson says the entry road is always plowed, as in spotless."

"Okay."

"That's not so weird except that no one has a contract to plow her property. People have checked into it, and no one has ever admitted to helping her."

"Maybe it's someone with a truck and a snowblade."

"Nope."

"Maybe she made them swear to secrecy."

"Yeah, maybe. Only no one has ever seen equipment enter or leave her property. The county plow says that every time he does the main road, her drive is always clean and there are no tracks leaving. I mean, she could be plowing the road herself, sure. It's just everyone says it's always clean right down to the asphalt, like a snowflake never touched it."

"Maybe the road melts it, like heating coils."

"I suppose. Only folks say it's been like that for as long as they can remember, way before technology like that was ever thought about."

Oliver's heard weirder things, but she has a point. He shovels the roundabout, but the road is always clear no matter what time he wakes up. And why is it that tracks disappear in the field even when it doesn't snow?

"It used to be, way before you and me were born, that people just assumed your grandfather was doing all the work. But then twenty-seven years ago he went missing."

Oliver does the math. His mom would have been ten years old—about the time she went to boarding school.

"I don't think anyone would've known about it since he was just as reclusive as your grandmother, but he was always the one that picked up deliveries and signed checks and paid bills. One day, it all stopped. Not long after, your grandmother takes his name off all the accounts, changes her will, and pretty much erases his name off the deed. People in town got suspicious, so the police went out to see if everything was all right.

"When they kept asking questions, lawyers started threatening lawsuits for harassment. Add to that your grandmother owns half the buildings in town and funds most of the schools, well, folks left her alone. After a while, they all just forgot. Your grandparents never hurt anyone, and they left it at that. But no one's seen him since. And that road is still clean."

He doesn't know much about his grandfather. Mom didn't exactly carry family photos. But as far as he knows, there are no tractors on the property, and he'd never heard anything clearing the road. He always assumed that whoever was doing it arrived early.

*Or at night.*

"What do you think happens?" he asks.

She takes a long sip and thinks. For a moment, she looks lost in the music. "Well, some people think she's got zombies. Others think it's robots or slaves. There's one group that believes she hypnotizes animals to do it."

"What?"

"Yeah. And hunters swear the closer they get to her property, the fewer animals they see."

The perfect silence on the property hits that urban legend close to home. He's never seen a squirrel or heard a bird.

"But the weird thing," she continues, "is that every deliveryperson swears there's something watching them as they drive up the road. There's always an envelope waiting on the front porch where they dump the supplies, but no one ever comes out. But someone is always watching."

"The house has this window on the top floor. Sort of looks like an eye, maybe that's what they mean."

"Maybe. Doubt it." She shrugs. "Here's another thing: she doesn't receive power from the city, or propane or wood from local suppliers. And there are no records the house has ever been on the municipal power grid since it was built in 1901. That wouldn't be so strange if she had solar panels or wind turbines, but no one has ever seen one on her property. I mean, it's possible she's got them away from the house, but you said yourself the windmill was frozen."

*Not frozen, but it's not supplying power. Something's supplying it with power.*

She sits forward. "Have you ever seen anything?"

He searches his memory for any sign of a reflective solar panel or wires running from telephone poles, but the house seems normal.

Big, old and cold, but normal.

"The house is sort of heated. The garage definitely is."

"That's what I mean. No one knows how her lights work or how she keeps from freezing. And that Google Earth thing? It sounds like magic, right? I mean, no one has figured out how to block Google Earth—not movie stars, drug smugglers, or the military. It's all there, except your grandmother's property. You got to admit, something doesn't add up."

Oliver takes the journal off the table and squeezes it with both hands. *When something doesn't add up, that means there are missing numbers.*

"Why doesn't anyone go find out?" Oliver asks.

"Most people are scared, I guess. Hunters don't go near her property. They say a compass doesn't work."

She fiddles with the plastic lid on her coffee. Maybe that's why she doesn't notice him turn pale. Compasses don't work, he knows that.

"They sneak onto the property with their guns and ammo and end up walking right back to their trucks like the trees led them out."

Oliver puts the book on his lap to keep her from seeing his hands shake. He'd seen that beaver-gnawed tree twice, and he knows he didn't get turned around. Now the weird feeling he left on the property has followed him into the real world.

Molly looks up as an Eric Clapton song starts. She closes her eyes; her lips move with the lyrics.

Then she says, "Why doesn't she let you stay out after dark?"

"What?"

"You said earlier that you had to do chores and exercise, but you had to be inside before the sun went down."

Before he found the hobbit house, he could've told her he didn't know without lying. But now he can't tell her that when the sun goes down, things come out. *Things that mess with your compass and move trees. And chase you.*

He shoves his hands under his thighs, but the nervous energy flows into his feet. He closes his eyes, momentarily, and counts his breath, hoping he doesn't hyperventilate.

"Sorry," Molly says. "Sometimes I say too much."

The conversation hits a long pause, the silence filled with Clapton's guitar. Oliver gets his nervousness under control, but the floor is slowly moving. Good thing he's sitting. Molly, head back on her chair, comes out of her music reverie and announces she's grabbing a refill.

"Do you want to read the journals?" The words pop out of his mouth. There's no taking them back. It's a stupid thing to say, but for once he feels like there's an anchor keeping his life from capsizing, and it's wearing a Ramones T-shirt.

"Um, yeah. You have them?"

"No. But I can bring them, you know, next time."

"And when's that?"

"I don't know..."

She tilts her head, exposing the gap in a churlish smile. "Text me, then. When you're in town, text me and I'll come meet you."

"Okay."

Molly snaps a photo of him sitting in the chair. She shows him the thumbnail. He looks like a ghost. Oliver quickly gets his phone out and aims it.

Molly jumps on the miniature stage and grabs the empty mic stand, striking a silent but shrieking pose. Oliver captures her in his contacts. He tries a sip of lukewarm coffee. She returns, and they talk for another hour. The Toye property is forgotten.

For now.

# 11
---

Three days later, it snows.

Oliver has completed his chores, but still isn't allowed to go outside. He walks the staircase and not because Grandmother told him to. If he sits too long, he starts thinking, and too many thoughts are not his friends.

Walking keeps his mind engaged.

That night, Oliver goes to his room early. This time, he leaves his door open and listens. When the last footsteps are heard and the last door shut, he sets the timer on his phone and waits an hour.

Occasionally, tree branches break in the distance.

He doesn't want to read, that will put him to sleep. He can't pace; his footsteps will creak. Instead, he counts his breaths so the thoughts don't pile up. At ten thirty, his alarm goes off.

He stuffs a journal down the back of his sweatpants.

His footsteps announce his journey across the third floor. He stops in the bathroom and waits a minute before flushing. He runs the water in the sink and, while the toilet is refilling, walks to the room at the far end of the hallway.

A rope dangles from the ceiling.

He pulls down the attic door and unfolds the steps, carefully climbing them just as the toilet goes silent.

The ceiling is pitched at an angle.

Pale moonlight beams through the circular window that faces the driveway. He shivers as he waits for his eyes to adjust to the lumps surrounding him. The ghosts transform into dusty sheets draped over furniture and containers.

His phone illuminates uncovered boxes labeled *kitchen* or *dinnerware* or *office*. Most are sealed shut. There's a bookshelf to his left. He takes a couple of surprisingly silent steps to flip through stacks of *Newsweek, Life,* and *Popular Mechanics.* The dates are only ten years old.

Grandmother must still be hauling them up.

That's when he realizes how large everything is. It's not just the containers, but dressers, tables and chairs. He tugs the sheet from behind a bookshelf. It's an armoire. *How did that get up here?*

The door is cracked open.

He dares another step and pries it open further. The armoire doesn't look old, but the clothing hanging inside does. Most are small dresses for a little girl. Maybe these were Helen's? Or maybe a little girl that died fifty years ago and lives in the attic waiting for idiots like Oliver to come snooping around about midnight—

He closes his eyes.

Counts to ten.

When his thoughts are calm, he steps away from the armoire and doesn't look at it again.

He goes to the circular window, where a wide coffee table is positioned. He notices, as he sits down, it's a perfect setup to watch the driveway, which is exactly what he wants to do.

The circular drive is still clear—Oliver shoveled it after lunch— but the entry road is buried. His breath is puffing white clouds in the moonlight. He vows to stay awake until midnight. If nothing happens before then and the road is clear in the morning, then he'll bring a coat up the next night. He'll set his alarm to watch it at different times until he's got all the hours covered.

He could just ask Grandmother how the entry road gets plowed, but he wouldn't believe her and still come up.

It made sense not to ask.

The road is lonely. What starts out tranquil turns to cold boredom in fifteen minutes. The journal, still tucked in his waistband, sticks to his skin. He lays it on his lap. The leather cover is the same as all the other journals, aside from three dots of ink splashed near the corner. The yellowish pages turn frosty in the moonlight.

Random doodles fill the first couple of pages, followed by several pages torn from the binding. About a third of the way into the book, he finds the first entry.

FEBRUARY *14, 1882*

*Nog always arrived after I woke. He'd slide into the room wearing a different coat—sometimes long and furry, sometimes short and smooth. He'd slowly circle the room, staring at me like he had x-ray vision, looking right into my bones. He told me it was February.*

*Months have passed. It feels like weeks.*

*I think I'm losing my mind again. I just want out. If I'm going to die without seeing you, then let it be with the sky above me, the wind in my face. I told him this. Told him I thought he was a hallucination and that I wanted to die.*

*The next morning I awoke to a very different room.*

*It was bigger than when I had gone to sleep, perhaps three times as long and twice as wide. Ice shavings dusted the floor, as if it was freshly carved.*

*There was a pile of clothing in the corner that included heavy sweaters and a coat with a thick pair of boots. Next to the clothing, protruding from the wall, were steel rungs that led up to a hole in the ceiling.*

*Before excitement could drag me from bed, Nog slid into the room. He was wearing white this time. "Good morning," he started. "I'd like to begin with apologies, once again, for the lengthy adjustment period."*

*He paused. I nodded. It was the best I could do. They saved my life, as far as I could tell. I couldn't be indignant about that. But there was a hole in the ceiling that, I knew, exited to the outside.*

*"Trust," he said, "is essential. Power," he said, "is intoxicating. And you will find plenty of power amongst my people."*

*He paused again. Maybe he was letting the words sink in, I don't know. He can be long-winded and often used words I didn't understand. I didn't want to extend the conversation with a reply, but then he said, quite suddenly, "Let's stretch our legs today."*

*I got dressed very quickly and climbed the steel rungs. I emerged on top of the ice. Outside. In the world. Alive.*

*And tears filled my eyes.*

*I began weeping like a child. The stars shone in the frigid sky, and the ice was flat as far as I could see. It was clean and spacious and free. If I could not die in your arms, then I would have gladly laid my body to rest in that moment.*

*I began to laugh. My bellows carried long and far, perhaps all the way to the water beyond my eyes' reach. I must've looked like a madman. Nog popped out of the ice. He just shot up like a cork. Others did, too. Three of them of the same size and proportion. Two were females with clean faces, one with a long gray braid that reached her feet. Nog stood next to this one and held her hand.*

*All of them wore white.*

*I had assumed Nog was the leader, but when the one with the braid, the one known as Merry, spoke, it was clear they deferred to her.*

*"We knew this time would come," she said. "We have aided the human race in ways you cannot imagine, and have wished to remain anonymous and peaceful. Perhaps, though, now is the time that we reconsider and join the human race." She paused before saying, "We are not so different."*

*There was a strange current in the air. I could feel something was about to happen. Merry spread her arms and said, "Welcome to the Elven."*

*And when she said it, they all came up.*

*Thousands of them, my love.*

*They were just as round as they were joyful, squabbling as they pressed near me, reaching out to touch me as if I was not the one dreaming, but they were.*

*I was overwhelmed. Tears, once again, filled my eyes. Merry said, above the melee, "Perhaps you would like to meet the one that saved you."*

*I expected someone larger than the elven, a beast maybe, because my memory of lying on the ice was that of a large shadow and hulking arms, something large enough to carry me against its chest and certainly the elven were not large enough for that.*

*But I was not ready for this.*

*As the snow began to swirl, I felt my knees weaken. My savior made these words possible. Without this one, there would be no hope that I would see you again.*

*Merry held out her hand. She was wearing a strange glove. I looked around for my savior, but no one stood taller than the elven. Then I realized she had something in her hand. It was an ornament, my love. A big metal ornament with the most beautiful designs etched into its surface. Excitement was all around, but I didn't understand. How could the ornament save me?*

*She tossed it into the air.*

*The elven scrambled away, giving it room to land in the snow. But it never came down. Instead, a cyclone of snow swirled from the ice, a frosty cloud puffed across my eyes. And when it settled, when the air was clear, I saw him, my love. I saw the creature that saved my life.*

*He was made of snow.*

SOMETHING CRACKS OUTSIDE.

*Someone's out there!*

The person is wearing a long black coat dragging over the snow; the head is hidden beneath a heavy cowl. A faint layer of gray is on the shoulders and hood—snow that's trickled out of the trees. The person is staring down the entry drive, where a cloud billows like an approaching dust storm.

Oliver is frozen on the coffee table, his heart thudding in his chest.

His neck muscles, rigid.

The snow cloud gets denser. Branches snap and drag. The black figure steps back before the thickening cloud engulfs him. Oliver can hear something coming, like a distant train.

And then he sees it.

In the depths of the burgeoning snow cloud, he sees the whirling ball of branches. It spins like a bristled sphere made of a thousand twiggy arms that grind through the snow and scrape the asphalt as it moves back and forth, back and forth. It reaches the roundabout and stops.

The snow clears.

The thing rests in front of the cloaked figure. Its body is a dirty, slushy snowball, a pincushion of coniferous branches, the ends softened with pine and spruce needles. Short stumps emerge from the bottom, like legs, and another set grows where arms would be.

Oliver stops breathing.

It's a snowthing, sort of like the snowman that saved him but different. It's thicker, rounder and shorter. The snow slurpy and lumpy.

The black figure flicks his wrist.

Had Oliver not noticed the figure's hand, he would not have leaped up, the journal would not have slammed against the window. He would have remained an anonymous voyeur. It was a gleam of metal.

Moonlight reflecting off a glove.

*Grandmother.*

Oliver did leap.

The journal did slam.

And the figure turns toward him. The cowl, deep and dark, does not fall away. The snowthing, however, is gone in a cloud, the branches and slushy snow swishing into the trees.

Oliver closes his eyes and holds very still. When he opens his eyes, the driveway is empty. He runs to the steps and climbs down, paying no attention to noise.

He pauses.

Motionless, his ears filter out the natural ticks and creaks of the house in search of a door opening or a footstep falling. He goes to the bathroom and, once again, flushes the toilet and runs the sink. If anyone asks, he's having a bad night. On the way to the bedroom, passing the stairwell—

A ghostly figure watches.

Oliver actually shouts this time.

It sounds like a small dog stepping on a thorn.

The surprise flings him against the wall, and, he realizes, there's nothing to drop or throw.

*The journal is still in the attic.*

Grandmother, clad in a flowing beige robe and fuzzy slippers, methodically climbs the steps, crossing through a slice of moonlight. She looks like she should be carrying a lantern.

"What are you doing, Olivah?"

"I had the...the bathroom." He rubs his stomach. "My blood sugar was...I think it was something I ate."

She looks like she just climbed out of bed. It couldn't have been her out there. She couldn't have gotten up the stairs that fast. She's not even winded. But her hair is pulled back in a tight bun.

*She doesn't sleep like that.*

"What makes you so afraid?" she asks. "The things you see?"

She looks in the bathroom, then at Oliver. It sounds like something is caught in her throat. She returns to Oliver as silently as she walked away and takes both his hands, turning them over like she's checking for stolen goods.

Or dust from the attic.

"I washed my hands," Oliver says. "I always do when I...you know, go to the bathroom."

"Do you think I'm a tyrant?"

He shakes his head, but she can see the truth. That sound returns to her throat again. *Is that laughter?*

"We know nothing in our little worlds." She pats his hands. "Only when we know everything do we realize we know nothing."

"Okay."

He waits for her to leave, to return to her bedroom on the first floor, but she doesn't move. Her icy stare is fixed on him, her eyes like black marbles. She appears to smirk, but he can't be sure it's not just the wrinkles.

"Goodnight."

"Goodnight." He goes to his bedroom.

"Oh, Olivah."

He stops.

"Be not afraid. It's only your thoughts that have come to get you."

The moonlight through the window catches the side of her face. Even from this distance, he's sure he sees it.

She's smiling.

He climbs into bed and pulls the covers over his head, thinking she must be sleepwalking. What disturbs him most, though, was the feel of her hands.

They were very cold.

---

## 12

Christmas arrives like any other day.

He opens presents with his mom. Grandmother joins them for breakfast. She wishes them a Merry Christmas, but no gifts are exchanged. Aunt Rhonnie and the twins arrive for tea. They all have new sunglasses and coats.

In the afternoon, the twins make their journey across the field.

Oliver says he's not feeling well, which he isn't. The weird has a stranglehold on him. He's woozy and dreamy. He tries not to think and sleeps as much as possible. The twins return before supper and leave early because Helen says there's a party that night and they must leave now.

Later, he realizes the chore board has been blank all day.

*Merry Christmas, Olivah.*

HE DOESN'T LEAVE the house for the next couple of days.

Oliver sleeps later than he should, and his blood sugar drops too low.

He does his chores.

He walks the steps.

And he avoids Grandmother.

Even at tea, he keeps his eyes forward, exerting perfect form and manners. On occasion, he glances at her when she looks away, careful not to make eye contact. But the old Grandmother is back. That smile he thought he saw in the moonlight is long buried. This is the one thing that gives him comfort.

*Maybe I was dreaming.*

Maybe he dreamed about everything, because pincushioned snowthings don't plow driveways, they don't take orders from old women...*they don't live!*

But no matter how much he throws himself into his chores or how long he sleeps, the world is still covered in snow. Every morning, he opens his eyes and he's still on the property. Things are not getting better.

Oliver thinks about Molly often, but it's so much easier to pretend none of this is happening. As the days wear on, the memories don't disappear, but they do fade.

In the middle of January, when normal kids have already gone back to school, Mom drops him off at the library. It was her idea. He waits for the car to leave. Instead of going inside, he clears the snow off a bench. With service, his phone downloads a list of emails and unread text messages. Five of them are from Molly.

The last one just before New Year's Eve.

Oliver can see the circulation desk through the sliding glass doors. Molly is helping someone check out. He stays outside long enough to become quite cold. When his phone buzzes, he pulls his gloves off with his teeth, but it's just an update reminder for one of his games.

He can't stop chattering.

It's late afternoon. Mom won't be back for another hour. Oliver wants to go inside, but if he does, he'll talk to her. If he talks to her, color and detail will return to the faded memories. He'll also get her in trouble with Ms. Chatty Pants. So he'll sit on the bench until his mom picks him up.

"Oliver? Is that you?"

Molly stands at the entrance without a coat. Her yellow and black rugby shirt is long-sleeved. She crosses her arms and walks beneath the awning. Oliver buries his hands in his pockets as his stomach drops twenty floors into fear and, for once, a little excitement.

"What are you doing?" she asks.

"Using the wifi."

"Out here?"

"My mom's picking me up. And I didn't want to get you in trouble."

"What are you talking about?"

He looks back. Ms. Chatty Pants is at the circulation desk. "There's no service at the property. That's why I didn't text you. I'm sorry."

"You're freezing. Come wait inside, at least. I know you're from Texas, but you know what cold is. Stay out here long enough and you'll be an ice cube."

Molly hunches her shoulders. She's already shivering.

"I...I'll go inside," he says. "In a minute. You should go before you get in trouble."

"You all right?"

He starts to answer, but words don't make it out. Just a funny sound. A knot lodges in his throat, pressure building in his chest. If he doesn't say something, he'll have to go home feeling like this. He'll have to sit in his room with it bottled up.

Still, the words don't form.

He looks at his boots, rocking back and forth.

"I'll be right back," Molly says.

She rushes for the doors. Maybe she's going to get a coat, or tell Ms. Chatty Pants to call 911. Or maybe she's not coming back.

"I saw a snowman!" He jumps to his feet. "I saw it. I saw all those things you talked about. You were right. And I saw a snowman."

The words had to get out.

He forced himself to say something, no matter what order they came out.

Before he exploded.

Molly stops under the parapet. Her cheeks are flush, but she's not shivering. Not like Oliver. Someone exits the library and goes to their car, looking back at the teenagers. Ms. Chatty Pants is looking at them from the desk, but he doesn't care.

He's got to get the words out.

He tells her about all the stuff in the attic and reading the journal and the snowthing cleaning the road. He tells her about his grandmother lurking in the cloak and the weird glove.

He doesn't stop there.

The hobbit house and the creatures and the snowman that saved him. When he's finished, when there are no more words left inside, Molly is still there. She hasn't moved. She just stares. He's afraid to say more, afraid he's already said too much. He's huffing to catch his breath.

"You think I'm crazy?"

She doesn't answer because this is the part where someone would ask if he's been dreaming or pat him on the shoulder or hand or, worse, the cheek and ask about his blood sugar because he's a diabetic, the shot kind. *There's no such thing as snowmen, Oliver. Not like the ones you're seeing.*

Molly walks over to the bench, arms still firmly crossed, and sits down. She says, "I believe you."

"You do?"

"You saw it, right?"

"But am I crazy?"

"Because you saw something? That's not crazy, Oliver. You had the balls to see crazy things and tell someone. That doesn't *make* you crazy."

He collapses next to her.

The words are out. He doesn't have to hide them anymore. Molly has them now. She heard them and believed them. And that, he thinks, is what will keep them from sticking in his throat again.

"There's more," he says.

"I know."

They stay on the bench until Molly begins to chatter. Oliver holds out his hand. She leads him inside where it's warm. They find a table at the back of the library. He tells the rest of his story, leaving no details unearthed.

Until he's empty.

# 13

February is warmer than usual.

Snow still covers the ground, but the melt glistens off the asphalt. That means no shoveling. Oliver walks down the middle of the road, listening to the trees drip until he reaches the main road. He shades his eyes.

The dashed line is visible on the main road.

He stands on the shoulder like a hitchhiker without a hope, waiting for a pickup truck to come over the hill. A red one. Eventually, he carves an indention in the snowbank and sits. He's almost asleep when the first vehicle passes.

It's not red. Not a pickup.

"You excited?" His mom is coming up the entry road, wearing a thick turtleneck and a long scarf.

"Just waiting."

Oliver shades his eyes to see her smiling. Casually, she walks onto the main road, standing on the dashed line to look in both directions. She looks like she expects something to come any moment.

"I used to come out here when I was little," she says. "I'd stare at the crest of that hill and wonder what was over it. How far did it go? Who was out there?"

She cups her eyes like binoculars.

"Sometimes, I'd pretend my real parents were out there, and if I waited long enough, they would drive by and recognize me, like they'd lost me when I was born and they'd been searching for me ever since."

She looks in the other direction.

"You ever feel that way?"

If he was honest, he'd tell her he felt that way once, when he stayed at his dad's in Los Angeles. But he couldn't tell Mom that. He couldn't tell her about the strangers that came to his house, the business meetings in the bedrooms, and all the times he turned on the television and told Oliver he'd be right back.

Sometimes the house was still empty in the morning.

She didn't need to know all that.

"I'm sorry, Oliver." She remains in the middle of the road. "I mean it."

What she meant was that she was sorry she was a bad mom.

Oliver made her stop saying that years ago. Now she just says sorry, like she's apologizing for his life. Somehow, she's responsible for his dad, for his diabetes, for his life. Somehow, if she could just get over that hill, she would find what she was looking for. But she'd gone over that hill, she'd seen what was over there. And she crested the next one and the next.

It was just more of the same.

*More hills.*

"What happened to Grandfather?" Oliver asks.

"Your grandfather?" She plops down next to him, sighing. "Well, my father, your grandfather, wasn't exactly warm and fuzzy. Ever since I can remember, he kept to himself. Usually, he was tinkering in the garage or hiking the property. He was a burly man, a real man's man. Definitely not a man for children.

"I had just gone to boarding school when Mother called, said she'd have someone pick me up at the bus station. I was at home a couple of days before I noticed he wasn't around. Mother never said anything until I asked. Then she just said he wasn't coming back."

She sculpts a snowball.

"It didn't matter, really. Another week and everything felt the same, with or without him."

She gets up and knocks the snow off her pants, clapping her hands. She was about to apologize again, but catches herself. Fact is, she had it just as rough. Maybe worse. She did the best she could.

She doesn't need to apologize.

A distant rumble comes from the left. They both hood their eyes to see the truck. Oliver jumps to his feet. They wait by the road as it pulls through the gate and stops.

Molly opens the door. "Need a ride?"

"Yeah." Oliver smiles. He opens the passenger door and waits.

His mom leans into the cab to introduce herself. It's the first time she'd met one of his girlfriends, because she hadn't seen her yet. And because Oliver's never had a girlfriend. Molly pushes the hair from her eyes—the candy-red strand dyed brown like her normal hair—and shakes her hand.

Mom steps back and squeezes Oliver's shoulder. "You go ahead."

"You sure?"

She's sure.

Oliver climbs into the cab, kicking empty Starbucks cups out of the way. Molly turns the radio down. Oliver watches his mom in the sideview mirror. She closes the gate. Maybe she didn't see snowmen when she grew up. Maybe she didn't see anything at all.

Maybe that was worse.

MOLLY SITS across the table from Oliver. She pulls at the stiff collar rising from her wool sweater and catches Oliver's glance before casting her eyes down.

"Tea is served," Mom sings.

Grandmother puckers her lips and reaches for a small plate of scones. Tea is poured in silence. The awkward silence rings in his ears. He stirs creamer into his tea and clinks the cup.

Molly, however, moves with precision as she pours her cup and lifts it, eyes cast down and pinkie finger drawn in. The china doesn't make a sound when she places it in the saucer.

"A lovely house, Ms. Toye. The orderliness is breathtaking."

A long pause hangs.

"Thank you, Molly," Mom finally says. "We work very hard to keep it this way."

Grandmother draws another sip, passing a sidelong glance at her.

"We're happy to have you come out," Mom says. "Aren't we, Mother?"

"Tell us about yourself," Grandmother says.

Molly takes a bite and doesn't speak until she swallows.

She grew up in town. So did her mom and dad. He's a cop. Her mom teaches high school history. "She'd kill to be sitting here, having tea with the Toye family. She says you're quite a mystery, Ms. Toye."

"Keeping to oneself is not outrageous," Grandmother says.

"Of course not."

"Why are you here?"

"Ma'am?"

"Your manners are perfect. Your flattery is charming. What do you want?"

"I don't want anything," Molly says without hesitation. "Your grandson invited me, and I like him."

Mom tries to interject. Grandmother holds up her hand. "Where did you get these manners?"

Molly swipes her scone with raspberry jam and chews slowly. She wipes the corners of her mouth while a knot grows in Oliver's gut.

"I learned about tea ceremony at the Zen Center of Denver. My mom would take me there when I was a kid. If I'm honest, it was boring. But now that I'm older, I appreciate the structure. As for the flattery, Ms. Toye, I was simply observing my surroundings. My hope is that you haven't lost sight of the historic beauty you have around you. I work in the library, so I appreciate order. It's where I met your grandson."

Mom hides a grin behind her teacup. Oliver sits on his hands. He taps his toe in a steady rhythm. Grandmother turns her head toward him.

He lifts his foot off the floor to fidget in silence.

"Honestly, I'm thrilled," Molly adds. "Very few people have seen the outside of your house. I would guess that fewer have seen the inside and had tea with you, Ms. Toye."

"Try none," Mom says.

"I'm honored to be here, sitting in the house your husband built in 1901 without any assistance from people in town."

Oliver didn't know his grandfather built this by himself.

"You are one of the largest donors to the Nature Conservancy," Molly continues, "and one of the largest private landowners in the state of Colorado. Like I said, I am honored. However, if I make you uncomfortable, I will leave."

Oliver is frozen.

His mom doesn't move.

Only Molly dares to sample her tea and take a bite while the silence hardens.

*Fearless.*

Grandmother stares ahead, then says, without looking at anyone in particular, "Very well. If we are to have company, it is perhaps nice to have someone that can appreciate what we do."

And that was it.

They talk about things like school and hobbies and hiking the countryside. When Grandmother finishes her tea, she wipes her mouth and announces tea is finished. She leaves the room in a way that Oliver has become accustomed to seeing. Strangers, he knew, would consider it rude.

Molly never flinches.

Mom lifts her teacup, finger hooked through the handle, and smiles at Molly. "It's so good to have you."

And she means it.

❄

"THAT WAS AMAZING." Oliver holds the back door for Molly. "How did you know?"

"Know what?"

"All of that during tea! You nailed it, said everything she wants to hear, even the way she wants to hear it."

"It's easy. Just look at the place. You live in a museum. Your grandmother donates to the community, half of it is done anonymously, but everyone knows it's her. She's a strong, assertive woman. I assumed she would respect strength and honesty. I just did the things that matter to her."

She made it sound easy.

They walk around the house. Before they reach the windmill, Oliver warns her. "It's electrified. Must be a loose wire or something."

"How do you know?"

"I touched it."

Molly's eyes wander to the top of the structure. Rust has chewed holes through the weather vane. A gust of wind hits the windmill's blades, and the squeal pierces their ears and gets under their skin. They both plug their ears with their little fingers.

"Well, it's not harvesting any wind," she says.

"Definitely not."

"No, I mean it keeps turning when there's no wind, so it must be using energy. But why?"

"Maybe Grandmother likes the way it looks."

Molly puts out her hand, lets it hover a few inches above the windmill's leg. She eases it closer. Oliver's fingers dance at his sides, but he resists the urge to pull her away. With a half-inch gap between her and the metal, her hair begins to rise. A few strands at first, then several fray out.

"That's weird," she says. "It's emitting a field or something. I don't think this is a loose wire."

Before Oliver can respond, she slaps her hand against it. Her hair flairs out below her stocking cap.

"Oh, wow," she says. "It's like I swallowed a tuning fork."

She sounds auto-tuned.

"I don't think that's a good idea." But when Oliver grabs her hand, the hairs stand on his arm. A current of helium fills the space between his eyes; he doesn't want to let go—can't let go—or he'll float away like a parade ornament.

Molly yanks her hand like a wet tongue stuck to cold metal. She examines her palm. Oliver feels planted on the ground, his head heavy again. She takes a lap around the antiquated structure and studies it from top to bottom.

"I don't think this is a windmill. Not anymore, at least."

"I don't care what it is; we shouldn't touch it."

"It's a disguise."

"For what?"

She shrugs. "Maybe this is why there's no Google Earth or cell phone reception. Maybe it creates a distortion field. You ever see it stop spinning?"

He shakes his head. "Why would she block cell phones? She's got a landline. What's the difference?"

"Maybe it's a side effect." She looks at the house and barely moves her lips, like someone might be watching. She whispers, "If you had a snowman, would you want the world to see?"

A chill wriggles down Oliver's neck that has nothing to do with the cold.

"What about the hobbit house?" he says. "There's reception in there."

"Maybe it has a deflector shield."

She chuckles, and he knows why. This all sounds like a Wachowski Brothers movie.

They venture out to the field but don't go very far—the hair still tingling on Oliver's arms—just far enough to get out of sight. He stops where the snowball had pulverized Henry, knocking the cap off his gel-sculpted head, and points to the exact spot where it was launched. Molly nods while he tells the story. Just as he gets to the part where Henry stops short of the trees, Molly wanders forward.

She touches the prickly needles.

"I swear he was right there," Oliver says.

"How do you know it's a 'he'?"

"It's a snow*man*. He, uh, told me."

She looks back. "He talks?"

"No, he doesn't talk. I just know."

"He wrote you a note?"

"No." Oliver sighs. This is when he feels the craziest. "I could feel it, like a thought."

"How do you know you weren't imagining it?"

"This was different, I swear. I was thinking about 'it' standing there watching me, and then I suddenly had this thought that told me he was a 'he,' not an 'it.'"

"Yeah, but maybe it's neither. It's like people call God a 'he.' Maybe God is both."

"You don't believe me?"

"I believe you." She means it. Mostly.

Molly steps into the dark between the trees like a foxhound with a scent.

"We won't find him."

"How far have you gone?"

"Pretty far," he lies. "I don't think we'll find him looking for him, I mean. He just showed up."

She's nodding, but looking as far as she can see. Which isn't far.

"I want to show you something."

Oliver walks just inside the trees. A few minutes pass before he sees the side of the garage. He waits for Molly to catch up, warning her to stay out of sight. The doorknob turns easily, and, as usual, a gust of warm, almost hot air greets them. The car is still spotless. Molly leans over the driver's door, inhaling the fragrant leather.

He warns her about the window, that if you stand in the right spot, someone might see her from the house.

"What will happen if she sees you?"

"I don't know." He knows. They both do.

Oliver pulls open the filing cabinet, third drawer from the top. It's packed with folders, the manila tabs bent and worn. They stack a handful on the bench and spread out the contents, Oliver keeping track of the order while Molly unfolds the plans. One of them looks like a space-age laboratory, the dome-shaped kind that could be erected on another planet.

"You sure he wasn't an inventor?" she asks. "These are like sophisticated plans."

"He was a mechanic."

She opens an eight-fold plan, smoothing out the wrinkles. The scale is larger, and the details easy to read. She studies it for several minutes while Oliver keeps the folders in order.

"Something's not right."

She slides her finger to the top right corner. The signature is dated back to 1920. The worn creases and yellowish color make it believable.

"He built this house before that," Oliver says.

"That's not it. This looks like plans for cold fusion and plasmic welding." She looks at the crescent wrenches and ball-peen hammers. "This garage is still in the 1940s. Besides, no one was thinking about cold fusion in the '20s and plasmic welding, whatever that is."

Oliver plunks the wooden orb on the plan. She compares it to the etching details on the paper. Oliver, however, doesn't tell her how the wooden orb feels when the snowman was near.

"This is a model." She rotates the wooden orb between her fingers and thumbs. "What do you think he was trying to invent?"

He knows what he was trying to invent. He knows what the wooden orb looks like—that drawing, too—but he's not ready to explain what he's read in the journal. *Did he invent a snowman?*

"No idea."

"You ever see anything like this around the house?"

"No."

She tosses it a few times before dropping it in his hand. "You know what I think it is? Some sort of power source. Look at the house. It's off the grid, remember? No solar panels and that windmill's not doing crap. Maybe this thing"—she thumps the plan—"is crammed in the basement or something."

But there's no basement door, not one Oliver's ever seen. And it's not in the attic.

"You see any plans for a metal glove?" she asks.

He hasn't. But there's a lot of paper in those drawers. Molly taps her chin, eyeballing the filing cabinet like a treasure chest.

"You want to read the journals?" he asks.

"They're out here?"

Oliver strips off his backpack and, stealing a glance through the window, digs out a journal from the inside of a *PC Gamer* magazine. "Come on."

She follows him beneath the workbench. Oliver shows her the footlocker, releasing the moldy smell of centuries-old fabric. Molly presses against him, looking over the rim as Oliver digs through the artifacts.

He hands her the journal.

She knows all the crazy things out there, but what's in the journals is the real test. *It's about to get nuts.*

She strokes the old cover. Oliver takes the phone and, while she's smells the leather, sets the timer.

"Just in case," he says.

The binding cracks like snapping twigs as she pulls the cover open. The pages are bright in the white light.

"Oh, man." Molly brushes the first page with her fingertips. "Oh, man."

He has the urge to put his arm around her, pull her warm body against his, but he's afraid. Her weight leans into his shoulder like she answers his thought.

"Read it." She puts the book on his lap.

"What?"

"I want to hear your voice. It's your great-grandfather; I want to hear it in your words."

Oliver sits up straighter, clearing his throat. Molly nuzzles up to him, tipping her head on his shoulder. An ache already throbs in his tailbone, but he doesn't move.

"Here we go." Oliver scans the page.

"What's wrong?"

"I just want to warn you. My great-grandfather was lost after his ship wrecked in the polar ice. He survived and wrote these journals. They're a little out there."

"I'm at the Toye Property. I expect it."

"I mean, like, *Alice in Wonderland* out there."

"Good. Stop stalling."

He feels her warmth. She leans her head back and closes her eyes. Oliver takes a deep breath.

And begins.


*MARCH 19, 1882*

*I grow weary, my love.*

*The elven have been most gracious, indeed. There is never a thing I want they don't provide—food, clothing, entertainment. Still, I grow weary. They cannot bring you to me.*

*There is discussion about me. Nog mentioned, when I asked the other day, they are considering chaperoning me back to civilization. They have been in hiding for 40,000 years. They roamed free during the Ice Age. I don't know why, all this time, they have chosen to remain separate, isolated in the Arctic Circle, hiding in the ice. Nonetheless, Nog said, they choose to watch the human race rather than join it.*

*What bothers me most is the implication of these discussions. I feel as if they are deciding whether I can return or not. I am in full health; there is no reason I should not return home, where I belong. In your arms.*

*I will be talking to the fat man very soon. If anyone should understand my plight, it will be him.*


SKETCHES FILL THE PAGES. While still abstract, he's become quite good at drawing. There's a haunting tunnel of ice filled with short, round elven and a large, fat man among them with a grizzled beard, his thumbs hooked in his belt.

"Can you tell me something?" Molly asks. "What are elven?"

Oliver explains. Molly hums along, eyes still closed. He waits, tensely. When she doesn't immediately leave, he breathes easier.

"Then who's the fat man?" she asks.

"I don't know."


MARCH 22, 1882

*There was a celebration yesterday.*

*It was good timing. I was feeling quite melancholy. There was quite a stir amongst the elven, though. I could feel the excitement building. Nog informed me we would see the rising.*

*I climbed onto the ice with only a thin coat. I have grown quite large and find that, with this layer of blubber padding my flesh, I need less clothing to stay warm. If the captain could see me now, standing in the Arctic with one coat, he would perhaps cry.*

*Most of the colony was already on top. There are thousands. I don't think they all live where I am. Some must have migrated from other locations in grand sleighs. The gold rails were curled and the bodies shiny red. I cannot say how they would fabricate such items, but nothing surprises me any longer. While there were reins tethered to the fronts of these grand sleds, there was nothing to pull them.*

*I can say, without question, there could not be a jollier lot. Even the fat man was above the ice, towering over the elven, his distinctive laughter carried above the celebration. I have not met with him, but I have been promised our meeting will be soon. I considered confronting him right then, but he is very popular among the elven. They all want his attention, and the atmosphere for serious discussion was naught. After all, he arrived much like I did, only he never left. He made this his home. But he came with his wife.*

*I would do the same.*

*A sudden hush fell over them. They faced east. I stood next to Nog, watching the sky lighten until the first sliver of the sun rose above the horizon. It did so to raucous celebration. The elven hugged and kissed, throwing their short arms as far around their tubby bodies as possible. They exchanged gifts and plates of food—cookies being the most popular. Music began to play, and the elven danced and sang. Later, I saw the younger ones remove their clothing to plunge into the icy water, rising up with laughter.*

*I, however, did not join, my love. I watched the sun continue its ascent, remembering the time we spent on the wharf that early morning in July, the morning after we wed. How we watched the sun rise. I thought, naively, it would never end. I believed we would be together forever.*

*I never should have left.*

THE FLAT LINE of a horizon bisects the page, a curved hump of the sun peeking above it. The scribbles of celebrating elven, spherical and jolly, arms raised, fill the landscape. Hovering above the sun is a mess of lines that, at first glance, appear to be a spray of clouds. Oliver begins turning the page when he recognizes the eyes, lips and a chin below the tip of a nose.

"Is there more?" Molly asks.

*APRIL 18, 1882*

*The fat man still won't see me.*

*My weariness has turned to worry. There are rumors that the colony is divided about my return. Some, I've heard, want me to remain in the Arctic, that life has been good without intervening with the human race. Others feel like now is the time to guide humanity, that our technology has become dangerous and without their wisdom we could cause irreversible damage.*

*I don't care about any of that.*

*I only want to see your face.*

*The claustrophobia has become unbearable. I can hardly sleep, but despite the fat that insulates me, I cannot remain above the ice indefinitely. I find myself wanting to tear down these icy walls, to be free.*

*Perhaps that is why Nog came to me yesterday. I believe he senses my unrest. He assures me, on a daily basis, that a decision about my fate will come soon. And daily, he brings no new news.*

*But yesterday, he suggested we do something different.*

*We journeyed topside. I thought, perhaps, we would ski the ice. I arrived on top of the ice in shock. I had to blink several times as the chill wind blew, but it did not dispel the mirage.*

*There, standing on four legs, was the largest reindeer in the world. Its rack of antlers spread the length of a full-grown horse. It pawed the ice while two elven stroked its front legs, as if they were the keepers.*

*"Where did it come from?" I asked.*

*The beast snorted, and its nose grew red as a flame, as if I had insulted it. When it shook its head, the antlers fanned the air. One of the attending elven said he lives on the mainland, where he feeds on lichen and such. That sounded impossible. How could a beast of this size reach the mainland? I asked that question, but secretive smiles were all I received in return.*

*I was not allowed to pet it. He can be temperamental, they said.*

*Nog asked that I step back. He pulled open his coat, revealing the magic bag on his hip. He still refuses to call it a magic bag; that is my name for it. Science, he insists always, is when you understand. Magic is when you don't.*

*But then he did something that explains why all those sleighs were at the equinox celebration. With the metal glove on, he reached—*

"THE GLOVE!" Molly smacks Oliver's arm.

His heart begins to quiver. It wasn't just "glove" that was written. *Metal glove.* The entry sounds like his great-grandfather has already seen it, like he knows what it can do. There must be an explanation in one of the other journals.

Molly shakes him. "Keep reading."

WITH THE METAL GLOVE ON, *he reached into the magic bag. As he's done before, he pulled something out that defies the laws of physics. This time it was a red sleigh. The golden-railed sled emerged at first like stretchy fabric, but it shook the ice when it landed.*

*They fed the reindeer another handful of green cubes. The beast minced the food without taking its wary eyes off me. They guided it to the front of*

*the sled. Nog explained, while they tethered it, that the beast had modified*
*organs, in particular a helium bladder. This had something to do with the*
*webbed hide hanging loosely between its legs.*

*I suppose I had some idea of what was about to happen, but, at that*
*moment, I could not think clearly. When Nog patted the seat, I sat without*
*resistance. I still believed this thing would gallop over the ice like a stallion.*

*The attending elven stepped back, and a buzzing wave rolled around us,*
*slightly distorting the horizon. "A shield," Nog said. "To protect us." Without*
*warning, Nog called to the beast.*

*"Onward."*

*My stomach dropped.*

*The world blurred into two colors: white below, blue above; the two*
*dissected by a fuzzy line.*

*The horizon, my love. I was looking at the horizon from above.*

*The reindeer soared in front of us, legs spread, the hide-webbing taut,*
*and its belly swollen. My head spun. I clutched the railing.*

*We were flying.*


The alarm goes off.

There are illustrations of the reindeer, the sleigh and the flight. He closes the journal, and they sit quietly—Molly holding his arm with both hands.

*She's still here.*

"Did he ever write about eating wild berries," Molly asks. "In any of the earlier ones?"

"No. Why?"

"Elven. Flying reindeer. Maybe these are hallucinations. I'm just saying."

Oliver wonders the same thing, and, maybe, he'd believe his great-grandfather had written these in an insane asylum, that maybe his mom made all this up to keep him entertained while they lived here.

But he saw a snowman.

And he hadn't eaten any wild berries that day.

Before they trek back to the field to return to the house, before they even crawl out from under the bench, Oliver indulges one last nagging feeling. He flips back through the pages and stares at the face in the clouds.

*My love.*

# 14

O liver wakes up at midnight.

It had become a habit, going to sleep at ten o'clock and waking up at midnight. He listens to the distant rumbling of the forest—branches snapping, ground thumping—thinking about Malcolm Toye's sketches and unrequited love.

It had been a week since he and Molly had sat under the workbench. She's coming for tea again. Grandmother even nodded and said, "That would be fine," when Mom told her. For normal people, that comment should be translated as, "That would be fantastic! I can't wait to see her!"

Oliver called her on Grandmother's landline, with her permission, of course. But without service, he can't text. He even began sketching her face into wispy clouds. He'd thrown all his attempts away. They were horrible, and he didn't need his mom seeing them. Grandmother, either.

*What if she recognized it?*

He's already read two of the three journals he took from the footlocker. The second one is still in the attic. He should've grabbed the other three when he was sitting right next to it with Molly, but he had other things on the brain.

It's windy everywhere, not just in the trees. The house pops and creaks with each gust. He tosses in bed as violently as the weather. Sleep is too far off, so he crawls out of bed and retrieves the two journals beneath the dresser. He reads them by the light of his cell phone, but he's been through them a dozen times. Nothing new.

It occurs to him that now is the perfect time to get the one in the attic. Why didn't he think of that before? Everyone's asleep. He'll get in, get out, and have something new to read.

He gets to his bedroom door in a few creaky steps and, with hand pressed around the metal doorknob, holds his breath. With an eye to the crack in the doorway, he searches for his grandmother waiting in the moonlight.

He walks to the bathroom, listening at the top step. Somewhere on the second floor, his mom softly snores. A gust of wind slams the house. Sleet smatters the roof like a handful of gravel.

A door slams.

Muscles coiled, ears tuned to every little tick—Oliver is catatonic. He can't be sure what he heard. It sounded like a door, but he's not certain. Maybe he left the snow shovel on the porch, and it fell over. Or an icicle dropped on the steps. He waits at the top step several minutes, counting his breaths. The distant noises seem right on top of the house.

Usually, he'd crawl right back in bed. But tonight, he refuses to run. It's just sounds he hears. Just thoughts that frighten. Now is the time to grab that journal.

He flushes the toilet, just in case, and hurries down the hall. His phone is back in the bedroom, and, without moonlight, the room is dark. He swings his hands like the rope's a piñata. He smacks the knob tied at the end and waits for it to swing back. When he has two hands on it, he begins to pull—

There's a flash outside.

Oliver jumps against the wall.

His heart swells with each beat.

At first, it seemed like lightning. But there's no thunder, just wind. Eyes wide, ears pricked, he watches the shadows play on the far wall.

The light dims but doesn't go away. He slides toward the window. It's black outside, the night sky capped with clouds.

Light beams from the garage window.

*Someone's in there.*

His brain aches to remember if everything got put away. An errant paperclip could expose him. A cold emotion splashes down his spine.

The light brightens like a power surge.

For a moment, the entire backyard is lit up, and then it goes back to normal. Oliver watches until his body aches. Nothing happens. Not a shadow, not a form, not a sound. A thought occurs to him, one that wriggles down to his toes.

*Who's out there?*

"It's only your thoughts that have come to get you," Grandmother had said. And it's his thoughts that have locked his knees.

*Just thoughts. There are no ghosts on the stairs, no wild things roaming the house. I'm just having thoughts something will happen. Just thoughts.*

It could be those things from the river. It could be the snowman. It could be anything. He should go back to bed and pretend like nothing ever happened. That's what he gets for leaving the journal in the attic.

*Not tonight.*

He wants to know who's out there. If Grandmother catches him in the kitchen, he'll say he needed a snack. He's diabetic, after all.

He squeezes the wooden orb. Courage seeps up his arm.

It takes all that courage to not pass the stairwell and flee for the room, but he makes the turn. One step at a time, he descends.

Standing at the sink, he can see the garage. The light is still on. Other than that, there's nothing out of the ordinary. Maybe Grandmother left the light on by accident. Another ten minutes at the sink and still nothing.

It's during those ten minutes that Oliver has another thought.

Never in his life has he done something like this. When his dad had parties, Oliver hid in his bed. When there was a bully after school, he stayed in the classroom. He played it safe. The chances of getting hurt are slim if you stay in bed.

Just ask Malcolm Toye.

But he made it to the North Pole. He met the elven.

Stay in bed and nothing happens. Ever.

*The journals.*

There are three of them out there. He could wait until tomorrow and find a way to get them. There's always tomorrow. Oliver's lived his whole life waiting for tomorrow.

He goes to the mudroom and slides on his boots, carefully closing the back door behind him. The night air seeps beneath his shirt. He folds his arms, eyeing the square of light splashing across the lawn. Oliver follows the maze of exposed grass, avoiding the snow. He stops short of the window.

Nothing inside moves.

He moves to the left, taking tiny steps, almost shuffling, until the edge of his boot is touching snow. From here, he can see almost half of the garage. No one's in there.

*The car is gone!*

The door must've been Grandmother leaving the house. She must drive the car when no one is watching. Molly's right; she's a private person. Maybe she does her joyrides in the middle of the night.

Again, this would be a good time to beat a retreat back to bed.

Oliver races around the garage, past the large door to the entrance. He opens it quietly. It's strange to see the car missing. The garage seems so big without it. And the concrete where the car usually sits is so clean and smooth.

He wipes his boots and ducks beneath the workbench. His breath is loud, and his heartbeat thuds in his ears. He digs past the coat and yanks the remaining three journals out, stuffing them inside his pants. Without breaking stride, he races out of the garage, leaving on the lights.

Quickly, he returns to his bedroom and slips the journals beneath the dresser. Adrenaline pumps through him. He should check his blood sugar, just in case. But for now, he lays in bed.

Something bothers him, something's not right.

He assumes it was the risk he took. It was stupid, but it worked.

In the morning, looking out the kitchen window as he rinses his plate, he realizes what was nagging him before he fell asleep. It wasn't the danger of being caught or the journals hidden beneath his dresser. It's the snow around the garage, just outside the big garage door where the car would pull out.

*There were no car tracks.*

# 15

Molly dazzles at tea.

She tells a story about a dog named Peanut at the shelter where she volunteers on Saturdays that only poops when no one is looking. And when she cleans it up, Peanut barks at it.

She actually used the word "poop." During tea. And Grandmother smiled.

*Remarkable.*

They go for a walk afterwards. Oliver stops about halfway to the main road and, sort of whispering, tells her about the car. The next morning, it was in the garage like it had never moved. Molly starts asking questions, and he gives her the quiet sign.

"Let's go somewhere safe."

He leads her through the trees until they reach the field. The windmill churns behind them. Snow is drifted in the shadows, but the field is exposed and sloppy. April has arrived, but winter refuses to leave.

"I brought something." Molly's got a magnetic compass. "I saw it at the store, thought we might test the hunters' theory."

Oliver knows exactly how that test will go.

He warns her about the sinkholes. They hike through the trees, every once in a while checking the compass. North is never the same direction. Sometimes the needle settles in one spot and, before she puts it away, moves to another.

Molly stops at a pair of maple trees leaning against each other. The bark is misshapen and molded into a grafting kiss where the trunks touch.

"Test one more theory." She unties two friendship bracelets from her wrist, putting the red one around the smaller tree. Oliver attaches the blue one to the other.

She stands back. "The kissing trees."

It has been over a month since Oliver has been this far.

Snowmelt has transformed the stream into a river. The icy blue water crashes off the rocky shores, carrying debris in the white-tipped waves. The river speaks through the earth. They can hear it through their feet.

"Be careful." Oliver stops several feet short.

They walk parallel to the river until the bend appears up ahead. This part of the forest still looks like Nature's battle zone, with branches spearing the ground or hanging from above. Oliver points at the stack of stones across the water.

"The hobbit house."

"That's it?"

"Yeah." He can feel the water's draft from where they're standing. It was dangerous the last time he crossed. This time it would be fatal.

Molly slips her fingers between his. "We don't have to go."

"I know."

But she wants to go. And she's not afraid, he can tell. She's not shivering, not like he is.

*One step at a time.*

But this isn't the staircase, these aren't just scary sounds. Not this time. Fall and bad things happen.

Oliver leads her through the maze of branches and up the stone steps. He stands on solid ground, an icy breeze rushing past him. The tree bridge is solid and the footing tacky with moss. He's afraid, though, that his knees will lock up halfway across and his legs, now numb from his knees up, will fold.

Molly squeezes his hand and walks onto the bridge first. She stops halfway and, with plenty of room on both sides, reaches for him. He takes a step.

Another.

Together, they cross.

"The door's in there."

They enter the dark hollow, hand in hand, with phones guiding them to the gnarly handle. The door opens as easily as it did the first time. Musty odor, like wet blankets, greets them. The room hasn't changed. Firewood is stacked by the hearth, charred logs inside the fireplace.

"Someone lives here," Molly says.

"I don't think so. My cousins come out here for the service." His phone signals new messages. "The only place on the property. Look." He steps outside, only a few feet from the threshold. "A signal in there, but not here. Weird, right?"

"I can smell the weird. It's got like a..." She makes a swirling motion with her hand. "A smell of alloy, like metal beneath the mold. Can you smell it?"

He thought she was kidding, but she's taking deep breaths. He's not smelling it.

"Who do you think built it?" she asks.

"I don't know. It was just here."

She strokes the rough stubble of the plaster walls. Her fingers follow a crack running behind the table. She puts her ear to the wall and knocks, then moves the table and taps the floor.

"What are you doing?"

"Maybe there's a secret door somewhere. You know, push on the right spot and find a tunnel. The electronics are somewhere. You don't get cell phone service through a tree. If you ask me, this place is too empty. Who do you think stacked the wood?"

"My cousins, I guess."

"Someone lives here. They just don't want anyone to know."

"Maybe we should go."

She pulls the mesh screen on the fireplace and throws a log inside. "I say we stoke a fire and stay a while."

A lump is rising in his throat. Crossing the river was one thing; making themselves at home in the hobbit house had other consequences. *If Henry finds out.*

Molly finds matches in the table drawer. Before long, the room is warm enough to take off their coats. She pulls off her boots and socks, stretching in the chair. They listen to the wood pop. Oliver fishes through his backpack and pulls out the journal.

"You read my mind," she says.

Oliver sets his alarm so they have plenty of time to return. He can't make that mistake for a lot of reasons. He turns to the first page and begins to read aloud.

*August 6, 1882*

*A decision has been reached.*

*The elven elders have debated my fate for far too long. Despite my protests, they urge for my patience. I suppose they saved my life, they have that right. But my patience has reached an inglorious end. It has been tested for an Arctic summer. So it is with great pleasure that I received the news that a decision has been made.*

*It has been several months since I woke in the ice. I'm afraid you would not recognize me. I am as round as a sow and hairy as a grizzly. This very morning, when Nog told me the news, I was on the ice with nothing more than a sweater. To avoid dwelling on the pace of life with the elven, I have dedicated myself to helping wherever I can. I discover something shocking every day. They know so much, my love, yet I feel I've learned little.*

*This morning, I was releasing solar dust. These are tiny particles, no larger than pollen, that hover hundreds of feet above the ice, absorbing the sun's heat and transferring it back to the colony in the form of energy. Can you believe this? They don't burn wood or fuel; they transfer it directly from the sun.*

*In fact, Nog let me use the magic glove. He still hates it when I call it that, and he shouldn't let me use it, but he, more than anyone, knows how difficult this is for me. He said he trusts me, and that is a sign the news of the elders' decision will be good. Or perhaps he was just trying to cheer me up.*

*I must say, the glove is more magical than scientific, I don't care what Nog says. It is made to fit an elven hand—not a full-grown man's hand—but when I slipped my fingers inside the small opening, it expanded in a way that swallowed my hand. The metal links squirmed across my palm, shifting and settling. There was a slight stinging, and then, just like that, I couldn't feel it anymore, as if it became a second layer of skin.*

*Nog taught me how to visualize what I wanted, to reach into the bag and find it. Energy cannot be destroyed, he said. The bag simply reorganizes it. On my first attempt, I retrieved a canister to store a batch of dead solar dust. Next, he showed me how to retrieve an abominable sphere. These metallic orbs do more than just allow a snowman to build a body, they store the memories of past elven. He described it as a computer, something that stores data. Then he tried to describe a computer, and I'm afraid I still don't understand. Nonetheless, the snowman orb can be dangerous. Elven can touch them without a glove, but humans he's not so sure. He thinks that one might absorb the memories out of me. I wasn't willing to test his theory, so I put on the glove.*

*Nog tossed one of the metallic spheres into the snow, and just as the body began forming around it, I opened my hand and the orb slapped into the palm like the glove was a super magnet. It was quite empowering.*

"THAT WOULD EXPLAIN your grandmother's mystery power," Molly says. "Maybe your great-grandfather brought back solar dust. And if he didn't, maybe there's something else even more futuristic. You ever see a strange cloud hovering over the house?"

"No."

He had searched for a basement door, and there is none—none that he can see. *Would we even see solar dust?*

"What about a bag?" Molly asks. "Ever see anything like that?"

Oliver shakes his head. "I've only seen her wearing the glove. She might've had a bag under her coat or in her pocket, but I don't know."

Molly throws another log on the fire.

"Let's assume she's wearing the same glove," she says. "I understand why she'd keep it secret. I mean, you can't let everyone have a magic glove, but why would she wear it outside?"

Oliver reminds her how she pointed at the snowman clearing the road. She was wearing the glove. Maybe she was controlling it.

"But why the other times?" Molly says. "It's like she's using it for something other than pulling sleds out of magic bags."

*Maybe it's a weapon.*

Malcolm Toye pulled the sphere out of the forming body. Maybe Grandmother could do the same thing if she saw a snowman, or one of those things at the river.

Oliver flips past more drawings. The last one is of a gloved hand beautifully rendered to highlight the metal gleam.


*September 24, 1882*

*It has been a month.*

*It has taken me that long to record my thoughts. I'm afraid these words will never reach you.*

*I have not eaten. Food is tasteless. Even when I force it into my mouth, my stomach curdles it like spoiled milk. I have lost so much weight that I've had to wear heavy coats to keep warm. Even bundled up, the cold never really leaves.*

*To be honest, I have avoided this journal. To write the words will make their meaning real. I wake each morning hoping I dreamed the event, that my imagination is a magic bag that can rewrite history if I just visualize it. But each morning, I am still here.*

*You are still so far away.*

*I think Nog knew the decision. I should've known. The morning he led me to the elven elders, I sensed a change in the colony. We passed through the commons, where many elven come to eat. That morning, few were there.*

*Naively, I had assumed they were preparing for a celebration, that we would soon climb to the ice to welcome a new era where elven and humans walked the same sidewalks and lived as neighbors, that I would lead them out of the cold and introduce them like family.*

*My delusions were reinforced when I entered the great hall—a circular room with seats filled with elven. In the center was a raised dais, where the elders were seated along with Jessica and Nicholas Santa.*

"Did you just say 'Santa'?" Molly sits up. "As in St. Nick? As in Santa Claus?"

Oliver reads the paragraph again. "It says 'Nicholas Santa.'"

"Why didn't I see this coming? Did you see it?"

Oliver shakes his head. He hasn't seen anything.

"Elven on the North Pole, flying reindeer, and now Santa Claus?"

"It...it doesn't say Santa *Claus*."

"Is there another Santa?" She has a point.

"You want to hear more?"

She closes her eyes with a fixed grin. "Absolutely."

Nicholas delivered *the message like he was cauterizing a wound. It was swift and clean. "We will not merge with the human race," he said. "It has been decided that the world is best served if the elven continue to exist anonymously. Humanity is still in its infancy. Elven technology would only thwart human growth."*

*The fat man said 'we' like he was one of them. He is still human, like me. He still stands so much taller than the elven, but he speaks as if he's been one of them all his life. I, for one, don't wish for such delusion. I am human, and their attempts to mollify my pain are patronizing.*

*He continued to explain that the decision was difficult, that he knows I am lonely, that I yearn for home, for my love, but it is best for me, for the elven and humanity that I stay at the North Pole. Perhaps, he said, the decision will change in the near future. Does he realize dangling that tempta-*

*tion before me is dripping lemons into the wound? A wound that's been open for so long that it will never heal.*

*I have waited too long, my love. And while the jolly spirit has returned to the elven colony, it is not contagious. Rather, it mocks my pain.*

*I would rather die in your arms than live long in the ice.*

THE FIRE POPS, and the logs settle.

Silence between Oliver and Molly hangs for a minute. Then two.

"Oh, my God," Molly says. "Your great-grandfather may be wacked-out of his gourd on crazy berries, but this story is breaking my heart."

Oliver closes the journal. "It feels...*real.*"

"I know what you mean. The emotion is right there, on the pages. And those sketches are raw suffering."

"And the science behind solar harvesting, he wouldn't know about that in the late 1800s."

"Assuming the journals are authentic. I mean, your grandmother could've made those up before you got here."

"Why would she do that?"

"I don't know. I'm just putting it out there." She begins pacing, her bare feet quiet on the wood floor. "It's just the whole Santa Claus thing is throwing me."

"It didn't say Santa Claus."

"For some reason, the elven evolving during the Ice Age and the magic glove had me believing. But Santa Claus?"

"He said 'Nicholas Santa.'"

"What's the difference?"

She pinches her lower lip, walking back and forth, deciding whether to believe this or not. Her eyes have the intensity of a hungry owl. He can feel the doubts grinding in her head, this fantastic story colliding with reality. He's been there, too. He survived. *Or it altered me, and now I can't tell the difference between real and fantasy.*

The smell of weird is all over the property, but the mention of Santa somehow short-circuited everything.

*Even the snowman.*

"Do you still believe me?" Oliver asks.

"Yes, Oliver. I believe you."

There's a difference in how she said it, different than all the other times. A sliver of doubt had wedged its way between them. Oliver has had splinters. He knew if they weren't pulled out, they'd fester.

Oliver's alarm sounds off.

They snuff the fire and clean up, leaving the hobbit house exactly like they found it, even dragging wood from the forest and stacking it on the brick hearth. No one would know they had been there. Not the twins or anyone else.

Oliver leads her over the fallen tree, reaching back to hold her hand. The compass isn't much help, again. Oliver senses what direction to go, can feel the pull of home. A few minutes later, they spot the twin trees up ahead. The friendship bracelets are still attached.

"Look, Oliver!" Molly trots ahead. She loops her finger through one of the bracelets. "They switched!"

He's not sure what she means. The colorful braided bracelets are still tied to the branches, one on each side. But then he gets it: the blue one is on the wrong side, and the red is on the other.

He doubts his orientation, wondering if he's looking in the wrong direction, but he can hear the river at his back. *They switched.*

"Smell the weird." Molly pulls in a deep draught of air. When she exhales, Oliver feels her sliver of doubt wiggle free. Perhaps not all the way, but the weird has pushed it to the side.

Oliver leads the way, following a sense of direction emanating from his gut, pointing like a magnetic needle unaffected by the forest. He brushes aside hanging vines, jogs around saplings like a hound following a rabbit. And then he realizes, the pull isn't in his gut.

He pulls his hand out of his pocket.

The wooden orb is warm. It hums, but not like his phone on vibrate, more like a caffeinated buzz in the palm of his hand. Like the sun rising on a cold day to kiss his cheeks.

They reach the clearing.

Oliver stops just inside the trees, eyeing the windmill across patches of wet ground and dying snow. The orb burns in his palm, the vibrations shaking his hand. He holds it between his finger and thumb. It sounds like a summer cicada taking flight.

"What's wrong?" Molly asks.

It pulls Oliver's attention away from the windmill. He looks to the far left of the clearing, just about where the mysterious snowball was launched. Something moves in the shadows.

Something massive.

It steps into the light, revealing its thick legs and barrel-shaped torso. One powerful arm hangs at its side; the other holds the nearest tree.

Across the distance, Oliver feels the needles from the branch he's holding as if they're pricking his own hand. His heart, for once, isn't beating like the heart of a frightened rabbit. It's calm and still. For once, maybe the first time he can remember, strength fills him from the inside, pouring through his hand like the orb is a spigot turned wide open. At that moment, he could lift a fallen tree.

The snowman steps back and then dissolves like he had once before, this time in a slushy stream that sifts between the trees. The orb falls quiet.

"Do you believe?" Oliver asks.

Molly's eyes are glassy. She wets her lips and whispers, "I believe."

## 16

---

Green grass and May flowers replace the snow.

Oliver holds the wooden orb. Ever since they saw the snowman, the day he took Molly out to the hobbit house, the day she held his hand, the orb had fallen silent. Now it's just a piece of wood. Oliver wishes for winter to return. Maybe not today.

Molly's coming.

Today they'll hike out to the forest flush with new growth and find the bracelet tree. They'll cross the bridge to hike beyond the hobbit house. If there's time, they can read another journal. Maybe the snow is missing, but the magic can still happen. And not the science kind of magic.

*That boy-girl kind of magic.*

He pulls on a sweatshirt and a clean pair of cargo pants, stuffing his phone deep in the side pocket. His boots are on the back porch. The backpack, though, isn't under the bed. He left it in the upstairs bathroom, tucked behind the toilet, to find the best journal entries to read. The ones in his backpack had more sketches and boring details about snow and daily chores—things about sustainable energy and food sources. Once he got to a passage that addressed the fat man—

the red-coated man named Santa—he slid a square of paper between the pages.

He promised not to read the last two journals without her. He scanned the pages to find the good parts, but he kept his word and didn't read them. Not all of them. But these are the last two. It was like coming to the end of a really good book: you want to read the end without the journey ending.

First things first.

*Rule #1: Nothing happens unless the chores are done.*

Oliver skips down the steps. Mom and Grandmother must be outside. There was talk about a garden and a shovel. Without a rototiller in sight, Oliver could guess who would be working the shovel. And what about mowing? Would he have to cut the pasture with a pair of dull scissors?

The chore board is clean.

Not a mark, not a letter. Nothing. His heart swells, but he holds his breath. Grandmother could be in the backyard, waiting to ambush him with a rusty pair of shears. *Get to mowing, Olivah.*

He'd have to think about this. Maybe it'd be wise to meet Molly at the entrance, hike through the trees to avoid the backyard; maybe load up his backpack for the day.

He closes the pantry door. *The backpack.*

It's sitting on the kitchen table, the flap flung open. The pockets are limp, the inside empty.

Oliver turns cold and not the kind nipping at your nose—the kind that reaches inside your belly, pulls your intestines into your throat, and wraps them around your heart like copper wire. Because it's not just the library books, the magazines and the *World of Succulents* that's missing.

"Where did you get these?"

Oliver jumps.

A sound escapes him, one reserved for cornered animals. Grandmother is wearing a black dress that reaches the floor, white frilly trim at the cuffs and hem. Clutched to her chest, her knuckles white around the spines, are the scuffed covers of the journals.

All five of them.

Oliver's chin begins to twitch. Lies tumble around his mind like a lottery wheel, but there are no words to get stuck in his throat. He's empty.

"*Where?*" Grandmother shouts. "Where did you find these? You tell me from where you took these books!"

Her voice has changed. It sounds small and scratchy.

The leather bindings creak under pressure, tendons stretching the thin and spotted skin on the backs of her hands. With them pressed to her breast, she reaches out with one hand, her fingers curled like talons, and crosses the kitchen. Her footsteps land like cinder blocks, shaking the dishes.

She catches his chin—her thumb plied to the left side of his jaw, her fingers clenching against the right. He falls back a step.

"This is not your property," she hisses. "I have locked doors in this house that you are not to open, places you are not to trespass. I made that very clear, Olivah. It was and is the first rule."

The pressure of her grip eases.

"How dare you violate my trust. Now tell me where you found these." Her eyes search his face. "Where are the other two?"

*Other two?*

She's holding five of them. If the one he dropped is still in the attic, that means there are seven journals. There were only six in the footlocker. He's sure of it.

"I want to know where you found these."

For a moment, it sounds as if she's asking, really asking where he got them. As if she doesn't know.

"Answer me!"

Her nails dig into his soft flesh.

"What's going on?" Mom is just inside the kitchen with dirt on the knees of her faded jeans.

"I have invited you to stay in my house, Debra. I opened up my life to you when you were in need, and now you have violated my trust."

"What are you talking about?"

"There are rules; I made that quite simple. All you had to do was follow them. Why is this so difficult? Why can't people simply *do what they promise?*"

It's not clear who she's talking to. Or about. A small squeak slips through her spastic attempts to swallow. She grabs the journals with both hands again, squeezing and pushing them up to her chin.

Mom looks at Oliver. "What happened?"

He clasps his hands behind his back to keep them from shaking. There's nothing he can do about his chin, still throbbing from Grandmother's claw.

"Answer your mother!"

"Mother." Oliver's mom holds out her hand. "Let's be calm."

"He took these. I found them in his bag."

"The blank diaries?"

The line between her thinning lips tightens. "No."

"What are they?" When Grandmother doesn't answer, she turns to Oliver, tells him to take a deep breath and relax. She just wants to know what's happening.

"Those are great-grandfather's journals...from the 1880s."

He adds more details about the journey. At first, his words blur together, but they become stronger the more he talks about the tragic journey and how great-grandfather survived because of the pendant around his neck.

He leaves out the weird parts.

Grandmother's eyes glitter as if a slick of tears has formed.

"Okay," Mom says. "Were they in your room with the blank one?"

"The garage."

"Liar," Grandmother seethes.

"Mother! That's enough!"

"That door is locked. It is always locked. No one is allowed in there, ever."

"I swear, it was unlocked," Oliver says. "I didn't do anything to—"

She starts for his chin. Oliver involuntarily steps back.

"Stop this!" Mom steps in front of her. "You will not touch him like that, Mother. And you will not speak to him like that, either. He is *my* son. I am *his* mother."

"Then act like it."

"And hit him? Berate him? Criticize him until he's nothing, is that what you mean?"

Grandmother turns her steely glare on him, the one that could pierce an armored tank. This time, though, it's lacking conviction. She walks to the other side of the kitchen, the books shielding her. The house is silent except for her wheezing and the covers squeaking beneath her palms.

"I know Grandmother's rules; I swear I never broke them." He winces, knowing he's broken more than a few, just not that one. "It was during the winter, when it was cold. I was looking for a place to store the snow shovel. The door was unlocked, I swear. I didn't think much of it. I wasn't snooping. But the garage was heated and I was cold, so I stayed until my exercise time was up. I didn't take anything."

He avoids looking at Grandmother because he *did* snoop—major league snooping—and he *did* take something. His hand moves over his pocket. Grandmother sees him feeling for the comfort of the wooden orb, reaching for the confidence that surges through his arm when he squeezes it.

"What do you have?" she says.

The blood drains from his cheeks, replaced by chilled antifreeze. Grandmother, walking silently this time, crosses the kitchen and pulls his hand away.

"What's in your pocket?" she asks.

He reaches to the bottom and pulls the pocket inside out. It's empty. *It's gone.* But he had it with him when he left his bedroom. He never goes anywhere without it.

"I just...I found the journals. They were interesting, that's all. I was bored."

"Why did you take them?"

He shrugs. "I was going to put them back when I was finished."

"Can I see them?" Mom asks.

"No," Grandmother says.

"Why not?"

"They are my property, Debra. Your son took them."

"If they're just diaries, why can't he read them, Mother? I'd like to know more about my grandfather. I'm sure that's why he read them."

Grandmother's grip tightens. Her chalky complexion turns pinkish then red like stage lights warming her face. She turns and, without a sound, leaves. The creaky floor tells them she's crossed the house.

Oliver explains to his mom, again, how the door wasn't locked. The door was indeed unlocked every time, the garage warm and inviting. As if waiting for him. Grandmother returns, her steps a little more forceful. She's pulling on a sweater. The journals are somewhere safe, unlikely to ever be found again.

"Come along." She gestures for them to follow as she trods—yes, actually trods—to the mudroom and out the back door. Mom watches her without moving.

A deep breath escapes her.

Grandmother is waiting in front of the garage, bare hands at her sides. No glove, this time. Oliver walks around the garage, his mom chaperoning like a prison guard. Nervous worms turn in Oliver's stomach as he steps into the shade. The mud squishes around his boots. Grandmother stands back, a grim frown pushing her chin forward.

Oliver reaches for the doorknob.

The metal knob is colder and harder than it should be. He squeezes it and closes his eyes. He turns it.

*Click.*

It hardly moves before catching the lock. It's followed by three more clicks as he tries again and again.

"Mom, I swear..."

Keys jiggle.

Grandmother pushes her way past them, avoiding the soft muddy spot where Oliver's standing. She removes his hand and, sorting through an old set of keys, some of them the old-fashioned skeleton type, finds a modern one. She slides it into the lock and, before opening it, drops the keys into her sweater pocket, but not before Oliver notices a smaller key sandwiched on the ring. This one is short and square, more like a peg with a glowing blue cube at the end, as if catching light in the shade. He's seen a key like that before.

*In the footlocker.*

Grandmother tells Oliver to remove his filthy boots. The garage is cold and dank.

"Grandmother, it was unlocked all the other times, I swear."

Her x-ray truth sensors tell her he's not lying about the door, and that's what bothers her. He was lying about something earlier.

"Where did you find the books?"

He points at the dark corner beneath the bench.

Grandmother investigates. "*Exactly* where?"

"In the footlocker. That was unlocked, too. I know I said I wasn't snooping, but I didn't come in here to do it. I was just looking for somewhere to put the shovel, and then I was going to leave. I just noticed the footlocker, and...and I got curious. I'm sorry, I really am. I didn't think I was hurting anything."

*That's where the six journals were,* he wants to say. *Not seven.*

A sick feeling fills his stomach. He was *curious* when he rifled through the filing cabinet and crouched beneath the workbench. But if he was honest, he was getting back at all the strict rules. The garage was his one safe place he could do stuff he knew he shouldn't be doing. He was hiding in the dark when she came into the garage wearing the metal glove, unlocking the door when she did and locking it when she left. But still, it was unlocked for Oliver. Somehow, it was always unlocked. This was his place to learn secrets.

Secrets no one was going to tell him.

He's not certain if that rotten sensation is guilt or sadness that it's over.

Grandmother walks away from the workbench and past the filing cabinets. The pinkish hue of anger fades from her cheeks. Her eyes dart around the room, her head turning like a bird listening for a worm. She pats her empty pockets. Her hand, the right one, the one that always wears the metal glove, flexes uncontrollably, like it's searching for something she can't reach.

Mom looks under the workbench. "What footlocker?"

"The old one." Oliver starts bending over, but now he knows. Maybe it's because the garage feels different—colder and darker. The look on Grandmother's face.

*Something's wrong.*

She walks around the shiny black car and pulls the garage door shut. Patting her pockets, Oliver thinks she's looking for the glove again, like the bulky thing was hiding in a secret pouch. Instead, she pulls out a cell phone and not an ordinary one.

*A smartphone.*

"Mother, what are you doing?" Mom asks.

Oliver doesn't notice that she's thumbing through contacts and searching for a number. He's still processing the vision of her holding a cell phone. And using it. She puts it to her ear, the black modern case clashing with the steel gray hair pulled back in a grandmotherly bun.

Grandmother answers his mom's questions, but Oliver is wondering how she's getting service. The rules prohibit Oliver from using electronics; he had assumed they applied to her, too. But if brought to a court of law, the rule clearly stated that *he* not use electronics.

"Hello," Grandmother says to someone. "Yes, it's Mother. I need you to come to the property tonight. Bring Henry and Helen."

That snaps Oliver back to the present moment like a fist in the midsection. It doesn't take long for the facts to tumble into place. If Henry knows he's been in the garage, when he finds out that he was reading the journals...

*He'll know I've been other places.*

## 17

---

Oliver adjusts his weight. The bottom step creaks.

Grandmother stands with her back to the front door. Despite spring's warmth, she hides her hands in the pockets of a dark wool coat.

"This isn't necessary," Mom says.

"Do you want to continue living here?" Grandmother takes her laser blue-green eyes off of Oliver. "If you do, there are rules to be followed. If you and Oliver do not follow the rules, people can be hurt. Or worse."

She puckers in consternation, lines of worry carving the flesh around her paper-thin lips.

"He said the garage was unlocked. He didn't take anything," Mom says. "I understand it can be dangerous if he gets lost on the property or stays out after dark, but you're overreacting, Mother. He was just reading journals about his great-grandfather. Maybe if the rules weren't so strict, if you let him use his phone and iPad, he wouldn't be looking for something to do."

Oliver shoves his hands deep into his pants pockets, searching for the comfort of the orb. He wishes he could find it. He'd squeeze it right in front of her, he wouldn't care. He needed it.

Grandmother turns her focused high-beam on him, as if sensing the untruth.

*I did take something.*

It never felt like he took it until she asked. The journals, those he took. But up until the moment she asked, the orb felt like it belonged to him.

"My property operates on rules. It is the sole reason I am alive today."

"What are you talking about?"

"Order, Debra. I'm talking about order and chaos. Without structure, there is chaos. You have to know your environment and the world you live in to survive. Despite your convictions, you know very little, my child. Chaos has not done you much good, I think you'll agree."

"Mother, can we just talk about the garage right now?"

"Do you want to stay in this house, Debra? Do you want to live under my roof?"

Mom's chin juts forward. She shakes her head, an expression Oliver has come to know as grim resignation. "I appreciate your hospitality," she says, the words being pushed out, "but there's no need to drag this out."

"Answer the question."

"Of course, Mother." Mom stands straighter. "We need a place for now."

"Then you shall follow the rules."

"And these are the same rules that Father followed before he left?"

Grandmother doesn't flinch. There's a long pause. Unspoken words hang between them, their long glares locking like horns.

"Your father broke the rules," she finally says. "And he is no longer with us."

Oliver fidgets, and the step sings.

"Olivah, keep your place and stand at attention. Keep your hands at your sides, no touching the bannister. You will remain here until further notice. Is that understood?"

He nods.

And then she says something that nearly buckles his knees. Not with fear, but shock and amazement.

"I love you both," she says.

*Love.* The word actually came from her mouth. Her lips formed it, her tongue spoke it. Hearing it was like swigging from a bottle of vinegar but tasting something sweet—it didn't compute. Even if she delivered the word with the synthetic emotionlessness of a computer, it still came out of her.

"But true love," she says, "has nothing to do with feeling good."

Oliver feels a wave of weird begin—his blood sugar is getting low. He'll let it drop. He used to do that when he was little, especially when he was mad at his mom. He'd let it go until he was shaking. It was his way of punishing her.

Grandmother slides her hands into her coat before walking to the kitchen. Mom watches from the front door, a grim smile dimpling her cheeks, her chin cocked sideways like she'd taken a right hook.

He knew this expression, too.

She's putting pieces together, hatching a plan. The last time he saw that look was in Texas, shortly after losing her job. Creditors had been calling, and the rent was due. There were few options for them, none of them good.

And then they came here.

She unlocks her jaw. With a brief nod, she climbs onto the bottom step, forcing him to move over. She takes a jagged breath, adjusting the kinks in her back before standing upright. A calm expression rises to the surface, placid and meditative.

Her next breath is smooth.

"We had to do this when we were in trouble," she says. "She would make us wait for our father. Sometimes it would be hours. When it was just me, the boredom was unbearable, but I became a pro at this. I learned to keep good posture. I hate to admit it, but it helps. Pretend there's a string pulling the crown of your head where your hair swirls. This will keep your back straight. Find a spot on the door and breathe through it."

She pulls an easy breath through her nostrils, lets it flow from her lips.

"And she always knew if we were touching the wall or the railing. And if we got the giggles, that was also more time on the step. The record was four hours, all the way until bedtime. And then we went back to the step first thing in the morning."

"What'd you do?"

"Doesn't matter." She shakes her head. "There are worse things than standing on this Godforsaken step, I suppose. Your grandmother never hit us, so there's that."

Oliver knew what it was like to be ignored. He knew what a fat lip was like, too. Given the choice, he'd take a shot to the mouth.

But neither was good.

Oliver tried her posture technique, imagining a string attached where the hair swirled on his head, picking a spot on the side panel of glass to breathe through. It wasn't long before his back ached. Worse, he thought about not seeing Molly.

That ached, too.

"Get off the step, Debra." Grandmother appears at their side. "Don't be silly."

Mom keeps her composure, quietly breathing. Oliver keeps his focus on the window. Several moments pass.

Grandmother stands at the side of the door, the sharp tip of her nose almost pressed to the glass. Oliver stares at the bun on the back of her head, not a single gray hair escaping the intricate web of pins and elastic bands. He inhales through his nostrils, imagining his breath pulling through her head like a cool breeze, her thoughts penetrating his sinuses like dust, swirling inside him.

Cold and empty.

He consumes her innermost secrets, or what he imagines them to be, picturing her up late at night, walking the property in search of something, the metal glove securely wrapped around her hand, the fingers arched like talons, the moon pale on her cheeks. Beneath her distant stare and hardened stance, he feels a great need, an unrequited desire for something she'd lost. Something she'd once had.

*Once loved.*

"What is love?" The words leap from his tongue, startling him like someone else said them.

Grandmother flinches. "Quiet."

"If it doesn't feel good," he continues, "then what is it?"

He was thinking about Molly, the way it felt when their hands were entwined, the warm swirl in his belly when they walked together. When he saw her, his chest opened and fireworks exploded. She was this star, this enormous field of gravity that he was hopelessly caught in, destined to forever orbit. If that's not love...

"It's a fair question." Mom spoke up.

Grandmother doesn't move, but her shoulders rise with a long, deep breath. "I didn't say it didn't feel good. The point of true love is not happy feelings. It's to do what is required in that moment. Good feelings may result, but that's not the point."

Colors spread across the distorted panes of glass as a car eases into the circle driveway.

"It is difficult to truly love." Grandmother opens the door.

Aunt Rhonnie is climbing the steps. The fair-headed blood-related duo is behind her. Henry is locked on him like crosshairs tracking a buck.

Breathing becomes difficult. It feels like a wool blanket has been pulled over Oliver's mouth. Each step his cousin takes, another layer is added.

"What's so urgent, Mother?" Aunt Rhonnie asks.

"Come inside."

She steps aside to let Henry and Helen go first. A smirk snarls deep into Henry's cheek, his eyes hooded like a viper. Aunt Rhonnie brings her open hand behind him, cuffing him in the back of the head.

"Stop smiling. Get in there."

Henry and Helen stand to the side, their shoes shiny and their clothes snug and wrinkle-free. Their fair skin appears to have avoided sunlight for too long, almost vampire-like in its paleness.

Aunt Rhonnie lowers her movie-star glasses and peers at Oliver's mom.

"What are you doing?"

"Reliving old memories."

Aunt Rhonnie's eyes narrow.

"What do you know about the garage?" Grandmother asks. Aunt Rhonnie turns, but Grandmother is standing in front of Henry and Helen. The twins exchange confused looks.

"Tell me. Now."

"There's a car inside," Helen says. "Is that what you mean?"

"Have I not told you to stay away?" They agree, in unison. "Have you been inside the garage, then?"

"No," they say.

"Have you ever tried to go inside?"

There's a pause. Without looking at each other, they decide not to test Grandmother's truth detector. Together, they nod.

"Mother, really?" Aunt Rhonnie says. "This couldn't be done on the phone?"

*Her death ray only works in person.*

"Olivah says the garage was unlocked for him." Grandmother leans closer to Henry. Her nose twitches like she's smelling the truth. "He took something that belongs to me. Something very special. What do you know about this?"

A dark shade falls over Henry. The joyless smile is replaced with grim focus.

"Well?"

"Nothing, Grandmother," Henry says. "We've never even smelled the inside of the garage."

She stands in front of him. Oliver, once again staring at the tight bun, feels Henry's eyes as if they are boring through Grandmother to latch onto him.

"What's the big deal, Mother?" Aunt Rhonnie says. "So they want to see the car. I hardly think this deserves an investigation."

Grandmother steps away; her hands fold behind her back.

Henry, his stare once again fixed on Oliver, says, "If I may speak?"

"Continue," Grandmother says.

"What else has he done?"

A cold shank of fear drives down Oliver's legs, spiking his heels into the step. He can't feel his thighs and knows to keep his knees locked or he'll fall like a boneless bag.

"I'd like to have a word with Henry and Helen," Grandmother intones. "Alone."

"Oh, for God's sake," Aunt Rhonnie mutters.

"Come along." Grandmother exits the foyer, quietly padding down the hall. Henry lingers after Helen until Aunt Rhonnie tells him to get his butt in gear. Oliver avoids looking at them.

Once in the kitchen, their voices murmur. Oliver, Mom and Aunt Rhonnie concentrate to make out what is so top secret until the back door closes. Silence falls like heavy snow.

"Get off the step," Aunt Rhonnie says. "You look ridiculous, Deb."

"That's the point."

Aunt Rhonnie cusses. "I need a drink."

She slams the front door on the way outside. The pointy ends of her high heels hammer the steps and chisel the sidewalk. Several moments later, the base line of a synthesized beat vibrates through the front door. Aunt Rhonnie sits alone in the car.

Mom begins laughing. "Come on."

She steps off and stretches. Fear punches Oliver between the ribs. His ears prick for sound coming from the back of the house, aware that old ninja shoes can still be watching. Mom pulls him by the elbow.

Surprisingly, he doesn't fold like a book. His legs are still solid.

She walks to the kitchen, rifling through the cabinets for a glass, whistling while she does it. *She's done this before.*

When Oliver gets the courage, he follows. Mom is in the dining room, but a glass of tea is waiting next to the sink. He's not thirsty, but takes a sip. He grabs something to eat to bring his sugar up. He'll need a blood test.

Outside, standing in front of the garage window with her back to the house, Grandmother is talking to the twins. Oliver jumps to the side and, a few seconds later, eases in view.

Henry is looking at him.

But that's not why Oliver's knees go limp-noodle.

*He's wearing a metal glove.*

# 18

Aunt Rhonnie sits in the car for hours.

She's on her phone with a cup of Starbucks. A grande. Occasionally, she walks around the circle drive with cup in hand, waving it in a slow circle. Eventually, she goes home.

The twins stay.

That night, dinner is quiet. Almost silent. Oliver doesn't look up from his plate. Henry and Helen clear the table but leave the dishes for Oliver. He doesn't mind.

Oliver locks himself in his bedroom. He searches for the wooden orb, yearning to feel the vibrations in his arm like a fat beetle shaking its wings. It's gone. *Where could it be?*

He hears footsteps outside his door in the middle of the night.

The next morning, the twins are gone. There are chores by his name. Henry's and Helen's names aren't on the board. That afternoon he sees them returning from across the field. Dinner is almost as quiet as the first night.

This goes on for a week.

Oliver stays in bed the next morning. He eats his stash of energy bars to keep his sugar balanced. It's not quite lunch when he leaves. He pauses on the second floor. The bedroom doors are open. The house, a veritable motion detector, popping when someone yawns, is silent. He backs up a step, then two. The blood pushes through his veins in gushing waves. He clutches the railing.

His socks, hanging off the toes, allow him to slide quietly, not silently, but quietly toward Henry's and Helen's rooms. He stops midway at the bathroom, listening before continuing.

Henry's room is first.

Oliver peeks around the open door. His head vibrates with excitement. He takes a deep breath and steps inside. The bed is made, the corners tucked and the bedspread smooth. The top of the dresser is clean, like the floor. No one would know someone lived here.

*Rule #980: Live like you don't exist.*

Oliver looks under the bed, where dusty bunnies have been exterminated. He doesn't touch the bed, afraid a wrinkle will give him away. After listening for signs of life, he crosses over to the dresser and pulls open the top drawer.

It's full of clothes.

All the drawers are full. The shirts are neatly folded, the pants pressed and creased. Even the underwear is organized next to rows of socks lined up like soldiers. At first, Oliver hoped to see something without touching anything. There's one thing he wants to find more than anything else, even more than the wooden orb. Something that would ensure that he wasn't imagining, that this isn't a dream.

*The metal glove.*

*Were they just pretending they couldn't go into the garage? It was one thing for Grandmother to get weird, but she acted like they were in on it. And Aunt Rhonnie and Mom still didn't seem to have a clue. But if I find that glove, it'd be proof the weird includes his cousins. If I find it, I could put it on.*

But it's not there. And he's not going to move a single sock. He's already beginning to wonder if he's left footprints in the hall. He eases the last drawer closed.

"There you are."

Oliver's heart rockets into his throat, bulldozing blood into his head. Darkness spills into his vision, and he steadies himself on the dresser, turning to see someone in the doorway. His heartbeat slams past his eardrums.

"Looking for your cousins?" his mom says.

"No," he says. After several breaths, but still clutching the dresser, he adds, "Not really."

"I need to talk to you."

Oliver slides out of the bedroom while she adjusts the headband that holds her hair off her face. She's wearing fewer earrings than usual, just a couple in each lobe. Oliver uses the restroom first, just in case Henry or Helen come upstairs and see them standing outside their bedrooms. When he comes out, Mom has her shirt tucked in.

"How do I look?" she asks.

"Good. Are you going somewhere?"

"Sort of. I've got a job at the bookstore down the street from that café you go to."

"Little Professor?"

"That's the one. It's just shelving books and running the cash register, but it's something."

His mom was never good with real jobs. She always got bored. It was the whole punching a clock and taking orders and evaluations. She referenced Pink Floyd a lot when she complained, that humans weren't meant to sit in rows and march in lines. Sometimes she got fired, but mostly she just stopped going. They didn't have much money, but that never bothered Oliver. He didn't know he was poor until he got older.

Texas, though, was the first time his mom borrowed money. The lenders were coming for everything. Hard to start a career when you're standing in a hole. Oliver often wondered which one was deeper: the one back in Texas or the one Grandmother dug in her childhood.

"Is that what you wanted to talk about?"

"Yeah. That and moving out of here. I looked around for apartments and figured we could live in town. It'd take a few months to get enough for first and last months' rent, but we'd be out of here. How's that sound?"

"Great." He didn't shout or jump for joy, but a smile crossed his face.

"I know, I know. It wasn't fair to bring you here. I mean, I'm used to dealing with your grandmother. I won't be making much money, so we'll have to eat ramen noodles for a while."

"I'll eat paper for dinner, I don't care. I'll brush my teeth with soap."

"All right, relax. We're not moving into a dumpster. I want to stay in town, though. Your grandmother is getting older, and despite what she thinks, she'll need some help—"

Oliver wraps his arms around her, so elated that if he didn't hang on he'd float to the ceiling. They'll move to town, where he'll get phone service, where he can walk to the library. Where he'll see Molly.

He never thought he had much of a normal life compared to others. After living with Grandmother, he realized he was much closer than he thought. And he'd get back to that. Nothing could stop them from leaving. Nothing could change his mind. Least of all Henry.

*He'll be happy we're leaving.*

If only Oliver could avoid him until then. But the streak ends that night. Oliver thought Henry would be the last person to change his mind about leaving.

It's almost midnight.

Oliver can't sleep. He's imagining a two-bedroom apartment. He could put posters on the wall, not make his bed in the morning or do chores. Excitement trembles inside him like a surge of caffeine.

The silhouette of the windmill is dim in the open field. There's no snow to contrast against, not even patches in the shadows. Winter is officially over. The river must be swollen. Maybe it's even reached the bridge.

Oliver looks at the dresser, the outline barely visible in the dark room. There's still a journal in the attic. He hadn't thought about it since Grandmother snatched his book bag, afraid she'd see the thoughts in his eyes. *What must be in them that made her panic? Maybe she doesn't want us to know mental illness runs in the family. The world knows without those journals, trust me.*

*And where's the seventh one?*

Maybe now would be the time to go to the attic. He checks the time, thinking he could get down the hall and back within minutes—

Tap. Tap. Tap.

Oliver fumbles the phone. His teeth lock together, clamped by the raw grip of fear. Someone knocked on the door, but not with a knuckle. More like a fingernail, each rap separated by a long second. The last one sent gooseflesh across his shoulders as the nail dragged across the painted surface.

Tap. Tap. Tap.

...scratch.

The previous gooseflesh transforms into full-body shrink-wrap. Eyes wide, he stops breathing.

"Ollie."

Henry didn't so much as say his name as he breathed it. And not through the heavy door, but under it.

"Open the door, Ollie. I know you're in there. I know you're awake."

Oliver presses his hands over his ears. He could sit there all night. Henry couldn't get into the room unless he had a key. Which he probably does because it's just an old-fashioned lock.

"Ollllllie."

If he's got a metal glove, he's got one of those keys.

"Open the dooooooor."

Scratch.

With jerky movements, he slides across the room. The knob turns against the lock. Oliver gulps for air, drawing deep, smooth breaths, feeling his pulse flutter in his neck. He slides his feet—his dead cold feet—and holds the doorknob.

"Open," Henry says, "the door."

Oliver turns the oval end of the key. The latch tumbles in the assembly. He pulls it open. Henry stands upright in the doorway. Oliver can see the perfect posture of Grandmother possessing his body. The dim light from the bedroom window reveals a spreading grin.

"What do you want?" The words lack the quiver in Oliver's belly.

Henry, wearing a white robe with wide collars and soft-soled slippers, walks forward. Oliver steps aside. In the dark, he paces around the bed, hands in the square pockets of his robe. He looks around the room, tilting his head toward the dresser, the nightstand and bed, as if he might see something in the dark. Maybe he smells the binoculars still hidden under the bed.

"What do you know?" Henry flips the pillow and rubs his hand over the sheet beneath it.

"What?"

"What do you know, Ollie? What have you seen?"

"I don't know what you're talking about."

Henry sighs. With his back to the window, he's a silhouette. "I know you and your girlfriend have been out to the room, the one in the hill. When I specifically told you not to, you went out there, didn't you?"

Oliver hopes Henry can't see his chin quiver.

"You went into the garage. You read the journals. You snooped around."

Oliver shakes his head. Henry lets the seconds pile up. His breath leaks through his nostrils like steam.

"You don't know anything, Ollie. You know nothing about this family, about the property or Grandmother. You and your gypsy mother wander in here like homeless tramps and think, because we share DNA, you'll fit right in, but you're wrong. Tell me what you've seen."

"I don't know what you're talking about."

Henry moves a step closer, his features still hidden in the shadows.

"Was it magical? When you saw him, did it blow your mind? Did you think he'd have a corncob pipe and a carrot for a nose? He led you into that garage, took you right to the journals, didn't he? He put them right in your lap so that you'd know the story, and you ate it up. If you think he cares about you, you're wrong. He doesn't care about anyone."

"How do you know it's a *he*?"

"Kiss the journals goodbye. The snow is gone; he won't be back. It's just you, now. No more friends to protect you. No mystery snow-balls flying out of the woods, no free rides to the open field. You're alone, Ollie."

"Why do you have a metal glove?" The cold quiver that usually buckles his knees is still there, but now there's an undercurrent of steel in his bones. His feet remain planted on the floor. He can feel the lines burning his palm as if he's squeezing the orb.

"It's not a *he*," Henry says. "Get it right; it's an *it*. And *it* doesn't like you."

"What's the metal glove for? Do you control them with it? I know Grandmother has one; I've seen her with it. Why does she have it? Why is the windmill charged and the forest shift and the garage locked? Why is all this a secret?"

The walls crackle. The momentum of courage pushes the questions out. He can't stop.

"What's the glove do?"

"You need to stop asking questions." Henry steps closer. Oliver can smell his mouthwash. "Nobody is ready for the answers, Ollie. Not you, not this town. Not the world. It's best if you and your mother be on your way. Before you get hurt, Ollie. It's not safe."

The menace dropped from the last line. There was no threat, like he actually meant it, he actually cared. Just for a moment. But the menace comes back in the very next breath.

"I know this is all wonderful and exciting. Everything is new and fun. There's so much mystery on the property, I get that. But it's not for you or your mother. You've got to go; it's for your own good. People disappear out here, and no one cares. You know that."

"I'm not scared of you."

"It's not me you should be scared of."

"We have a right to be here."

"I'm trying to help. Why can't you see that?"

"I don't think you are. The snowman doesn't, either. That's why he pulverized you with the snowball."

Henry hesitates. He doesn't move. And in that long moment, Oliver senses doubt covering something up.

"You're scared of him," Oliver says. "That's why you want us to leave."

"You have no idea what there is to fear."

"You're lying. He doesn't hate me, he hates you. And that scares the crap out of you."

It makes sense now. The snowman showed Oliver the journals. He kept Henry from taking his stocking cap and protected him from the things in the woods. Henry's not trying to protect Oliver; he's trying to save himself. Grandmother, too.

"You're forgetting something." Henry takes another step, and Oliver backs into the wall. His mouthwash smells like medicine. "Without snow, there is no snowman."

Oliver's hand is balled into a fist, aching to feel the grooves in his palm. He relaxes his hand, but reflexively squeezes. If he concentrates, he can feel the rough surface, sense the confidence surge through his arm. Cradle his chest.

Henry steps back and looks down.

Oliver doesn't realize he's staring at his clenching fist. Oliver finds himself cornered between the bed and window. He raises two fists and squares up.

He's never been in a fight, never thrown a punch. His dad taught him how to stand, how to hold his hands, but that was it. He smacked Oliver in the head, called him names, and laughed in his face. His dad bragged that Oliver couldn't even make him spill his drink.

Truth was, Henry was going to pound him, right there in the bedroom. Oliver could cry for help; his mom would come. She pulled him out of school and called the parents of a bully that took Oliver's lunch; she cussed out his dad when he came home with bruises on his arm. But for the first time, Oliver didn't want her to save him.

He was making a stand.

Henry catches Oliver's arm and, in one swift motion, twists it behind his back. Pressing his thumb into Oliver's wrist, he pries open his fingers to find an empty palm.

He shoves Oliver in the corner.

Oliver's huffing, fists in front again. He's bobbing on the balls of his feet. Next time Henry reaches, he'll crack the top of his head.

"Where is it?" Henry says.

"What?"

"You know. Hand it over."

"I don't have anything."

"Where'd it go?"

He shrugs. "Depends on what you want."

"Don't play, Ollie. You shouldn't have it."

"Have what?"

"The wood ball." Henry looks back at the door. "You don't know what you're doing, Ollie. You don't know anything. Now where is it?"

The truth would make this easy. It would be safe. Oliver shifts his feet, bends at the knees, and tightens his fists. He wishes he had the orb, wishes he had something to protect, a reason to tense for a battle. If he did have the orb, he'd like to see Henry try to take it from him.

Henry makes a move, but it's a feint to flush Oliver out of the corner. Oliver doesn't buy it; instead, he lunges. Henry's caught off guard but quickly regains his balance, avoiding Oliver's swing, shoving his face into the down comforter. With Henry's knee in his back and a mouthful of fabric, Oliver panics to breathe. He wasn't ready to hold his breath, and his chest is already on fire.

"You think you're special?" Henry says in his ear. "I've been out here since I was born. I've been waiting for that snowflake to give me the orb, and you come out here with your dirtbag mother two months and I get a snowball in the face..."

Oliver flails, but Henry holds him down. It's almost too easy.

"It's not going to work that way, Ollie. We'll decide where the magic happens."

His words are hot on Oliver's ear, but the air sizzles in his head as he tries to breathe. Henry twists Oliver's arm, and, automatically, his fist opens.

"Where is it?" Henry's knee thuds in Oliver's back. "Where is it!"

"Enough," someone says, drily.

Henry leaps off.

Oliver rolls onto his back, sucking air while tears stream over his cheeks. Grateful it's dark, that maybe they can't see him cry, he wipes his face.

Grandmother stands in the doorway; Henry's next to her. His hair isn't even messed up. He bends slightly. Grandmother whispers in his ear. Without a glance back, he swiftly leaves. Oliver, still laboring to breathe, listens to him descend the stairwell to the second floor.

Grandmother closes the door.

Calmly, she crosses the room to stand at the window. Her steps, silent as always, are shorter and slower—an old woman rather than a taskmaster faces the view of the open field. The moonlight highlights her stoic features. Tonight, however, her cheeks are burdened with emotional weight. Her eyes catch the bluish light.

"Does your mother know?" she says just above a whisper.

"About what?"

She turns at the shoulders, her neck stiff. It's clear what she means. *The snowman.* Oliver shakes his head.

"I need to know the truth, Olivah. Does she know?"

"No."

"Then you will do me a favor?"

"Yes."

"Keep it that way."

She contemplates the view with her hands balled in the pockets of her sweater. Henry came for the wooden orb. She was waiting for it.

"I know the stories," Oliver says. His voice is shaky. "I read about the elven and Santa in the North Pole. The snowman, too. Is it all true?"

"Do you have the orb?"

He pauses. "I had it. But it's gone now."

She doesn't bother asking where the orb is. She knows.

She knows what he's seen. When she found the journals, she thought, perhaps, he was just prying where he shouldn't be. She was angry at the betrayal, but something else, too. It wasn't just reading the journals, it was that he found them. And maybe what else he might've found, such as the orb.

*Is she scared? For me or herself?*

"I saw the glove," Oliver says. "I've seen you wear it when you're outside, when you go to the garage. I've seen you with it late at night, out by the driveway. I know something haunts the property, that the woods shift and animals don't live here. The old windmill is powered by something I can't explain, and the house doesn't get electricity from the city. None of this makes sense any more than the...what I've seen out there."

*Snowman,* he thinks. But he can't say it.

"It's best you don't know what happens out here. Trust me, Olivah. Your mother, too." And then she whispers, her lips barely moving, "He should not have come to you."

"Who?"

Her eyes darken. Lips purse.

"He saved my life." Oliver's breathing is normal, but his heart still racing. "That night I was out past dark, I found the little room in the hill, the one Henry and Helen go to. There were things that came to life, that chased me. The snowman saved me, I think. I don't know what they were, but they were going to hurt me. Is that what you mean? Is that what you're protecting us from?"

Her eyelids fall for a long moment. She shakes her head.

"He saved me. He picked me up and carried me to the field right before you found me." Oliver steps closer but resists the urge to reach out. "What is he?"

"There are things in this world better left alone. But once discovered, there is no going back." She turns to him, struggling to hold that perfect posture. Moonlight glistens in her eyes. "We can only limit the harm."

She crosses the room. With her hand on the doorway, she says without looking back, "You'll move out, Olivah. I'd prefer it that way."

Silently, she disappears into the dark hallway. Even the stairwell doesn't betray her descent.

Oliver remains at the side of his bed. There are lines pressed into his palm as if he had been squeezing the orb. *He should not have come for you.*

It doesn't feel like a bad thing. The snowman is anything but that. But Grandmother seemed so concerned, so worried for him.

And his mom.

Oliver never thought he'd feel this way. Staring out the window, he can't help feel the weight of sadness Grandmother left behind.

*I'm not the only one that wants to leave.*

# GRANDFATHER

## II

*Not all grandfathers are great.*

## 19

A little bell rings.

Oliver ties a bandana over his head. It keeps his hair—bleached by the summer sun—out of his eyes when he leans over the sink and the sweat from running down his cheeks. For a while, he tied it back in a small ponytail, but once, in the middle of July's heat wave, when temperatures reached one hundred degrees three days straight, he had to dump a cappuccino when sweat dripped in the foam.

"A large latte with soy." Cath slaps the order on the counter. "The double cap ready?"

"Almost," Oliver says.

"We're backing up, O."

He doesn't tell her the frother is partially clogged because she didn't clean it when she closed up the night before. Instead, he pours the espresso in a circle—his signature—in the white foam. Cath pops her gum, her gothic eyeliner giving her black eyes.

The line at the counter is five deep. Oliver grabs the next ticket in line.

"Need some help?" Ms. Megan, a short woman with bobbed black hair that has the texture of straw, is pulling on a second sweater. It's September—two-sweater weather.

Oliver slides over two tickets. He always feels funny passing work off to the owner of the Smile Café, but she once said she didn't open the place to stand around. Not many bosses work harder than their employees.

"Can you close tonight?" Ms. Megan asks. "I forgot about my daughter's recital. I'll make it up to you."

"Yes."

"You sure?"

"No problem, Ms. Megan." He and Molly were going to the movies, but they could do that tomorrow.

"You're a lifesaver, O. What would I do without you?"

Ms. Megan locks her elbow around his neck and pulls him down to plant one on his temple. She didn't kiss Cath like that. Maybe that's why the eyeliner queen always looked like she was sucking a lemonhead.

Not many bosses had an employee like Oliver.

Homeschooling let him work whenever he wanted. And living in the apartment above the café didn't hurt. They had lived there all summer and hadn't missed rent yet. Ten months without being late was the best they'd ever done. Now that he was working, too, they would shatter that record.

He texts Molly about the change of plans. She texts back a sad face. "Stop by," he texts.

A happy face comes back.

It takes half an hour to catch up with the morning rush. Once the tickets are cleared, Ms. Megan sneaks back into the office to catch up on paperwork. Cath files her black nails. Oliver cleans out the frother in time for the next wave of commuters.

At times, he misses the property. Even Grandmother.

When he was sweating in the July heat, he imagined hiking through the cool shade and the spring-fed waters of the stream. He had only been out there once since moving out last May. The open field was a wildflower wonderland. He didn't explore it. He had tea with Grandmother, instead.

She looked tired.

Her cheeks were rosy where she'd applied makeup, but ashen beneath. She made very little eye contact. When tea was finished, she escorted them to the door, said she was tired. Oliver watched the windmill churn its slow grind in the sideview mirror.

"Non-fat, no foam, chai tea latte. Make it hot," Cath says.

Oliver goes to work. He doesn't have to look at who placed the order—Ms. Vera had not changed her drink since late May. Even in July, she liked her drink smoking hot.

He puts it in the microwave for thirty seconds and burns his hand taking it out. His arm begins to tingle. At first, he thinks maybe he caught his elbow on the counter and hadn't noticed. He'd done that once before, so focused on what he was doing he didn't realize he'd cut himself.

Not this time.

The burning creeps past his elbow and into his shoulder. He rubs his biceps. The tingling spreads across his chest and begins to hum around his heart. He hasn't checked his blood sugar since he woke up, but he'd never felt this before. Not even the time he forgot his supply pack and the car broke down on the interstate. He went hypo when his blood sugar soared and woke up in the hospital.

This is more like a stroke.

"O." Cath waves a ticket in his face. "Wake up."

He hands her Ms. Vera's chai latte and swallows. His throat is slightly numb. The room feels darker and the windows brighter. He could definitely use a stocking cap instead of the bandana.

Art, a heavyset regular, stomps his feet at the door. "It's going to be a long winter."

Art greets everyone on his way to the counter, wiping sawdust off his sleeve. No need to write down his order—three shots of espresso and extra foam. Oliver's hand throbs like he pulled a metal pipe from a bed of coals.

"Summer was hot enough to melt the shingles off a tool shed," Art says. "Now Old Man Winter is in town like he's pissed."

The rotund litigator's bald head looks damp. He blows into his hands.

"They're talking six inches," he adds.

Cath turns around. The frother is still quiet.

"Take a break, O." Ms. Megan tickles his back. "I got this."

Oliver takes a deep breath. He goes to the bathroom, splashes water on his face, and washes his hands. The tingling fades, but it's still wrapped around his chest. Even the bathroom feels dim.

He grabs a small coffee and heads to the front of the shop to get some fresh air and test some blood. He was up late the night before, texting with Molly and scrolling through social media. He'd already had a cup of coffee that morning. Sometimes he gets the jitters. *This is different.*

He steps outside and realizes Art wasn't brushing sawdust off his sleeves; he wasn't sweating.

It's snowing.

Large snowflakes are coming down. Oliver brushes it off the small metal chair outside the door. First snow since he left Grandmother's. And now his chest humming. His hand burning. He packs a snowball and holds it until his fingers are numb.

His hand still burns.

THE LIGHTS ARE OFF.

The fluorescent closed sign reflects off the dark windows and The Black Keys thump in the café. Oliver cleans the frothing nozzles. The counters are cleared except for a skinny latte in a to-go cup.

He loves to close. It's his little secret. He likes to pretend Ms. Megan sold the place to him and he lives upstairs. He comes down whenever he wants, makes killer coffee for his mom, and hangs out after hours with the music turned up. He wouldn't change a thing about the place, except maybe add a few more loungers. If code would allow it, a fire pole would make it easy to slide down from the apartment.

He washes out a cup and turns it upside down in the sink. He's maxed out on caffeine for the day, especially after that burning episode. He feels normal except for his hand. He touched the frother while it was steaming.

*That doesn't explain the lines.*

There's a light rapping on the window.

Molly is at the front door, huffing on the glass and drawing a smiley face, her finger poking through brown gloves with the tips cut off. She dyed her hair black and frosted her pigtails pink. Large snowflakes stick to her coat.

Oliver goes to the front, drying his hands. "We're closed."

"I need to speak to the manager."

"Password?"

"The what?"

"The password."

She pinches her bottom lip, thinking. "The pearl is in the river?"

Oliver turns the locks and sticks his face in the narrow opening. "Do you mean 'zee pearl iz in zee river'?"

"Ahoy, matey."

She plants a kiss on him, her lips moist with chapstick. Oliver pulls the bandana off his head and opens the door. The streetlights glow in the halo of falling snow. Four inches cover the sidewalk.

"Love what you've done with the place," she says, unwinding her scarf.

Oliver returns to the sink. Molly cradles the to-go cup and inhales the latte before sipping. She closes her eyes, a foamy mustache on her lip.

She tells him about her day at school: an upcoming homecoming dance and the football cheerleaders and the jocks that love them. Afterwards, she worked a shift at the library. Oliver wipes down the counters and equipment as she tells him about a storyteller that entertained a bunch of grade schoolers.

She stops to sing along with the Pixies.

Oliver runs one last pitcher of water through the frother. Fueled on non-fat latte, Molly tells him the storyteller's story—"wide... mouth...frog." She's on the last chorus as the frother runs out of steam. He turns the knob—

And jerks his hand back.

Oliver massages his palm when the sensation crawls up his arm again. A tingling net falls over his chest and tightens around his heart —warm, protective but stifling. A storm thrums in his head.

"Oliver?"

Molly's by his side. He's missing a chunk of time, long enough for her to come around the counter. The storm continues howling in his ears. He rubs his chest and throat.

"What's wrong?" Molly asks. "Your blood sugar low?"

He dosed himself just before she got there. Besides, this isn't diabetes; at least nothing he's ever experienced. He describes the sensations, says it happened that morning, too. Maybe he's dehydrated. He hasn't had water, come to think of it. Or tinnitus, Molly says. She's heard of people getting hit with mysterious ringing.

"Maybe you need a doctor," she says.

"I'm all right. I'll drink water."

Molly helps turn over the last couple of chairs and hang the damp wash towels. He takes a breather, downs a bottle of water, and he's already feeling better. Besides, he doesn't want to ruin the night.

He stands up, gives it a second.

"Sounds like an allergic reaction," Molly says. "Better check what you're drinking."

She's got a point. They cracked open a new brand of coffee beans that morning. He needed to ask Ms. Megan if anyone else feels this way. It would kill business if they did.

Oliver grabs his book bag and slings it over his shoulder. Molly's waiting by the front door. The flap is unzipped and spills books.

He freezes in the grip of another tingling wave.

There's a book on the floor. One he didn't pack.

A book he hasn't seen since last winter.

He squats down to pick it up, staying on one knee as he brushes the leathery cover. The bottom corner is broken with three spots of spilled ink on the edge.

*The journal from the attic.*

"Where'd you get that?" Molly asks.

"I don't know."

His hand throbs. He turns it over. In the red glow of the CLOSED sign, they see a pattern in his palm.

*The intricate lines of the orb.*

## 20

The next day, the snow becomes slush.

Molly waits on the sidewalk. Snowmelt drips from the café awning. Oliver leaves with a dish towel over his shoulder. His hair curls from beneath the stocking cap.

"You all right?" she asks.

He turns his hands up. The redness has faded, but the lines are still there, like he'd been squeezing the orb. The warm tingles have disappeared, but the invisible net of claustrophobia remains. Oliver looks down the sidewalk. The Little Professor sign hangs four doors down. Mom won't get off work for another hour.

"You ready?" he asks.

Molly nods.

Oliver clutches the book bag in one hand. It hasn't left his sight.

There's a green door around the corner and a flight of noisy stairs. The oak door slams behind them as they run up the steps. The apartment is down a short hallway, first door on the left. He holds the door open for Molly. Inside, it smells like a coffee grinder. The couches and chair were all purchased from garage sales. To the left is the kitchen where the refrigerator rattles.

Nothing matches the olive green walls.

"There's not much time." He slings the book bag on the couch. A dust cloud wafts into a beam of light. Oliver slides the journal out. He feels slightly dizzy.

"I still don't get it," Molly says. "How'd it get in your backpack?"

He had told her that he recognized the journal. It's the one from the attic, the one he dropped when he saw Grandmother in the driveway. And this buzzing sensation, he says, that's what he felt whenever he squeezed the orb or when the snowman was nearby.

*Without snow, there is no snowman.*

"Snow." He turns toward her. "There hasn't been snow since we moved out, not until yesterday. I think my hand started burning when it started snowing."

"And the journal shows up?"

He shakes his head. "I don't know."

"I think he's looking for you. He wants you to know something."

*He never should've come to you.*

Grandmother said that, she thought the snowman had come for Oliver. Henry did, too. He was angry that he'd been out there all his life and never got the orb. Grandmother, though, wasn't jealous. She was worried. He didn't know if she meant for him to hear that. Maybe she thought once he was off the property, he'd be safe.

*Maybe she's wrong.*

The binding cracks as he opens the journal. The coarse pages are musty. Oliver reads aloud the portions he had seen while in the attic, about the day his great-grandfather, Malcolm Toye, first left the ice room. He went above to see the elven. And met the one that saved him.

Made of snow.


*It stood ten feet. Maybe fifteen.*

*Its legs were thick like timber, the long arms bowing from a stout chest that pulsed not from the beat of a heart but something more precise and mechanical. The head was wide like a turret and featureless except for two indentions where eyes would be.*

*I expected its steps to crack the ice or, at the very least, make the world shudder. But it was soft and silent. The elven reached for it as it passed, clinging to its legs and hanging from the swinging arms, laughing as they fell and rolled.*

*So powerful and intimidating, like a creature carved from a nightmare, that I expected to quiver as it neared, but I found myself smiling. A feeling of warmth radiated inside my chest, pulsing in waves corresponding with the thumping of its chest. There's no other way to describe what I felt when it stopped in front of me.*

*It was love.*

*"He is an abominable," Merry said. "He protects us, but he has limits. He risked his life to find you, Malcolm."*

*Life? I thought. It wasn't breathing, and it was made of snow, but she acted as if it was alive. How could I argue? It stood over me, filling me with a sense of belonging.*

*"Why?" I asked. "Why would it do that?"*

*"Love is powerful," Merry said. "Love is why we exist."*

*I remembered the locket when she said that, wishing I could see you one last time. Did the snowman know that?*

*"Does it have a name?" I asked. It seemed a silly question, to ask if it had a name.*

*"Flury," she said.*

*"Flury," I repeated, and tears filled my eyes. He was a giant white blur when I reached for him and said, "Thank you, Flury."*

*He embraced my arm, and the wind began to whip around us. The elven began to cheer, and when I looked up, three more just like him had appeared as if the snow simply swirled up from the ice. They were distinctive in shape, but all massive.*

*And the feeling around my chest, the love that had ensnared my heart, made me think that whether they were made of snow or flesh, these creatures were more human than anything I had ever met.*

"OH MY GOD." Molly is limp on Oliver's arm. "Not in my dreams, I never would've thought..."

She leaps up, fanning her face.

"I think I'm going to cry. Don't look, it's not pretty."

There's a lump in Oliver's throat. He's not about to cry or admit it, but the passage was devastating. The handwriting started crisp, as usual, and slowly turned shaky. At the end, it was almost illegible. He must've been crying when he wrote it.

What's more, Oliver knew what he felt. There was a connection inside him. It was that buzzing vibration that was netting his chest, as if synchronizing with the towering snowman that looked intimidating but, the closer it got, was soft and warm.

*Love.*

"I believe." Molly's hiding her face. "I believe all this. Do you?"

A snowman and mysterious burns are on his mind. And something about the quiet footsteps, the way the snowman walked so silently. It reminds him of Grandmother.

"Expect the unexpected," he mumbles.

The apartment walls shudder.

The door at the bottom of the stairwell had slammed. Mom's heavy steps echo in the hallway. Oliver shoves the journal under the couch cushion and scrambles to find the remote. Molly grabs it from beneath the coffee table, pushing the buttons as she collapses against him. The journal crackles beneath her.

Keys jingle.

The door opens.

"Hey," Mom says. "What's going on?"

Oliver and Molly, sitting upright and stiff, both say, "Nothing."

"Nothing? I thought you were working?"

"Lunch. Molly and I are just chilling, getting away from the café for a minute, you know."

"Oh, yeah?" She points at the television. "Just catching a little *Dr. Phil*?"

Dr. Phil was introducing owners and their pets to a psychic. And Molly was wiping her eyes.

"It's sad," Molly says. "They lost their beagle for a year, and now he's back, and...he said he missed them."

"Really."

"And I'm on my period."

"Okay."

Molly blows her nose. Oliver's arm is caught behind her at a weird angle, but he's not about to move. Mom goes to the bedroom. They can hear her laughing. She's smiling when she returns with a folder. "I'll be back in half an hour, just need to drop these off. You two be all right?"

"Yeah," Oliver says.

She grabs a bottle of water from the fridge. "Why don't you watch *Ellen*. It's a little more upbeat."

They remain still until the steps are quiet. The pictures on the walls shudder when the street door slams.

"Period?"

"I panicked. She thought we were doing stuff. I was under pressure. I think it worked."

Oliver knows it didn't, but if his mom thought they were getting down on the couch, he was all right with that. It was better than the truth. He stalks to the door and makes sure the stairwell is empty, swinging his arm around to get the feeling back. Molly blows her nose and balls up the tissue.

"I'm all right," she says. "Let's read before she gets back."

"You sure?"

She nods. They pull the journal from beneath the cushion. The cover is creased. Oddly, he's worried Grandmother will be mad. *That would be the least of my troubles.*

Oliver lays the journal open, and Molly leans into him.

The entries follow his daily life. He's rarely alone, always surrounded by elven that, apparently, are the happiest beings on the planet—constantly playing and singing. Malcolm soon yearns for solitude. *It's like living with puppies,* he says. He frequently complains about being trapped, how the elven never answer his questions about home. Once he mentions Santa, the fat man, but doesn't get to see him. *They don't trust me.*

His spirits pick up when he's assigned to different areas of the colony. To stay, he hopes that's not what they have in mind. Toward the end of the journal, he visits the energy production division, and things get interesting.

APRIL 6, 1882.

It's become clear that the human race knows nothing.

Whenever the elven explain something, they speak like it is common sense, yet I understand nothing. They push buttons and light appears. Magic happens. Nog continues to correct me, saying magic ceases when understanding arrives. Then it becomes science.

They don't burn coal or wood. They use the sun and wind and ocean currents, somehow converting these natural resources into power. I suppose that makes sense, but then they took me to the science lab.

In the science lab, I was hunched over to avoid the low ceiling, eventually getting on my knees while Nog slid next to me. Fascination kept the impending sense of claustrophia at bay. These elven wore long coats. They were much more serious than all the other elven, and I liked that. Too much joy only makes my heart heavier. Their efforts to raise my spirits only sink them deeper. Do they not understand you are my only happiness?

Our last stop, though, something felt strangely familiar. There were four spherical objects suspended in the air. They were about twice the size of my fist and gleamed like polished steel with intricate designs carved into their surfaces. They felt like the abominables.

"Each one is at the heart of their body," Nog said.

He went on to explain that the sphere creates an electromagnetic field that pulls snow around it, forming a body of sorts. The spheres also served as power storage, achieving enough density that their low-end gravitational field allows them to generate power and something about fusion. He pulled a sphere from his pocket, one small enough to fit in the palm of his hand.

"This," he said, "could power London." He claimed that houses could be automatically heated in the winter and cooled in the summer. He said there was more they could do with a power source like this, but it was beyond my imagination. Perhaps he doesn't realize they had already exceeded my imagination when I arrived.

*Nog pocketed the smaller sphere and put on his special glove before extending his hand. One of the spheres floated to him. He held it like a crystal balll. "This is more than a snowman," he said. "When an elven passes from this world, he or she is absorbed inside. Their wisdom is contained in the heart of the abominable. It's what allows the elven to grow, to remain peaceful. To learn."*

*I will tell you this, my love. Standing in the presence of the spheres filled me with peace. I do not want to admit this, but in that moment, I wished for nothing. I felt no yearning to be anywhere else but here. That this moment was perfect, with or without you.*

*And I hate myself for feeling that.*


THEY FLIP THROUGH THE PAGES, stopping at some of the sketches. Molly continues to sniffle. The apartment rattles. His mom returns, and they're sitting on the couch, the journal beneath the cushion and the television off.

She doesn't ask why.

Before he goes back to the café, Molly says, "I want a snowman."

*Me too,* he thinks.

# 21

---

Town Square is a long rectangle of paths and cozy benches beneath a grove of shade trees, where locals sat on a patchwork of blankets to listen to a string quartet on Wednesday nights in summer while kids played.

Oliver leans his bike—a beater with knobby tires he found in a dumpster—against a beech tree where initials are carved into the elephant-skin bark. He drops his book bag on a bench, the boards partially decayed with lichen clinging to the armrests.

Mom is at Grandmother's house for Sunday afternoon tea. "Grandmother," she said, "thinks you're too old for tea. I don't know what that means, but you don't have to go."

He knew exactly what it meant: *It's not safe.*

The trees are dripping. The four inches of snow had all but melted. Oliver leans forward, cold snowmelt thwapping the back of his weatherproof jacket as he kneads his palm. The pain is gone, but not the lines.

Thoughts rattle in his head. A landslide of ideas and emotions keep him buried. They roll him upside down until nothing makes sense.

"Hey." Molly's wearing a short-sleeved Clash concert T-shirt with a wool scarf dangling over the handlebars of her mountain bike. Her hair is tied beneath a red bandana. "How's the hand?"

He displays his palm, fingers spread. She bends over and squints, tracing the intricate pattern. "It looks like a brand. Does it hurt?"

He shakes his head.

Oliver pulls his stocking cap over his ears. Side by side, they pedal out of Town Square. A mile down the road, they turn onto a path and grind their way into the countryside. By the time they reach a meadow, their backs are spotted and their tired legs splattered with mud. They spread a blanket and lay out sandwiches, chips and dip with a thermos of dark roast coffee. The journal is placed in the middle like the guest of honor, a giant crease in the cover.

They eat in silence, letting the coffee hum through their exhaustion while staring at the Rockies, clouds sitting at the peaks like fluffy halos.

"I thought about your great-grandfather all night," Molly says. "I don't think I slept."

She digs a spiral-bound notebook from her backpack. The pages are filled with sketches and notes in bubbles and arrows connecting thoughts. It's half full. The first page is a diagram of the property, with house, garage, windmill and hobbit house all labeled, and the river running through it.

Oliver didn't sleep much, either, but he didn't write anything down. Wouldn't have made sense if he did.

"Let's start with the property." She drops a finger on a square. "There's the house and mysterious power and there's Flury. I think it's obvious, don't you?"

"What?"

"Your great-grandfather brought back one of those orbs."

"How?"

"I don't know, just saying one of those orbs solves the power mystery. The journal said one of those small ones would power London. That explains why your grandmother has never paid a power bill. It might also explain how the trees shift and compasses don't work."

"It does?"

"It seems like magic, right? Maybe that just means we don't understand, like Nog said."

"But my orb was made of wood."

"Prototype." She flips a few pages, taps a sketch. "All those plans in the garage looked like someone was designing an orb. Your grandfather was a mechanic or engineer or something, right?"

"Yeah, but those are my great-grandfather's journals. And maybe he built the orbs instead of stealing them."

"I didn't say he stole them. Maybe the elven gave them to him and sent him home."

Oliver retreats into his thoughts. Molly was being nice. She's thinking the same thing he is: there's no way they gave him an orb. They claimed to be reluctant to join the human race. It seemed unlikely they'd give him something that could power London and wish him a Merry Christmas.

*That means he's a thief.*

"Maybe he invented one," Oliver says.

"The journals are in the early 1880s. He built the house in 1901, so that means he returns within twenty years. People were still riding horses, so I doubt he invented a cold fusion power orb. Maybe he carved the orb you had, but it's more likely he brought back a functioning orb."

Oliver rubs his palm, wishing the evidence wasn't pointing in this direction.

"Look, we don't know if he stole one or not, so let's not assume." She rubs his shoulder.

"Okay."

"What we do know is that one of those orbs can power the house. It would also explain how a snowman can be running around the property."

"Abominable."

"Right. Abominable. Your great-grandfather brought back an orb and that explains Flury. So, the question is this: did he bring back more, and where are they?"

"Running around the woods."

"I doubt it. You read what that lab looked like when he saw them as power generators. I think they're hiding somewhere on the property."

"You think there's more than one."

"There's one in Flury, but I think there are others for power. It's just a guess, a weird guess. But I consider us experts in the weird. So let's assume there are more than one. Where would they be?"

"The woods. They chased me that one night."

"Maybe. But there's something different about them, I'm guessing. Your grandmother seems kind of scared of them."

He's not so sure she's not scared of Flury.

"The garage."

"Wrong." She turns to an elaborate sketch of the elven science lab. "I told you, I didn't sleep much. This is what I think the lab looked like. Those orbs were levitating on special equipment to generate power. I doubt she has them on a shelf behind a bag of peanuts."

Oliver describes the house. There's no basement that he knows of, and none of the rooms are suspicious. "It's got to be the garage."

"I know what you mean, I can smell the weird in there, too. But I think it's just a place your grandfather tinkered and kept the journals."

"But the footlocker wasn't there." It's logical, he knows, but his gut feeling tells him there's more to the garage. Grandmother didn't know those journals were under the bench.

"Right," Molly says. "Which makes me think..."

She goes back to her master sketch, accidentally smudging it with hummus. She thumps the far off circle.

"The hobbit house?" Oliver says. That nook definitely smells weird—a bunker in the trees with wifi. And the twins go out there most of the day. "I guess. But there's nothing out there, either. We searched for secret doors and didn't find one, remember?"

"I know, but maybe we missed something. Think we can get back out there?"

"Grandmother letting me explore the property?" He chuckles. "There's a better chance I'll turn into a snowman."

She lies her head on his lap, eating chips. "Maybe you're right, it was just your grandfather's man cave, a place a guy can go to hang with his snowman. You know, kick back, play a little catch...or whatever you do with an abominable. What would you do? I mean, besides throw snowballs and fly and pummel things."

"Protect," Oliver says.

"Protect what?"

"I don't know. That's what the snowmen did for the elven. Maybe grandfather has one to protect him against those things in the trees."

Silence stretches out as they recede into their own thoughts. At one time, Oliver would have wanted Flury to protect him from Grandmother, but he'd seen her when she was vulnerable. She was scared. *Maybe she's not scared of Flury. Maybe it's those things in the woods.*

"Last thing." Molly tosses the notebook on his lap. The windmill is circled with question marks. "What's that for? Because I know it's not about the wind. It turns like a clock."

"Maybe that's the power center."

"That's what I'm thinking. Maybe those orbs are under it. Is there a door or anything under it?"

He shakes his head. "Just dying grass."

"Maybe that's why it's dying."

They watch the clouds float past them, each one looking like a snowman. Her breathing turns heavy, and Oliver shuts his eyes. He's falling under the temptation of a dream, the sun on his cheeks and birdsong in his head.

"I know one thing," Molly says.

"Yeah?"

"Flury needs you."

Oliver remains awake with that thought, but sleep eventually pulls him under, and he dreams of dark rooms and silver orbs. When he wakes up, he's heavy with a thought, a realization that's finally come to the surface.

*Flury needs help.*

# 22

Oliver ends up reading the creased journal nine times.

He sneaks it into the bathroom in the mornings, takes it to work, and reads it on breaks. At night, he reads it by the light of his phone. Each time, he feels empty and sad when he finishes.

Helpless.

*What good was a great discovery like the elven (and a man named Santa) if the price was separation from the one you love?*

"Can I visit Grandmother with you?" he asks his mom one morning.

"Why?"

"No reason. Haven't seen her in a while."

Mom adjusts her headband. "Let me ask her. She hasn't been feeling well this summer."

*This summer?*

She's in her eighties, so it could be that. Or the lack of snow.

October is dry and warm; not a single snowflake falls. His hand returns to normal; the lines vanish. Oliver reads the journal five more times. He and Molly refine their theories, but there's little they can do when Grandmother "doesn't feel like company."

Halloween falls on a Thursday. Oliver is wiping down tables, a black eye patch to go along with his red bandana and the plastic sword on his hip, when Mom walks through the café door.

"Want to come?" she asks. "Just dropping off some groceries, we won't be long."

"Grandmother said it was okay?"

"No. But it'll be quick."

He takes an early lunch and grabs a few packets of pumpkin-flavored tea. Mom's car is parked at Town Square, where straw bales, scarecrows and various stuffed displays haunt the grounds. The roads are steep and curvy. He remembers feeling carsick when they first arrived.

*It's almost been a year.*

The gate is closed, but Mom has a remote. A chill crawls down his back. Unlike the vibrating hum back in the café, this sensation injects an inky cloud of fear beneath his skin. A second wave of creepy-crawlies hits him when the house comes into view. There's no need to decorate it—*it is Halloween.* The sunlight falls around it, not on it.

Mom swings around the circle drive and, unlike a year ago when she strangled the steering wheel, begins humming.

"Did you ever go into the garage when you were little?" Oliver asks.

"All the time."

"Anything weird?"

"Unless you consider tools weird." She finds a tube of chapstick in her purse. "She means well, Oliver. I think she had a hard life, a lot of buried pain. You got to remember, she grew up in a different era. Love was different back then."

"Is that what it is?"

"We all have unmet needs. Until we recognize them, life is hard."

"That doesn't make you angry?"

"No one can *make* me angry, only trigger angry thoughts."

"You don't have angry thoughts?"

"Oh, I have plenty."

She pats his knee and gets out. He grabs a box of groceries from the back seat. Mom rings the doorbell. A year ago, she waited for Grandmother to open it. Now she walks in.

"Mother?" The silent house answers with a groan.

Oliver takes the box to the kitchen. The smell of old wood mixed with shadows makes for a distinct brew, what Molly calls "the weird." *I smell it.*

Mom calls a few more times. She begins unpacking the box and finds the pumpkin tea.

"Did you bring this?"

"Yeah."

"Oh, that's sweet of you."

"I thought she might like it."

"She'll hate it."

"I know."

The house groans again, unfamiliar with the sound of laughter. Mom gives him a quick hug. "See if your grandmother is upstairs."

Oliver lets her finish unpacking the supplies. At the staircase, he stops on the bottom and looks at his hand—no redness or swelling. No lines.

*No snow.*

He studies the old framed photos on his way to the second floor, stopping at the illustration of a shipwreck. *How did he get back? And why doesn't anyone know about it?*

History books don't mention any survivors beyond the initial ones. No reports of a deckhand returning home months later—fat, healthy and hairy. It's like he snuck back.

*And if he had an orb, why didn't he share it with the world?*

Grandmother isn't on the second floor or the third. Oliver goes to his former bedroom. The bed is made without a wrinkle, as if no one ever slept in it. It seems like just yesterday he was trapped between the bed and the window, Henry pushing his face into the pillow, driving his knee into his back, searching for the orb.

*What was he going to do with it?*

The shrill cry of the windmill calls. The rusted blades make a quick turn in a rogue breeze before resuming their methodical rotation. Across the field behind the autumn foliage, the hobbit house is hidden and the stream runs cold and deep. There are no tracks in the snowless grassy field.

Oliver reaches under the bed blindly and finds the binoculars still wedged in the bedsprings. The trees are too far to see much, even with the binoculars. If the orbs were hidden in the hobbit house, why weren't there lights or heat? Molly and he decided one late night in the café, on their third latte, the orbs weren't out there; she had checked for secret doors. It had to be at the windmill since it carried the strange current.

He aims the binoculars at the corroded structure. A gust of wind comes across the grass and swings the windwheel one full turn. The windmill cries out. There's no room in the structure for a door. The grass around it is shorter and tanner than the surrounding field, like a blast of radiation. There could be a hidden entrance in the sod, but there are no outlines or handle. He could thump the ground for a hollow sound. It might be hard to explain what he's doing. *Just searching for a secret entrance, Grandmother. You know, where you hide the orbs great-grandfather stole.*

He focuses directly beneath the windmill, hoping to see the faint outline of a trapdoor or the loop of a handle. There's neither. He sweeps all around the legs. It's the third time around he sees something.

It's not what he's looking for.

There, leaning on the back side of the nearest footing, is the corner of something tan and rectangular. He checks the other legs for something similar, maybe a strut that's come loose or wooden block. It's hard to tell from the bedroom, even with the binoculars. It's the color of worn leather.

*The sixth journal.*

There are seven of them. Grandmother has four, the fifth one is in his backpack.

Oliver forces himself to walk quietly down the steps. He's halfway to the kitchen when he realizes he's still holding the binoculars and tucks them under his belt. The smell of pumpkin is in the kitchen.

"She's not upstairs." His voice is slightly pitched. "Have you seen her?"

"No, I haven't," she says from the pantry.

"I'll look outside."

"Check the garage."

He moves to the sink, keeping his back to the pantry so she doesn't see the binoculars bulging under his shirt. He can see the far wall of the garage. *The car is gone.*

"I'll go look."

Oliver rushes to the front of the house. After a quick scout around, he begins walking. Once he's in the open, in full view of the family room picture window, he sprints. The little square is still at the foot of the windmill, and the closer he gets, the more he's convinced.

It's a journal.

He picks it up. *Has it been out here since the last snow?* He slides it under the binoculars. Using the heel of his boot, he thumps the ground in search of a hollow sound or the hard panel of a hidden door. He doesn't quite make it to the center when something moves near the garage.

Oliver turns sideways behind a leg.

It's like trying to hide a jelly bean behind a toothpick, but the figure walking toward the house cuts across the grass in evenly measured steps. *Grandmother.*

Her head is slightly bowed, watching the grass in front of her. Oliver is too close to the coarse iron leg, the waves of power twisting his stomach like a carnival ride. He dry heaves but stays in place. She appears lost in thought, not looking up until she's reaching for the back door.

As soon as the door closes, he's on the run.

The windmill sucked the strength from his legs, and he stumbles. Regaining his momentum, he runs a crooked line to the car without another fall and stashes the journal and binoculars beneath the seat. He takes a moment to catch his breath. Thankfully, a bag of apples is still on the back seat. He can use that as an excuse for going to the car. With his heart pounding in his throat, he stops on the porch.

The car wasn't in the garage. And it didn't drive up.

Another frigid wave passes through him.

He goes around the right side of the house and stops before walking through the backyard. There's a stitching pain in his side. He takes several deep breaths with his hands on his hips. He's got to look normal, just a casual walk across the lawn. They'll see him from the kitchen. He counts to ten. Still slightly dizzy, he steps into the open with a bag of apples in one hand.

And stops in the middle of the yard.

He meant to just take a glance, like he was looking for Grandmother. But once he can see inside, his feet turn to concrete.

*The car is there.*

## 23

O liver parts the curtains.

Sleet ticks off the glass, settling on the window ledge and frosting the sidewalk around Town Square. Someone is parking right below their apartment. An older woman gets out and goes into the café.

The journal sits on the coffee table. *Number six.*

The leather is in worse shape than the previous ones, the surface water stained and scratched. *How long had it been out there?*

Oliver flips through pages. This one is thicker than the others. He resists the urge to turn the pages slower, to stop at random and read a page, just one. But he promised he wouldn't.

He looks at the time.

After another ten minutes of pacing, the apartment walls rattle. Having second thoughts, he stuffs the journal under the cushion. There's light tapping on the door.

Molly slowly opens the door.

"What took you so long?" he says.

"I got hung up. You didn't read it, did you?"

"No. No, I swear. I'm on break, but Ms. Megan's getting impatient."

"You closing tonight?"

"Yeah, but I've been taking a lot of breaks lately."

It has been a few days since his boss said, "What would I do without you, O?"

"Let me see." She strokes the cover like a delicate fossil. "I can't believe it."

He had texted her on the drive home. Molly made him swear not to read it. He hid it beneath his bed. It wasn't easy waiting.

"Did the windmill shock you?"

"Yeah." He explains the dry heaves and dizziness, stopping short of using the words *radiation sickness*. But they're both thinking it. "I don't think there's a trapdoor, though."

"It'd be hidden if it was, take more than your boot to find it." She places the journal on the coffee table. "And it was just leaning against one of the legs?"

"It was hidden pretty good. Lucky I saw it."

"I don't think it was luck, Oliver."

"I think it's been out there a while." He points at the water stains. "Anyone could've seen it."

"Who was going to see it?"

"The twins. Grandmother."

"I thought she didn't walk the property."

Not as far as Oliver knew, she didn't. And it took a pair of binoculars for Oliver to see it when he was looking directly at it. Grandmother could've been standing right next to it and missed it, especially the way she looks now.

They had stayed for tea. Grandmother took one look at the pumpkin tea and gave it back. It was Earl Grey or nothing. Her shoulders were slumped but not from a curvature of the spine. It was exhaustion, the same tiredness a coating of blush couldn't cover. Even her lips weren't as stiff as wire.

"And no car in the garage?" Molly asks.

"Not when we got there."

"Positive?"

"Stick a needle."

Molly continues petting the journal. She was thinking the same thing as Oliver: *Where did it go?* There was only one way into the garage, and he didn't hear or see the car. The trees on the other side were so dense a bicycle would have a hard time getting through. And what about those bright lights late at night.

"We got to get in that garage," Molly says.

"We?"

"Never mind. We're wasting time." She pats the couch cushion. "Let's read."

He's barely welcome out there. There's no hope for her.

Oliver props the journal on his legs and cracks it open. The smell of vintage paper fills his head.

And the weird escapes the pages.


NOVEMBER *15, 1883.*

*It has been quite some time since I last wrote, my love.*

*This is partly because I have been busy with this new life in the ice. The elven have gone out of their way to accommodate my needs. Summer was much more interesting. The sun never sets.*

*But that is not why I have avoided writing.*

*It aches too much to speak to you. Even though you are a world away, this parchment and ink spans the distance between us. These words bring you back to me. I see you in my dreams, hear you in my sleep, smell you when I wake. And yet, for all these blessings, I still cannot touch you.*

*And you are not here.*

*But to forget you is not my salvation. I think that is what the elven want, perhaps. They want me to file you in the past, to move on. Now that it is winter and the days are dark, I think of you more often. I dream of you in every step.*

*I spend my days walking the ice. The abominables come with me. The polar bears are hungry, and I would make quite a meal. Sometimes all of the abominables come, but most often it is just Flury. His footsteps are so stealthy that I forget he is with me at times.*

*He is an amazing creature. I have to remind myself, though, that he is not a creature at all. He is not the snow that makes up his massive body nor a mind inside it. He is a metallic sphere engineered in the science lab to contain elven memories. There is nothing real about him, yet when he is by my side, I don't feel so far away from home.*

*I worry that you would not recognize me, my love. I am the size of a walrus with a beard like tumbleweed. The Arctic cold affects me no more than a blustery autumn day in Colorado. Strange how relative experience is.*

*There are days Nog comes with me. Where ice is exposed, he slides with little effort. He has given me flexible soles to put on my feet that would allow me to do the same, but I resist. I'm afraid, as every day passes, I am becoming one of them. That worries me.*

*And that is why I am writing again.*

<br>

DECEMBER 5, 1883.

*Something happened today, love.*

*I hesitate to write my thoughts, but Nog assured me there is no prying into my personal journals. And I have learned the elven are as honest as they are long-lived.*

*My walks above the ice have gotten longer. Sometimes I am just lost in thought and wander until someone comes for me. But lately I find myself walking with a purpose. I watch the horizon and pretend I see land. Each day, I walk farther, hoping that each step will bring something into view, a dash of terra firma, a shoreline besides ice. I fall into trances, I think, because hours feel like minutes. Sometimes Flury stops me to turn around.*

*And today, something happened.*

*I was focused on the horizon, placing one foot in front of the other, when a chill set upon my bones. I turned to see Flury a hundred steps behind me. He stood there, inanimate. I realized that it was the distance between us that brought about the biting cold, for I feel warmth when he is near. I went back for him, but no matter how much I coaxed him, he would not go further. It was today that I realized I had been walking for several hours. How far I had gone, I don't know.*

*But I reached Flury's limit.*

*I thought, perhaps, he had read my thoughts because, at that moment, I was thinking it was not possible for me to walk to land. No matter how well insulated my body has become, I still have human limits. But Flury could carry me. He brought me to the colony.*

*He could take me home.*

*I learned later the untruth of this. It was Nog that provided an explanation. Flury reached his limit, he said. The abominables can only venture so far away from the colony. What keeps them from going too far, he did not say. Nor did I ask. That would have certainly given away what I am thinking.*

*It was later I learned of the homing device kept at the colony that limits them. If they venture outside of it, they lose power. But if the homing device can keep them from leaving, there must be a way to turn it off.*

*And there will be no limit to where they can go.*

"I GOT TO GET BACK," Oliver says.

"Oh my God, really? Call in sick or something. We can put a hot rag on your head, work up a fever. I've done it like a hundred times. You can't leave, not now."

He doesn't want to, but Ms. Megan will be upset. If he's honest, he likes those kisses on the forehead. He's also getting uncomfortable. This is his great-grandfather. His pain, for some reason, feels like Oliver's. It's nice having Molly to share all the weird, but he'd like to digest it alone. Get a grip.

He stashes the journal under his bed. "We can read the rest tomorrow."

When they get to the street, the sleet has turned into snow. That night, when he's closing the café and he's all alone, when it's just him and the journal, he breaks his promise.

THE LIGHTS ARE OFF. The music plays softly.

Oliver hikes his feet on the counter and leans back. No one sees him get the leather-bound journal from his backpack. Beneath a buzzing light, he reads the entries from that afternoon again, hoping the lonely ache of his great-grandfather's pain will settle. And like a fully loaded truck braking on ice, he blows right through the last entry he and Molly read.

And into the next.

DECEMBER *21, 1883.*

*I could hear them below.*

*The entire colony was celebrating the holiday season. Strange, they're a culture completely removed from the human race, arguably not even human, yet they have similar customs. They were exchanging gifts. They called it the Christmas season and why not. This is the North Pole, and they are elven. Nog once explained that many of our customs, habits and even language originates from the elven.*

*I have become numb to these propositions.*

*Some mornings I wake believing this is a dream. And then I walk onto the ice with Flury by my side to live another day. Have I lost my mind?*

*So I could not celebrate this holiday season without you. Nog and Merry had given me a pair of fur-lined mittens since my fingers are the only things that still get cold. I took them above the ice and watched the Northern Lights. The urge to walk had died inside me. Now that there are limits to Flury's range with no way to turn them off, as far as I know, I could only go so far. That took the life from my legs.*

*Killed my hopes.*

*I heard my name. It was a soft voice, and, for a moment, I thought the dream of you had come to visit me before slumber. But when I turned, I saw Jessica on the ice. Nicholas was with her.*

*The Santas are human.*

*I had gotten to know them in the summer. I didn't see them much. Nicholas is in some ways the leader of the colony. How he came to be that I have never understood, but it is clear that all the elven respect him.*

*They are as fat as me, my love. Nicholas maybe more so. His white beard and thick hair hang in large curls. Jessica's hair is gray. It is rare that I see them, but when I do, Nicholas wears a ceremonial red coat. There are sleigh and flying reindeer, my love. There is a man named Nicholas Santa that the elven sometimes call Claus. I haven't seen him deliver toys, but all the other stories are true.*

*They arrived at the colony seventy years ago by accident. The details of their journey are strange, indeed. But strange has become normal. Nonetheless, I thought perhaps I heard that wrong because they do not look old enough for that period of time to pass. Somehow, they have taken on the age-defying ability of the elven. Will they live thousands of years like the elven? They're not even sure why they have stopped aging like other humans. I plan to ask Nog how that is. And whether it's happening to me. Because if there's one thing worse than living without you, it is doing so for thousands of years.*

*They had come up to soothe my loneliness, I believe. They spoke of the wonders of living with the elven, the peace and wisdom that accompanies such living. Adjustment, they admitted, is difficult at first. But they insist it is essential to understand this life because of the potential the elven possess. I had assumed they meant the technology sitting next to me: the snowman whose body was drawing snowflakes to it like metal scraps to a magnet.*

*They encouraged me to come back to the celebration. After much talk, I relented. Afterwards, I journeyed back to the surface to be alone. The Santas had intended to set my heart at ease, to bring peace to my tangled mind. Instead, they brought clarity. I understand now, perhaps now more than ever, I am never going home.*

*I understand, now, what I must do.*

OLIVER CLOSES THE JOURNAL.

He sits in the empty café, suppressing the urge to weep. Not in sadness for his great-grandfather and the long suffering he endured. Oliver fights back tears because clarity has come to him as well. After everything that's happened, and all that he's read, he knows something without a doubt.

*Malcolm Toye stole Flury.*

And there's a dreaded sense that his escape, in more ways than he can comprehend, has brought pain to everyone.

# 24

---

Wednesday evening at the library is busy.

Oliver stops inside the front doors with his thumbs hooked under his backpack straps. Molly's truck is in the parking lot. He sees her reshelving DVDs and walks down the adjacent aisle, dragging his fingers over the stacks of movies, stopping in front of the T section and checking out *Transformers*. She looks up for a moment, then goes back to her cart.

Oliver puts the movie back. "I'm sorry."

"You promised you wouldn't read it."

"It put a spell on me," he says with a chuckle.

Molly moves to the end of the row. There are two people in the aisle and another one behind them. Oliver drops the backpack and unzips it. Carelessly, he pulls out the battered leather-bound journal and holds it out.

"Take it."

"What are you doing?" She shoves it against his stomach. "Are you crazy?"

"No one knows what it is. You deserve it. I let you down."

Molly takes it and casually slides it back into his backpack, but not before stroking the cover. She remains kneeling, head down. "I can't take it."

"Yes, you can. We're in this together."

"It's yours, Oliver. Flury wants you to have it."

"No, I think he wants *us* to have it."

"Will you just let me be a baby for a minute?"

He doesn't know what that means.

Molly pushes the cart to the M section, slamming a copy of *The Matrix* into place. Two more movies abruptly find their rightful spots before she stops.

"I'm hurt." She doesn't look at him. "I'm hurt, and I'm jealous because you've got the family and the property and the journals." She points blindly at the backpack. "And I'm working in a library. Let me pout in peace."

*Jealous?*

No one in the history of humankind had ever been jealous of Oliver Toye, the kid with the hippy mom and the crappy dad. The kid with diabetes, the shot kind. They had no reason to be; he never had anything to covet. Still doesn't. His cousins are psychopaths, his great-grandfather is possibly a hallucinating bipolar hopeless romantic, and his grandmother a manic depressive. And there are things living in the trees that, he's pretty sure, want to eat him.

Jealousy is new ground.

"I need your help," he says.

"Not reading the journal, obviously." She stops the cart. "Sorry."

"It's all right."

"What do you need?"

"An obituary."

She files five more movies. Ms. Chatty Pants, the head librarian, is watching. Oliver is about to grab a copy of *Blade Runner* and thinks maybe he'll check it out, watch it for the fiftieth time, before hearing Molly whisper.

"Meet me in the computer room."

IT's past dinner when a terminal opens up.

"You looking for your grandfather?" Molly pulls up a chair.

"Great-grandfather."

Her eyebrows arch. "Hadn't thought of that."

She leans into Oliver. One of her pigtails brushes his cheek like a feather duster, leaving a clean trail. She mutters while typing, pulling up a website that tracks obituaries through databases that include funeral homes, churches, guest books, death certificates, birth certificates, and census records.

"His name is Malcolm Toye?" she says.

"Yeah."

"That's your grandfather's name, right?"

"He was a junior."

Several Malcolm Toyes come up. Oliver doesn't remember if his grandfather had junior in his surname or a fancy Roman numeral. Molly narrows her search but doesn't find any birth or death certificates.

"Where was he born?

"I don't know."

"What about your grandfather?"

He shrugs. His family tree has been pruned many times over, and no one knows where the branches belong. She plays with the criteria, moving the cursor too fast for Oliver to follow.

"There." She taps enter. "That must be him. Look at the dates."

*Malcolm Toye, 1860 to unknown.*

"Definitely not your grandfather."

"There's no death certificate?"

Molly clicks the name and sorts through the following lists. "Doesn't look like it. Says here he was born in Charleston, South Carolina."

"Is that the right one?"

"I think so. I found his voter's registration in the local district in 1912. Says he joined the Navy in 1877 and was assigned to the historic journey to the North Pole. Doesn't say anything about him returning, which is weird." She clicks a few more times. "Think there was more than one Malcolm Toye that went to the North Pole in the late 1880s?"

Oliver points at the screen. Molly clicks the links. There's a brief summary of his duty in the navy, how he was selected for the journey. They follow another link to an account of the ship's disastrous destiny and the crew that survived. Malcolm Toye was not one of them.

"Look at that." Molly highlights a line of text. "'Malcolm Toye, originally thought to have perished during the journey, reappeared twenty years later in a small town in Denver. Initially, he eschewed questions pertaining to his whereabouts and how he returned, but eventually conceded that he had been back in the United States for nearly fifteen years and wished to have his privacy.'"

Molly flips her pigtails around and frowns.

"Maybe it's not him," she says. "Look at the citations."

There are several references to the source's legitimacy. One citation even questioned whether Malcolm Toye was ever on the voyage. *Rumors.*

"But he got here in about 1888?"

"That's what it says."

"Where's the death certificate?"

"There isn't one. But that just means it wasn't recognized by a doctor or church. Maybe he died at home and got buried out back. That's probably how he'd want it. You should ask your grandmother."

*Rule #892: Mind your own business.*

"I don't see a birth certificate for your grandfather." She clicks around. "I mean, if your great-grandfather lived here in the late 1800s, I'm guessing he was born here."

"Maybe he was born at the house."

"Maybe. No death certificate, either. That could just be country folk; you know, live and let live." She clicks around. "What's your grandmother's name?"

"Virginia."

"That's weird."

"What?" And then he sees where the cursor is hovering. He

wishes, for a moment, he could turn the screen off and erase every-thing. But it's too late, he'd already seen it. And it felt like missing that last step at the bottom of a staircase, the sudden rise in your gut when the ground lurches up and you're not sure, for just a tiny moment, if you'll land on solid ground or just keep falling.

"It says here," Molly says, "Virginia married your great-grandfather."

"Look." She highlights the marriage announcement. *Malcolm and Virginia Toye were wed at the courthouse by a justice of the peace in 1905.*

Oliver keeps falling. "That's got to be wrong."

"I know."

"She'd have to be..."

"Like one hundred fifty years old."

"Oh, man." He sits back when the room spins inside his head and all he can smell is the weird. This feeling couldn't be cured with a dose of insulin. "Oh, man."

"What do you think?" Molly asks.

He knows what.

The pieces begin to click, and he knows. It bothered him the way Grandmother tearfully cradled the journals after she found them in his backpack. There was a sense of longing and loss. Malcolm Toye was his grandfather's father. Grandmother was not blood-related to his great-grandfather. Her pain didn't make sense. Why would she care about great-grandfather?

Unless she loved him. His great-grandfather, not his grandfather.

And that was impossible.

*Unless.*

"I got to go." He shoves away from the computer.

"You all right?"

"No. I just...I got to think about this."

"Hey." She grabs his sleeve. "Call me. I'm in this with you."

"I know."

Oliver keeps from running, even though the lights feel dimmer and the air denser. Despite the falling temperatures outside, he opens his coat before he passes out. His bike is where he left it. He rides home in the dark without a light. Even if he had one, he would've left it off. He doesn't want anyone to see him. He can't keep a secret like Grandmother. If someone saw him, they'd know it just by looking at him.

Malcolm Toye isn't his great-grandfather. He came back from the North Pole. He stopped aging when he did.

*Malcolm Toye is my grandfather.*

And it didn't stop there. Oliver has a suspicion, a gut-feeling, his grandmother stopped aging, too.

# 25

"Of course I don't mind." Mom paces the faded kitchenette linoleum, never known to stand still when on the phone. She rolls her eyes and says, "I can pick up a pumpkin pie on the way, but Mother won't be happy with store-bought, you know that."

The scarecrows in Town Square have been replaced by bundles of cornstalks and Thanksgiving displays. Oliver stares through the television. His feet already ache in the dress shoes. The Dallas Cowboys take the opening kickoff to midfield when his phone sounds off.

"Wish I was with you," Molly texts.

It's Thanksgiving. He didn't want to go out to the property without her, but like every family in America, she'd eat turkey with her relatives. They'd stuff themselves and fall asleep in front of the television. They'd hug, they'd kiss, they'd say goodbye at the end of the day and give thanks for the company. They'd walk Molly's grandmother to the car because she's ninety years old. That's how old grandmothers are.

*Not one hundred and fifty!*

He didn't have proof his grandmother had been alive since the late 1800s, but he knew it in the pit of his stomach. It's the way she dresses, the way she never smiles, the way she talks. Great-grandfather...no, *Grandfather* returned from the North Pole with the elven's secret to aging. They lived thousands of years, he said in the journals. Somehow he brought that secret back home with a snowman and gave it to his love.

*Grandmother.*

He couldn't look at the journal, not since putting the pieces together. He just wanted to forget. Why was this the tipping point and not a walking, talking snowman? Because this is real, this hits home. Somehow, Flury and the journals and the hobbit house all felt like a dream, but a one-hundred-and-fifty-year-old grandmother?

That was the pebble that tipped the bucket.

"Okay, sure. I'll let her know." Mom wanders over to the window and pulls the curtain aside. "That shouldn't be a problem."

Oliver texts Molly. "Wish you were here, too."

"Aunt Rhonnie has car trouble," Mom says. "She's not going to make it, so it's just me and you, kiddo. What'd you say?"

"Good."

"You all right? You've seemed a little down the last couple of weeks." She places her hand on his forehead. "You feel a little warm."

"I'm all right."

"You've been working a lot; maybe you should take a few days off."

"No, that's not it. It's fine."

"You and Molly all right?"

"Yes, I swear. Just a little tired, that's all."

Mom gives him a chance to talk. He hugs her. When he needs space, that always works. She squeezes back and goes to the refrigerator to get a cherry pie, stuffing and casserole. It all fits in bags that Oliver can carry. He throws on his coat and takes the food to the door.

"We don't have to spend the night." Mom grabs his arm. "If you feel like coming back, just let me know."

That's good, because he's not positive he even wants to spend a minute out there. But he remembers something a teacher once taught in class. She believed in reincarnation, that when we die we come back to learn the lessons we missed. She figured that if she quit on life, committed suicide or just wasted away, she'd have to come back and do it again.

So she may as well do it now.

Flury was calling. Maybe he needed help. Maybe he needed Oliver. If the teacher was right, he'd have to go out there sooner or later. May as well do it now.

"Zip up, kiddo." Mom grabs her keys. She wraps a scarf around his neck. "It's really starting to snow out there."

THE DRIVEWAY IS BURIED, including the circle. Oliver will shovel that before dark. The rest will be clean by morning.

His palm begins to warm as they approach the brooding house. It still looks like Halloween. The smell of turkey won't change that. Oliver kneads his palm without looking. Mom carries the cherry pie up the steps.

Oliver lags near the car, pulling the rest of the dinner from the back seat while staring across the field of snow. The silence is stifling, interrupted only by his breath. That familiar warmth tingles up his arm and gathers around his chest, this time not so sudden. This time it's a welcome embrace.

*Welcome home.*

The faint lines have returned to his palm. He traces them. The indentions are slight. He looks around, but nothing is watching except the window from the third floor.

And the old woman at the door.

Grandmother is wearing a black dress that brushes the floor. White buttons are snug on her neck. A tan shawl is draped over her shoulders. Her sense of style is outdated, but not for someone who once rode horses to town and pumped water from a well.

Oliver slides his shoes off on the porch.

"And what did you see?" Grandmother closes the door behind him.

"Snow."

Oliver tries not to make eye contact, but she doesn't move. Her complexion is still ashen, perhaps more pale than before. She's a grandmother, that's why. Grandmothers are old. *But one hundred and fifty?*

For a moment, all his convictions, his steel-cable theory about great-grandfather and anti-aging and elven all buckle and tilt.

"What do you see?" she asks again in that question-within-a-question sort of way.

"Nothing."

"Ignoring what you see doesn't change it, Olivah."

*Is she telling herself that?*

She points to the kitchen. Mom has the turkey on the stove. The smell does nothing for his appetite, but he helps prepare the side dishes and set the table. Later, they sit down to a traditional Thanksgiving.

They eat mostly in silence.

Oliver shovels the circle drive after cleaning the kitchen. It's dusk when he finishes, stopping just short of the drive that heads out to the road. He goes straight upstairs to shower and stay in the bedroom until morning. There will be chores, but he's due at the café by noon.

On the way up, he stops just short of the third floor. The creepy old pictures and paintings, as usual, seem slightly different, as if they're replications that someone didn't get quite right. The painting of the ship has been moved. It used to be closer to the second floor.

The rigging is barren, and the crowd of people at the bottom of the rampart appears to be travelers recently disembarking from a long trip.

He leans closer.

The painting seems significant, that's all. Something is calling to him, a detail out of place. *What is it?* One of those men must be Grandfather. He'd bet his life on it. The details are too vague to tell. Besides, he doesn't know what he looks like.

*The child.*

All the travelers are men, except for the fat little child. She's standing amongst them, not holding anyone's hand. As if she's a paying customer. She looks...familiar.

The bottom step creaks.

Oliver hustles up to the third floor. He gets to the shower before anyone comes up. By the time he returns to his room, the house is silent and the windows black.

A nearly full moon casts shadows over the snow. The skeletal frame of the windmill lays over solitary tracks already disturbing the pristine wonderland, wandering aimlessly into the field. The sun is down, and the weird is out.

Oliver sits on the edge of the bed. When he's certain everyone is asleep, he sneaks down the steps to look at the painting again. He knows why the little girl looks familiar. He saw that dress. It's short and wide, black with white frilly trim.

It's in the attic.

TAP, tap, tap.

He wakes up shivering.

His breath is foggy and his palm throbbing. He doesn't remember falling asleep. He had lain in bed trying to get the courage to wander down the hall and search the attic. That dress is hanging in one of the armoires, he's sure of it. He saw the strange clothes when he snuck up with the journal.

And now it's midnight.

What bothers him most isn't the dress or the painting of the ship with men and an obese child. It's the nagging feeling it isn't a child. *He brought back an elven. And her clothes are in the attic.*

But where would the elven be? Does she live in the hobbit house? Does she go with Flury? He's dozing again, the questions carrying him to sandy beaches and soft clouds, where the surf is warm and the water salty—

Tap, tap, tap.

He bolts up, sits quietly, wondering if he heard that or dreamed it.

The house makes sounds all the time. Grandmother might be at the door. The house is still silent except for the occasional snaps and pops. And far away, deep in the trees, the branches crack.

He opens the door. The hallway is empty—

Tap, tap, tap.

*The window.*

Oliver feels like he's holding a glowing coal. The lines are raised on his palm like a brand. He holds still. The window, though, is still black with night. Anything that might be looking through his third-story window would mistake him for a shadow, but no frosty face is peeking inside. No Jack Frost tugging at the pane.

Tap, tap, tap.

It's the window frame, not the glass. It sounds like a stick, but there are no trees near this side of the house. He waits through another stretch of silence, and it happens again. Oliver creeps across the room, his steps so slow that the floorboards hardly creak. He leans near the window, searching the lunar darkness, cupping his hands to the glass. The moon is brighter, and the tracks across the field numerous. If someone, or something, knocked, it would have to climb—

Tap, tap, tap.

His heart thuds.

He sees it. There, lying in a track carved into a shelf of snow just outside the window, is a wooden sphere.

*The orb.*

It takes an aggressive shake to loosen the window frame in its tracks, but he lifts it a few inches. A draft blows snow on the floor. The orb rolls across the sill, and Oliver catches it.

It fits in his palm like a puzzle piece.

He feels the etchings fall in line with the marks on his hand, and like the turn of a key, his body hums. No more discomfort, no more swelling—just raw assurance that he's connected to something greater than himself.

*How did it get here?*

Oliver squeezes the orb. The house rattles. He's filled with a pulse of warmth. The pressure surges up his arm, emboldens his heart.

There's another sound, this one from downstairs. Oliver feels a slight change in air pressure, followed by a distant rattle.

*The back door.*

Oliver pulls open his door and, stepping ninja-silent, ventures down the empty hallway. Pausing at the top step, he listens for any signs of life. He dips into the bathroom and climbs onto the edge of the claw-footed tub to look out the window. The garage is dark, but, in the moon's glow, there are tracks in the snow.

He waits. Nothing stirs. No lights appear.

The orb heats up, and his hand tingles when the garage window illuminates like a square of light, for a moment hovering in the night. There's a bright flash.

And then, once again, darkness.

It takes a moment for his eyes to adjust. Nothing has changed. The tracks still lead to the garage. Oliver steps down. He stands in the bathroom with the orb humming in his palm. He knows why it appeared on his bedroom window, why it woke him up in time to hear the door close.

*To see the light flash.*

He leaves without flushing the toilet. With the orb in hand, with courage rushing through him, he races down the staircase.

He doesn't notice how silently he moves.

# 26

Oliver stands in the backyard.

His loosely tied boots are fitted into a lone set of tracks. The snow is several inches deep, and Grandmother dragged her feet, making it easy for him to follow. He remains solid and still, moonlight casting his shadow in front of him.

The seconds fall like drifting snowflakes that never seem to reach the ground. Minutes crawl past and accumulate too slowly for him to stay out much longer. He shivers in waves; his teeth chatter. Only his hand remains warm.

The orb is full blaze.

The garage appears abandoned. The moonlight, however, reveals the empty space where the car should be. Once again, there are no tire tracks leading out of the garage.

Oliver waits.

In the distance, a tree falls into water.

Just when he can take no more, when he can no longer feel the end of his nose or stand the sound of his teeth rattling in his head, the light returns. It bursts from the window like a spotlight. By the time he blinks the world back into focus, the light has dimmed. Grandmother is climbing out of the car's driver seat.

Like a two-legged gazelle, he lopes ahead, plunking his boots into every other hole. Snow tumbles into his boots and packs against his socks. He bounds around the corner and plunges into the trees' shadows just before light slices through the dark.

He holds his breath.

Grandmother emerges from the garage. Keys jingle in the lock. By the light of the moon, she steps around the garage a bit livelier than the sluggish tracks she made coming out of the house. Oliver lets his breath leak out, listening for the back door. It takes too long, and he imagines her coming back, following her footsteps and noticing the errant ones heading into the woods.

But then he hears it. The door closes.

Oliver waits.

He begins shivering again, thinking of the warmth of the garage. If it doesn't open, if he's locked out, how long will he be stuck outside? And what if the back door is locked? He hadn't thought of that. He cups the orb to his face, but the heat doesn't transfer like a hot coal.

Oliver comes out of hiding.

Without hesitating, he turns the doorknob, and like all those other times, it opens. He's greeted with warm, dry air.

He opens his coat and paces around, letting the chills settle. The triangular blocks are wedged against the car's wheels. The engine is quiet, not ticking as if it were cooling from a long drive. Or even a short one. Oliver touches the driver door, realizing he's in view of the house. If Grandmother were to look out the kitchen window, she'd see him opening the door.

The leather is warm.

There's nothing special about the dashboard. The speedometer and radio and gears are exactly where they should be. He considers pushing buttons. Maybe the radio raises a secret door. But the chocks against the wheels won't let it roll anywhere, and there's no key in the ignition.

*The ignition!*

That's the weird thing, the one weird thing about the car. It's not a slot for a standard key but a square. *Like something for a small cube.*

The corner of the footlocker is visible. He crawls under the workbench with his phone lit up, pulling the old coat out and pushing items aside. He finds the key in the corner and holds it up. The cube casts a blue glow like distilled moonlight.

With the orb in one hand and the key in the other, a current flows through his arms like positive and negative posts of a battery. Somewhere in the middle, right around his heart, the current chases the chill out of his chest.

Oliver climbs back into the driver's seat. The cube is no longer glowing but rather shining. The light streams between his fingers. And the ignition is glowing, too. The key gravitates toward it, pulling harder the closer it gets. It nearly slips from his fingers. The cube falls into the square hole.

*Click.*

He's thrown into the steering wheel as the car tips forward. For a moment, it felt like it was falling. A blinding light sears his vision, explodes inside his head. His ears ring.

The car begins rolling.

He can't see where he's going—he can't see anything—but the car is picking up speed. He's soaring downhill. Hair whipping across his forehead, Oliver latches onto the steering wheel as his stomach rises into his throat.

The car levels out. Images form in his visual whiteout.

*A tunnel.*

The walls are solid and gray—concrete, maybe—and curved like it was bored from the earth. Bands of light encircle the tunnel at intervals like he's flying down a particle collider. His hair snaps around his ears, and tears stream down his cheeks, but the engine isn't running, and none of the needles on the dashboard have moved. Oliver still has both hands on the steering wheel.

He's dropped the orb.

The tunnel begins to cool about the same time the car slows. The air feels heavy. Ahead is a steel wall. Oliver throws both feet on the brakes, but the car stops on its own. Oliver strains to see the outline of a door directly ahead. He rubs his eyes, head still thumping.

He clears his throat. The sound echoes behind him where alternating bands of light and dark vanish into the distance. *How far did I go?*

He went straight for quite some time, but how far and how deep? Time gets distorted when you have a death grip on a steering wheel. But there's a bigger question.

*How am I going to get back?*

This could be a one-way ride. There's not enough room to turn the car around. Besides, he didn't drive it. The thing moved on its own and stopped, too.

Something thuds on the floor mat. The orb rolls against his boot. He dropped it when the rollercoaster began. He sweeps it up and gets out. The sound of the door closing echoes deeper in the tunnel.

The dead-end wall is dull gray, the surface smooth and hard. At one time it might have been polished. The door is nothing more than an arching seam. What he thought was a doorknob is a spherical indention. Nothing to grab or turn. He reaches for it, his fingers brushing the inner surface.

"Ow!" He jerks his hand back, fingertips tingling.

It didn't exactly shock him, but there was some sort of charge inside it. At the same time, the orb begins vibrating. The indention in the door isn't smooth like he thought. There are imbedded lines that rotate and merge and divide into various designs.

Oliver holds the orb next to it.

Like the ignition pulled the blue-cubed key when it neared, the hemispherical indention grabs the orb and sucks it snugly inside, turning and shifting.

*Pop.*

The seal around the door jolts. The orb spits into his hand. Intense light seeps out. Oliver covers his eyes and steps back. The door swings away from him, opening into a larger room. Light bursts down the tunnel, and Oliver turns away to keep his retinas from frying.

He feels the light in his bones.

It's a higher form of tingling, similar to the orb.

He should be running away, screaming for help or, at the very least, struggling to breathe. But his heart isn't even thumping. He feels stronger. No, not stronger. There's an absence of quivering in his belly. He doesn't feel the weight on his chest, the lump in his throat, the weakness in his spine. He feels so present.

*No fear.*

That's what it is. He's not scared.

The light's intensity seems to diminish, or maybe he's adjusted. Oliver slowly turns toward the doorway. The room is a large dome, another hemispherical shape with equally burnished surfaces. He's seen this before. It was on one of the plans he pulled out of the filing cabinet in the garage.

Unlike the outer wall facing the car, these walls inside the dome are covered with wires and pipes snaking around like circuitry on a motherboard, sinking into random ports, each pulsing in synchronized rhythm. Somewhere beyond the wall, above the dome, water trickles.

*Not circuits. Arteries.*

They all reach the apex of the dome some twenty feet above him where a large metal post is attached.

The post, anchored into the shiny floor, gleams like newly forged steel, reflecting distorted images of the circuits and objects around the perimeter. There's a thin rod in front of the post, about the diameter of bamboo and pointed. Suspended inches above the needle-tip is a metallic sphere about the size of an overinflated basketball. The complex design of etched lines glow on its perimeter as it hovers in midair—a supersized version of the orb humming in his hand.

*The elven sphere.*

Each step closer to the sphere makes his bones sing louder. He stops a few feet away when his teeth vibrate; he tastes metal. He holds up the wooden orb, comparing the etchings. The metal sphere is different than the one in his hand. *Is this Flury, or another abominable? Why does Grandmother come here every night?*

*If this is where she comes.*

It is. This is it. He feels it.

His bones feel like forged iron, his skin like impenetrable fabric, his muscles like cords of steel. The weird feeling that hovers over him, the one from the threat of blood sugar imbalance, feels nonexistent. This is where she comes to stay young. She bathes in this room like a fountain of youth.

*This is what makes her about one hundred and fifty years old.*

He tries to get closer, reaching for the floating sphere, but a force repels him. The energy is too intense, pulsing inside the bones in his hand. Would it dissolve him if he grabbed it? Maybe that's what the metal glove is for.

He can't touch it. That's what one of the journals said, humans can't touch a sphere or it will...what? Suck their skin dry? Erase them?

He can't remember.

The rest of the room is a mad scientist's lab: workbenches cluttered with scattered parts and stacks of tools and crackling lights. There doesn't seem to be a light source, as if the walls are glowing. Water drips.

A small puddle is near his boot. He follows it to a bundle of conduit—veins or arteries or whatever they are—snaking across the dome's ceiling.

Pockets are set in the wall above the workbenches. Inside each one is a sphere similar to the super sphere, smaller in size and dull. While there are etchings, each one unique, they lack the glimmer and pulsing light. Oliver doesn't feel any life when he raises his hand over one of them, pulling it out of its display.

It's cold and heavy.

There are dozens of them, all lifeless metal spheres of various sizes. None are wood. Some of the pockets, however, are empty. He puts the cold, dead sphere back and trips over a plastic bucket filled with dented, scratched orbs. These are smaller, about the size of the wooden orb, but all metal. He finds an empty bucket next to it and, on a whim, slides it over the puddle.

The next drip thuds the bottom.

For the first time since arriving, his heart jumps with fear. The door is closed and sealed. But it's not the same door he entered. The dome is disorienting. The super sphere is on the other side of the post. The entrance is across from it, the door still open. The car is waiting.

This is another door. And another lock.

He didn't bring his phone. It's impossible to know the time, but he left the house about midnight. It's already late.

The orb fits snugly in the lock.

The door pops open, releasing a gush of cool air. Inside, a steel spiral staircase twirls up into the darkness, the quality dull like the walls of the dome. Oliver looks up, then steps back. Stepping into a lighted dome is one thing, climbing into the unknown is another.

Every instinct tells him to return to the car. Maybe if he puts it in reverse or inserts the key again, it'll take him back. He would've done just that—in fact, he might've run through the tunnel had the orb not hummed in his fist, sending a jolt through his chest. Warmth spills through him, relieving him of tension.

His boot lands on the first step and sends a clang into the darkness.

The railing quivers in his hand.

One step at a time, he pulls himself into the unknown, clenching the metal rail with one hand, the orb with the other.

The heavy, cool air becomes colder. The light is below him, but he can see his breath. There's a dim light above. He continues his ascent. *To the light,* he thinks. *Just to the light.*

But the light, like the lab, doesn't emit from a source but rather glows from the walls. He reaches up and scratches the metal surface. Below, the light reflects off the railing and bottom steps. He starts to descend—he'd kept his promise, after all—when he notices the steps above him have ended.

*The top.*

There's nothing there.

He feels around for a depression or knob, but the staircase

appears to end at nothing. Perhaps, he thinks, this was a future project. His sweeping hand drags over a series of bumps.

The silence is broken.

The wall moves, and damp, earthy scents rustle his hair. Outside, the tunnel is dark. There's a dim opening several yards ahead. He takes a tentative step. Outside, the walls are no longer metal but crumble like clay. Roots dangle from the ceiling.

Foliage thrashes ahead.

Oliver takes a few more steps, waits and listens. He can see the trees beyond the opening and hear rushing water. There's something familiar about the smells and sounds, but it's not until he passes the L-shaped branch extending from the wall that he recognizes it.

*The hobbit house.*

The car went across the field. Of course it did. He didn't feel any turns, and it's pointed directly north. Once he put the key in, it dropped through a tunnel and raced underground. *But why so far?*

Debris showers the opening.

A cascade of leaves and snow whump down.

Oliver jumps back.

Among the twigs and sooty debris, something spherical catches the moonlight. *It's a sphere!*

He steps closer, but the pile begins to rise. Two legs raise the mass of dirty snow. Oliver backs up a step, then two. One of the legs—leaves falling from it—plods forward. The body undulates; broken branches, rocks and rotten wood ooze to the surface.

Arms extend.

Oliver turns for the staircase. He hears the sticks scratch the wall and leaps three steps at a time, spinning around the center pole as he descends. Above him, the door slams. Thuds echo down the spiral staircase chamber.

The thing hammers the other side.

Oliver jumps off the bottom step and collapses. The pounding fades. He curls against the wall, the orb cupped against his pounding chest.

The car is waiting.

The sphere hovering above the pointed rod vibrates through him but offers no confidence as he passes. He's prepared to run down the tunnel if that's what it takes. It would only take ten or twenty minutes.

He'd run an hour if he had to.

He slips into the driver's seat and turns the key. The car begins to move in reverse. Oliver watches the door close as it shrinks into the distance. It only takes minutes before he feels the ramp leading up to the garage. The floor lifts into place and the chock blocks slide under the wheels.

Oliver sits quite still, watching the house through the window, waiting for the kitchen light to turn on or the back door to slam.

His arms and legs are numb.

His head, spinning.

Now it makes sense why the concrete on that side of the garage is a slightly different color, why there are never any tracks outside the garage.

The back door to the house is unlocked.

Oliver turns the knob very slowly, knowing every click will echo. He closes it even slower. Tossing his boots and coat in the mudroom, he stops in the kitchen. If he hadn't stopped in the kitchen or dropped his things in the mudroom, maybe things would've been different. Maybe nothing bad would've happened and Christmas, a month away, would've passed without incident and no one would get hurt and everyone would be happy.

But standing at the open refrigerator with a carton of orange juice in his hand, he hears someone behind him. It's not the footsteps that give the person away. In fact, he didn't really hear anything.

He felt it.

"What are you doing?"

A month ago, if Grandmother had done exactly that, sneaking up behind him, the orange juice would've ended up on the ceiling. Instead, he pours a swallow into a glass and, after a sip, says, "Sugar a little low."

Grandmother watches him rinse the glass and place it in the sink. Oliver leaves her in the kitchen, wishing her goodnight. His steps make very little sound as he works his way up to the third floor and slips into bed. Staring at the ceiling, thinking about the jilted reality he's entered, he doesn't worry about whether Grandmother will see the snow on his boots or notice the distorted footsteps leading to the garage. He only thinks about the things in the woods and those pockets on the dome wall that contain spheres. It's the empty ones he thinks about as sleep falls on him. He knows where the missing ones are.

And why Grandmother doesn't let him stay out after dark.

## 27

"Y ou sure?" Cath had shaved the sides of her head and dyed them green.

"Positive," Oliver says. "I like closing."

"All right."

He wipes down the counters while Cath looks through her handbag. She finds a tube of lipstick and applies a thick coat of bright red, popping her lips in a small mirror. This goth queens celebrates Christmas.

Only a week had passed since Thanksgiving. The stalks of dried corn and all the hand-turkeys Ms. Megan's kids cut out and taped to the window have been replaced with ornaments and garland. Red and green strands of lights flash in the window; traditional Christmas music plays.

"You sure you're okay?"

"Yeah." Oliver moves the miniature tree to wipe the counter. "I'm fine."

"You don't seem fine."

"Well, I am."

"Fine." It takes another twenty seconds and half a dozen cuss words for Cath to find her keys. "Merry Christmas, O."

The bell rings and the door slams.

Oliver turns the chairs and makes another pass over the counter. Cath rarely leaves the café once, always forgetting something. This time, she doesn't return.

*A Christmas miracle.*

He drapes the damp rag on the counter and makes the last two cups of coffee for the night. Sliding them on a round table in the back corner, he leans back and lets the caffeine lift him from a long day.

He pulls the orb from his pocket.

It rolls across the table, gravitating to the other coffee mug. The wood never discolors in his pocket. Lint never wedges inside the etchings. He palms it, feeling the comforting warmth vibrate through his arm.

Molly's aunt passed away over Thanksgiving. Oliver got the text when he returned from Grandmother's. She would be staying in Illinois another week. "How'd things go at the property?" she had texted.

"Tell you later."

Bing Crosby is crooning when the bell rings again.

Molly slips inside.

Pausing at the unlocked door, she gives a short wave, the stiff-fingered kind that makes Oliver's heart thump. Her boots thump on the old wood floor. When Oliver stands up, she jumps into his arms.

She smells like Molly.

Bing Crosby is done singing when they finally let go.

"I missed you." A thick stocking cap hides her eyes.

He pulls her close again. It's clear how much he missed her.

They sit at the table, pulling their chairs closer. He asks about her family, the trip, and the weather. The talk is small and the pauses long. Their mugs are half empty when he says it.

"I found it."

"Tell me."

It takes longer to get started than he expected. He'd been holding it in all week, and now the details are stuck. Emotions swell in his throat, and for the longest time he rolls the orb between his fingers. She covers his hand and gently squeezes.

He tells her everything.

The more he talks, the more it feels like the trapdoor on reality that was sprung beneath his feet when he stepped into that car begins to close. With Molly to hold onto, his feet are back on the ground. She listens, just listens. When he's empty, when all the details of that surreal trip are in the light, he discovers something.

"Sadness."

"What do you mean?" Molly asks.

"The room, the...lab. It felt sad."

"How does a room feel sad?"

He shakes his head. When he stood in front of the super sphere, he felt something deep in his bones, something he couldn't identify. It was sadness.

*The super sphere is sad.*

"Does your grandmother know you found it?"

"I don't think so. We had tea the next day and went home. It all seemed so normal."

"It sounds serious, is what it sounds. That super sphere is a nuclear reactor or something. You remember the journals, where the elven used it for cold fusion. I think your great-grandfather has it wired up."

"Grandfather."

"What?"

"He's not my great-grandfather. He's my grandfather, remember?"

"Right." She hesitates. "Doesn't matter, that super sphere sounds dangerous. You felt it rattle inside like x-rays. I don't think you should go back."

She's right, he could feel it. And all the cables that looked like arteries, that had to be the power grid.

"This is no joke," Molly says. "If that thing ever becomes unstable, that could be a disaster on a national scale. We got to tell someone."

"What, that my grandmother's hiding a nuclear power plant stolen from the North Pole? Besides, Grandmother's not doing anything wrong."

"Tell them about Flury and the snowman-things..." She waves off. "Never mind. I just heard myself. What if you tell your mom?"

"No, I can't. Grandmother acted like she was protecting her."

"You can't do nothing."

They sit quietly through a bluesy version of "Baby, It's Cold Outside" and sip coffee. Oliver squeezes the orb like answers will leak out.

"If I ask you what needs to be done," Molly says, "what's the first thing that comes to you?"

*Sadness.*

That's what comes to mind, and that's what bothers him most. It's not the jilted reality or the crimes hidden on the property, it's palpable sadness. The essence saturated him, and he can't rinse it out.

"It's a prisoner."

"What is?"

"That super sphere. And so is Flury. They're sad because they're trapped."

"But Flury isn't."

"I think he is. I know he's running around, but somehow he's trapped on the property. The windmill is keeping him and everything else there."

"The windmill?"

He waves his hand. It's just a guess. "Just trust me, they're trapped."

"Well, maybe that's good, with those things on the other side of the river."

But that's the thing: that snowthing felt sad, too. That lumpy, dirty, leafy snowthing that rose up at the mouth of the cave and chased him down the spiral staircase was menacing, wanted to hurt him, but beneath the rage and hate there was a deep misunderstanding.

There were wounds it couldn't heal.

"We got to let them go," he says.

"We need to tell someone is what we need to do."

"First we got to release Flury."

"How?"

When he reached for the super sphere, it burned his hand like radiation. Malcolm Toye had written in one of the journals that he wasn't allowed to touch one with his bare hand or it would do something bad. But there was a way.

"We get a glove," he says. "If I get back down there, I can pull the super sphere off that rod. I think everything loses power after that, including the windmill. And the super sphere will be free."

"Why will it lose power?"

"Nuclear fusion, remember?" He describes the cables running across the ceiling. "That's got to be it."

"You could get hurt."

"Not with a glove. That's what he used in the journal. I can pull it out of the lab, and Flury can take it."

"Where?"

"Home."

"Where's that?"

He finishes the last swallow. "The North Pole."

---

## 28

The snow begins coming down in the second week of December.

By the third week, twenty-two inches accumulate.

When Oliver isn't working, he's sitting in the apartment watching snowplows search for asphalt. Unsuspecting parked cars become dormant lumps. Only the regulars within walking distance stop by the café for the morning grind.

Oliver keeps himself busy, but the coffee machines can only be cleaned so many times. Ms. Megan lets him put in hours even though she doesn't need him. The money is nice, but more importantly, his mind is occupied. Because when he's upstairs, he thinks about his plan.

And how flawed it is.

First, he has to find a metal glove. Grandmother doesn't exactly leave it around the house.

Next, he'll have to take another trip to the lab, assuming the key is still in the footlocker, assuming the footlocker is still under the bench, and assuming the garage is unlocked.

If all that comes together—the glove, the car, the lab—and he frees the super sphere and he doesn't kill himself with radiation or nuclear waste or whatever's cooking inside it, Flury will take it back home...*to the North Pole!*

In his mind, Flury would fly off like a magic unicorn while he and Molly stood next to the windmill and music played them into the sunset. She had asked about the magic bag; did he see one in the lab?

No.

Actually, he forgot about the magic bag. Even if he remembered to look, he'd still have to find a glove, still have to learn how to use it, still need a reindeer...

*Yeah. The plan has flaws.*

THREE DAYS BEFORE CHRISTMAS, Molly trundles across Town Square with her father's snowshoes. Mariah Carey sings through the café's speakers about what she wants for Christmas.

Molly will surely retch when she hears it.

Oliver considers walking to the back room to skip the song, but then the red and green strands of lights flicker out and the music dies. The café goes dark. So does the restaurant across the street.

The power outage lasts into the night.

By morning, half of the town gets their power back. Molly's house is one of the lucky ones. Town Square, however, is still cold. That's when Oliver and his mom pack up for the property.

The road is barricaded between walls of dirty snow. It's doubtful the car will make it. Colorado was built to withstand this snow—even small towns—but now power complicates matters.

*Failed transformer,* the gossip goes. *The backup, too. Waiting on parts.*

Here it is, two days before Christmas and it seems Grandmother has no choice but to let them stay over for the night. Or two.

They reach the property entrance.

The snow has been blown off the wrought-iron gate; the road beyond is clean. Just the slightest hump of snow runs along the pavement's edge. Grandmother waits on the porch, hands stuffed in a mink hand warmer. She looks shorter, her hair grayer.

Very few words are shared.

The chore board is long. At the top, in bold letters, is a statement. A rule.

*NO GOING OUTSIDE.*

That night, Oliver stands in his bedroom. The clouds turn the landscape ashy. He can't see the trees shake on the other side of the field, but hears the thumping, the limbs snapping. The wooden orb hums in his hand with each crushing blow. The fresh snow has renewed the battle of mystery.

Midnight, he goes to the bathroom.

The floor is unusually silent beneath his footsteps, as if he's somehow gained the ability to walk without sound. The garage, half-buried in a sloping drift, remains dark; no hints of a trail lead out to it.

Even Grandmother has abandoned the trek.

He wakes late the next morning feeling sugar-weird and injects insulin in his leg. Garland corkscrews around the bannister all the way to the bottom floor. Something smells good. Mom is whistling at the stove, and Oliver steals a muffin on his way to the chore board.

A new list is waiting.

In the living room, just below the wide picture window, is the miniature Christmas tree his mom bought last Christmas and had put on his dresser. Red, green and blue pinpoints glow on the tips. The tree is matched in height by six gifts, three on each side and brightly wrapped.

"You didn't think Santa forgot us, did you?" Mom says, drying her hands.

She goes back to baking and whistling.

Oliver stares out the window, a pristine field of white lays beyond the slow-churning windmill, not a single track spoiling its splendor. He spends the rest of the morning in that room, smelling the cookies and listening to Mom's happiness. Ever since he arrived at the property a year ago, the house has been a symbol of oppression and sadness, a place where joy withers in a never-ending winter. Yet, that day, this Christmas Eve, he had never felt so warm and comfortable.

So at home.

About midday, right before tea, a car door slams. A bean of excitement leaps in Oliver's stomach. He hadn't seen or heard from Molly since the power went out, which, according to Mom, has been restored. They'll go back Christmas day.

*Tomorrow.*

When a second and third door slam, his excitement turns frosty. Aunt Rhonnie's hollow laugh penetrates the door. When Grandmother opens it, his aunt has her phone against her head. She makes a grand entrance in a sleeveless top and tea-saucer-sized sunglasses. Her elbows are as sharp as window panes; more ribs push against him when they hug.

The twins follow like ducklings.

"Merry Christmas!" Aunt Rhonnie shouts. "Oh, Merry Christmas, Merry Christmas!"

The house silence is shattered by cackling laughter and the sharp command, "Put them in the living room, Henry. Now."

Helen is absorbed by her phone, and Henry carries presents while staring knives into the back of Oliver's head, shredding the magical spirit of Christmas Eve, killing the intoxicating cookie smell that dares to linger.

Henry and Helen are putting on their boots.

"Where are you going?" Aunt Rhonnie says.

"A short walk," Henry says.

"No, you're not. It'll be dark soon, and we're opening presents."

Oliver is washing dishes when Henry comes through the kitchen, brushing against him on the way to the living room. Did they think they were going to cross the field and back before night? More importantly, do they know about the lab?

*Of course they do. They go out to that hobbit house and sneak through the secret entrance, I'll bet. But do they have a key?*

Oliver pats the bulge in his pocket, as if the orb could suddenly vanish. It had done so once before. He couldn't stop it from doing it again.

The doorbell rings.

Oliver's hands are deep in the sink. The front door opens, and his mom bursts out, "Oh, Merry Christmas!" There's shuffling in the foyer, shoes falling on the floor, and giggling. Oliver dries his hands.

"You're not going to open presents without me." Molly walks into the kitchen. Her hair is tied on top of her head, red and green striping her hair. A black scarf is wrapped once around her neck, hanging to the floor.

"Nice hair." Helen strolls through the kitchen.

"Nice scarf," Molly quips.

Helen stops in the doorway. They stare without blinking. Henry comes to his sister's side, like a shark smelling blood. His hair is stiffly sculpted into place.

"I think it escaped the zoo," Henry says.

Helen smirks. It's a deadly smile, the corner of her mouth jabbing into her cheek as her eyes darken. It turns Oliver's stomach cold.

Molly throws her arm around Oliver. "Better hide your eyes, kiddies. The animals are going to play rough."

She growls, biting Oliver's neck and tickling his ribs. They break out in laughter. The twins walk off.

"I missed you," she whispers.

He doesn't need to open presents.

Christmas is already perfect.

MOM LIGHTS CANDLES in the living room.

The warm light lifts the gray pall from the faded wallpaper. U2 is singing about Christmas on Helen's phone, the sound tinny and small on the built-in speaker but better than the silence. Grandmother sits in a rocking chair facing the window, the rails slowly creaking.

The field is still white. Still perfect.

The presents, meanwhile, have quadrupled. Aunt Rhonnie, with a Santa hat flopping over her ear, drinks her special coffee and sorts through the gifts. She claps as she hands them out. Mom has a matching Santa hat. For the first time, they look like sisters, act like twins. The wrapping paper is torn, folded and stuffed in a plastic bag as each gift is opened.

"Hug your cousin," Aunt Rhonnie says to Helen. Then, "Hug your grandmother."

Oliver barely makes contact with her.

Grandmother doesn't even bother hugging back.

The ritual continues until all the gifts are open. Aunt Rhonnie hugs them all, leaving a trail of expensive perfume that will need to be showered off.

The sun has dropped behind the mountains, and the day is quickly fading. The windmill is a skeletal figure. Oliver will have to risk leaving his room tonight if there's any chance of seeing the lab. He can't do it now for a lot of reasons, especially since Molly's here. The plan was bound to fail, he'd accepted that. She didn't need to be around when it did.

He can set his alarm for the middle of the night, long after everyone is asleep, during the hour Santa is laying presents under trees. If the footlocker is there, he can grab what he came to get. And go where he came to go, do what he came to do.

And hope he finds a metal glove somewhere along the way.

"What's that?" Aunt Rhonnie reaches behind the little tree. "Is this yours?"

"No," Mom says. "I didn't wrap that one."

"It's for Oliver."

"Maybe it's from Santa." Mom passes it across the room.

The gift is half the size of a shoebox. The wrapping paper is red. There's no ribbon or tag, just Oliver's name scrawled in the middle.

"Open it," Aunt Rhonnie says.

He pulls the tape from one end.

The windmill begins to squeal when he slides out a brown box. Oliver folds the wrapping paper and hands it to Mom. With eyes on the box, no one looks up when—out of nowhere—a gust of wind batters the window with sleet.

He pulls off the lid.

The candlelight captures the dull silver inside. Nestled in a fold of tissue paper, neatly lying flat, is a single glove.

*A metal glove.*

"Where'd you get that?" Helen asks. "Who is it from?"

Grandmother stops rocking. Expressionless, she watches him lift it from the box. It moves like thick silk, cool against his fingers.

"What's going on?" Helen asks.

A snow flurry blows across the open field.

The whiteout engulfs the singing windmill.

The house shifts in the blustering squall.

"Olivah." Grandmother is reaching, hand open. "Give it to me."

His hand aches to slide inside the smooth glove, to feel the snug fit, the metallic grip.

"Olivah."

Oliver rubs the interior, smooth on his fingertips, just like he thought. The glove's hem closes around his fingers and begins to work up to his knuckles.

"You don't know what you're doing. Hand it to me now."

The house shakes.

Nothing is visible past the window but a white cloud, bits of ice ticking off the glass.

"Honey, let me see it," Mom says.

Henry lunges.

Oliver twists away and gets to his feet.

Henry latches onto his wrist, but Oliver pulls away, backs against the wall. Effortlessly, almost of its own accord, the glove slides over his hand. The dull surface brightens like polished steel. A light warms him from the inside. The room flickers with candlelight, but the flames look bright, feel warmer.

And the wooden orb vibrates.

Henry gets to his feet.

Oliver reaches for his pocket.

"Stop," Grandmother says. Henry freezes, his knees bent and loaded. Grandmother leans forward and pauses before standing. "Olivah, listen to me. You do not know what you are about to do."

"He needs to be free."

"There are other things to consider."

"I can't leave him. He needs me."

"He needs all of us. Stop what you're doing. Hand the glove to me."

The raging squall rattles the window.

"I can't."

"Trust what I'm saying."

She takes half a step, hand extended. Even in candlelight, her cheeks are pale. Her eyes, tired.

"Olivah."

Strands of gray have pulled free from the eternal bun and wave over her forehead. She waits for him, openhanded. Oliver's fingers inch away from his pocket. He doesn't want the glove or the orb. He just wants to do what's right, wants to relieve Flury's suffering, wants to extinguish the sadness below ground.

"No!" Grandmother shouts.

Henry launches.

Oliver leaps backwards. His gloved hand instinctually seeks his pocket, sinking deep inside. Henry grabs his sleeve with one hand and thumps Oliver's chest with the other.

Oliver falls back.

His fingers dig deep.

The wooden orb leaps into his gloved palm.

A bolt, a current, a flash of energy fills him. Henry is knocked back. Grandmother falls back into the rocking chair. Aunt Rhonnie's Santa hat tumbles across the room. The miniature Christmas tree falls over, wrapping paper swirls in a sudden draft like the storm outside has found its way into the living room. Oliver swells with life, with energy.

Electrified.

His hair tingles.

Oliver pulls his hand out. The orb is locked into the glove. The storm dies inside the room, wads of bright paper wedged beneath the chairs, pushed against the walls.

The squall outside dies.

The flurry settles.

The windmill emerges from the whiteout. A path is dug from the field, wandering all the way to the distant trees. Walls of snow have been thrown to the sides like a commercial snowplow passed through. And in the middle, limping near the windmill, walking toward the house, is a figure hunched in a hooded cowl. Things move in the mist settling around the figure.

Disfigured lumps of snow.

"Henry," Grandmother says. "Let your grandfather inside."

## 29

"What?" Aunt Rhonnie says. "What did you say, Mother?"

The hooded figure makes his way toward the house with a slight limp. Oliver had assumed, when he snuck into the attic, that it was Grandmother in the driveway. Of course, there could be another black cloak, but the frail nature of the man she called his grandfather matches what he saw that night he watched from the attic. And those things in the field, the ones behind him, the creatures that chased him at night...*the snowthings*...they're with him.

A dozen of them line the gash cleaved across the field.

They don't march like soldiers but slide like half-baked snowmen, bodies slushy and gray. Leaves, branches and gravel are packed into their bodies; their throbbing heads are without features except for a single, dark hole.

"Tell me what is happening?" Aunt Rhonnie says. "Tell me who that man is and what those things are and what is happening, Mother!"

Her voice rises, each word building on the one before it until she sounds like something at the zoo. The long spikes of her heels hammer the floor. Her arms are inflatable appendages with lives of their own.

"Aaaaaanswer me!"

Grandmother turns. "Open the door, Henry."

Aunt Rhonnie storms out.

Molly's hand finds Oliver's. Their fingers entwine.

His mom stands behind them as the back door opens. There is a short bout of muttering, followed by boots hitting the mudroom floor. Henry returns to the living room. His pale face is as white as winter.

Oliver's fingers ache in Molly's hand.

The hooded figure stops in the doorway. He lifts his right arm; a spotted hand with knobby, curled fingers emerges from a hanging sleeve to push back the cowl, revealing a bushy gray beard and sagging eyes.

"Hello, Virginia," he says. There's a smile somewhere behind the whiskers.

Grandmother says nothing.

Aunt Rhonnie clops back into the room. Her drink tumbles on the floor. She lifts her hand, the painted nails trembling over her red lips. "Oh, my..."

"Father," Mom whispers.

"Hello, girls," Grandfather says. "It's been quite a long while."

"What are you...where have you..." Mom stutters.

"That, my dear, is a long story that I'm afraid I haven't time to tell."

"What are you doing here?" Aunt Rhonnie says.

He turns his stiff neck toward her. "Your mother knows why I'm here. I won't stay long, but some tea would warm these old bones, if you have some ready. And I know you do."

When no one moves, Oliver starts for the kitchen. "Not you, Olivah," Grandmother says. "Helen, prepare a cup for your grandfather."

"Bring sugar," he says.

He favors his right leg.

Stopping near Mom, he reaches with his right hand, the arthritic fingers incapable of straightening. He stops short of touching her cheek. Again, the grin returns somewhere behind his beard, his eyes scrunching.

"Debra," he whispers.

Mom's grip on Oliver's shoulders tightens.

Grandfather pauses at the picture window, running his curled fingers over his thinning scalp. The snowthings patiently wait near the windmill. Helen returns with a saucer and cup. He thanks her, dropping three sugar cubes into the tea. The tongs shake in his feeble grip.

He sips.

They watch him stir in three more cubes.

Wistfully, he stares outside. "I thought my gift might ruin your Christmas."

"You gave me the glove?"

"I've given you many gifts, my boy."

"The journals?" Oliver asks. "The footlocker?"

His eyes twinkle over the rim of the teacup.

"This, too?" Oliver raises the orb.

"Not that, my boy. I needed you to find that for me."

"Why?"

He reaches for another sugar cube and groans. "You look good, Virginia. Don't you agree, children? For her age, I mean. No one your grandmother's age looks that good."

The silence is filled with Grandfather sipping. The hidden grin dances in his eyes. He shares a thousand emotions with Grandmother without saying another word.

"Am I going crazy?" Aunt Rhonnie mutters. "Someone tell me what in the world *is happening!*"

"He left," Grandmother says.

"Wrong!" The word is surprisingly powerful, exploding from the frail old man's grizzled beard. Everyone jumps, including Grandmother. "I *never* left, Virginia. Now tell them what happened."

The silence swells.

"Tell them!"

Grandmother sits with perfect posture, hands folded on her lap.

"Mother?" Aunt Rhonnie asks. "Why would you send us to boarding school and not tell us Father was alive, and why is he here now, and what the hell is out there?" She jabs at the snowthings. "Will you talk for once in your life!"

"Mother?" Mom says. "What's happening?"

Grandmother remains unmoved.

The frail woman has hardened beyond anything Oliver has ever seen. She says little because she knows a lot. And they're about to find out what she knows.

"You never were very good at explaining things, Virginia." Grandfather sighs. "Perhaps you can explain it, Oliver?"

"Me?"

"Would you mind?"

All eyes land on him. Molly pulls closer. Mom throws her arm across his chest.

"I don't..." His throat tightens.

"Come now. You've read about it. You know the story. I believe you know why I'm here. Out with it, my boy."

The light that had twinkled in the old man's eyes is, once again, snuffed by sudden impatience. Oliver peels his mom's arm off and moves away from her and Molly, as if distance between them will keep them safer.

Because he knows why Grandfather is here.

*He's come for someone.*

Oliver squeezes the orb with the gloved hand, hoping the storm that shook the room will return and knock the old man through the window. But the power he felt earlier has diminished by his presence.

"Oliver?" he says.

"Grandfather was born in 1865."

If there was space for more shock to enter the room, it would have settled in between the pauses. But there is none.

There was nothing Oliver could say that could surprise anyone, not when snowthings are watching, not when a previously thought dead man is sipping tea.

Oliver continues.

He recounts the trip to the North Pole, the discovery of the elven and their advanced technology. He explains what the orb does and the glove he's wearing and the snowthings. Mom and Aunt Rhonnie are the only ones staring. Henry and Helen listen without watching him. Some of this they know.

Maybe all of it.

Grandfather nods along, occasionally sipping, but mostly staring at Grandmother.

"He stole from the elven," Oliver says. "He took their abominables and made those things out there."

The snowthings move closer, as if they heard. Aunt Rhonnie shuffles back.

"Very good, my boy. A quick study, you are. You are not a disappointment." Grandfather glances at Oliver's cousins. "I am over one hundred and fifty years old, but your grandmother is much, much older. I look like this because, if she had her way, I would be dead. That's what you had hoped for, isn't it, Virginia. You wanted death to solve your problems. But death has always been our problem, hasn't it?"

He swirls the cup. There couldn't be anything left but a slurry of sugar. Oliver's grandparents share a long, knowing glare. So much left unspoken.

"Girls," he says, "I know I just returned, but I have to go. Perhaps another time I can explain." He groans as his back refuses to straighten. "Come along, Oliver."

"You can't take him," Grandmother says.

"Nonsense."

"I will not allow it, Malcolm. Take what you want, but you will leave Olivah."

"You can't stop me, Virginia. Perhaps you should have been more active in seeking my death. It's too late now."

Mom pulls Oliver behind her.

Grandmother remains still.

They stare like gunslingers, fingers dancing, waiting for a move.

When it comes, Grandmother reaches for her sleeve, but Grandfather merely flicks open his hand to reveal a metal glove. Oliver's fingers are pulled open by some invisible force, releasing the wooden orb from his grip. Instead of bouncing on the floor, it shoots across the room and slams into Grandfather's palm with a dull clink of wood on metal.

Wrapping paper rustles.

Grandmother retrieves a metal glove from her sleeve. But it's too late.

Grandfather holds the orb between finger and thumb and sighs. He rotates it, admiring the intricate etchings.

"I made this, but it was Flury who put part of his soul into it." He squeezes, and a mild whirlwind tosses loose items across the room.

"You have it now," Grandmother says. "Now go."

"Oliver will come. I'll need him."

"It will work without him."

"No, it won't."

"I'll go." Henry steps closer. "I want to go, Grandfather. Take me with you."

"I'm sorry." He drops his bare hand on Henry's shoulder. "Flury knows your intentions are no better than mine. Your mother was always selfish, and she passed those traits onto you and your sister, I'm afraid."

"That's...well, that's just not true." Aunt Rhonnie raises her hand to her heart. "I'm very unselfish. I don't know what you're talking about."

"Flury picked Oliver," Grandfather says.

Aunt Rhonnie looks around. "Who the hell is Flury?"

Grandfather chuckles. Henry and Helen don't have that question in their eyes. They know. They've seen him.

"He is something you wouldn't understand, darling. He is someone that trusts youth and innocence. He sees the inherent goodness in a child of a certain age and offers his magic, gives his soul. Which, as it just so happens, is also the key to my freedom."

He displays the orb again.

"But he's a prisoner on this property, just like your mother and me. Right, Virginia?"

Grandmother flexes her gloved hand.

"We didn't mean to become prisoners," he says. "We brought him to the property and held him captive."

He gestures out the window. No one would guess he was referring to the slow-churning windmill except Grandmother. But Oliver knows what he means; he knows that the windmill is the homing device that limits where Flury can go.

"If he leaves, he melts, so he locked us out of the lab. Revenge, I suppose. Can't blame him." Grandfather shrugs. "That was a problem."

"You started aging," Oliver says.

"My boy, you are the smart one. We started aging"

Grandmother's shaking her head. Her lips remain tight.

"Truth is, if we leave, we become ordinary. As you know, ordinary people don't live to be one hundred and fifty. We are as much slaves to the windmill as he is, so you see I needed Flury to return, needed him to give me the *lab I built with my own hands.*"

The teacup shakes. He puts it down, grimacing, wiping away the memories that rise in his voice. He looks at the snowthings pulsing.

Waiting.

"We knew the key to Flury's heart was children. We knew he'd give his soul to one of you." He displays the orb. "And his soul would open the door. So we had kids."

He nods at Oliver's mom and Aunt Rhonnie.

"We had you to get the key, so that we could free ourselves from the windmill. But your mother had a change of heart just when you were about the right age. Not you, I'm afraid, Rhonnie. Flury wouldn't have trusted you. Your sister, though."

He nods at Oliver's mom.

"I think he would've come to you, Debra. Your mother knew it, and that's why she sent you away without my knowledge. And while I was gone, Flury betrayed me, tried to destroy me, and your mother watched. If it wasn't for my babies..."

The snowthings swell, drawing surrounding snow into their sloppy bodies.

Aunt Rhonnie tries to say something, to ask anything that would make sense. But she doesn't understand. How could she know what an abominable is and that Grandfather somehow used it to extend their lives like the elven? *How could she even understand what an elven is?*

But that technology, that power, turned dark. Maybe because he was never supposed to have it. Maybe that's why the elven didn't want him to have it. Flury must have known; he must've locked them out to stop them.

*To stop Grandfather.*

Grandfather reaches for Oliver.

Molly grabs Oliver's arm.

Mom stands in front of him, hand out to stop her father. Grandfather's dark laughter rattles in his throat. In the moment of distraction, Henry reaches for the wooden orb clutched loosely at Grandfather's side.

Grandfather doesn't try to elude his grasp, he simply squeezes the orb, and Henry turns solid, his outstretched fingers within inches of the gloved hand. Choking sounds gurgle from his throat; spittle rises on his lips.

Aunt Rhonnie screams.

Henry backs away, his feet sliding across the floor as if an invisible force drags him by the throat.

"Not all youth are innocent," Grandfather says. "Not all are good."

Henry falls next to his sister.

Aunt Rhonnie rushes to their sides. That's when Mom is pushed to the side by the invisible hand. Molly unwillingly lets go, shouting as her fingers untangle from Oliver's hand. Both women struggle, both curse, but the orb in Grandfather's gloved hand cannot be denied.

The candlelight flickers on Grandmother's softened expression, glinting in her eyes.

"I'm sorry," she says.

"You should be," Grandfather says. "You knew this day would come."

The snowthings begin their irregular sliding, advancing toward the window. Their forms loom in the dark.

Grandfather pulls a handful of objects from his pocket that clink in his palm. He drops them on the wood floor. The metal bearings roll in all directions. Once again, the wrapping paper begins to skid over the floor, only this time it wraps around the little metal balls.

*Tiny spheres!*

Tissues shoot from a box, envelopes slide off the coffee table, a scarf creeps over the couch. They collide with the metal balls, reform around them until several little forms rise up from the shuffling mess.

The oddball little creatures, no taller than a hiking boot, march to Grandfather's side.

"They'll stay," he says to Grandmother. "Until we're finished."

"I never wanted it to be this way."

"I think you did, Virginia."

"Flury is only trying to help."

"He's in the way."

"You don't have to do this."

"You know I do."

"We can end all this. It doesn't have to involve them."

"It's too late. I think you know that." Grandfather reaches for Oliver. "Help an old man, my boy."

Oliver takes his grandfather's arm and guides him to the kitchen. He's not forced to help him walk through the back door, where a path is carved through the snow. He walks willingly, knowingly.

He helps an old man limp to the garage.

# 30

Grandfather stops behind the car, his eyes walking over the shiny exterior. It takes several short steps for him to reach the driver's side, exhaling like a dying engine. Oliver wonders if he might expire before falling into the red leather seat. He caresses the steering wheel, twisting the grip.

"Get in."

Oliver is obedient.

It would do him no good to disobey—Henry tried that—but a small part of him wants to get in the car, wants to go with him.

*Flury picked me. Why me?*

Grandfather begins to wheeze, coughing uncontrollably. Oliver thinks this time he'll crumple, but the old man recovers, pulling a key from his pocket—one with a glowing blue cube—and inserts it into the ignition.

Once again, the ride steals Oliver's breath.

When they stop, the wall is looming. Grandfather tries to get out but needs Oliver's help. The old man shuffles to the door. Ogling the wooden orb one last time, he hands it to Oliver.

"Go on."

Oliver knows what he means. When he takes the wooden orb, his body tingles. "It won't work for you?"

"Open the door, my boy."

"What if I say no?"

Grandfather guides him by the elbow. "I can take the orb back. You know what I can do with it."

Pressure closes around his throat just below the chin, triggering a fierce headache. He's released from the grip and, hunching over, gasps for air. The ache continues splitting his head.

The orb is pushed into his hand.

"Don't test my patience, my boy."

Oliver inserts the wooden orb.

Turn. *Click.*

Hands on his knees, he squints to see Grandfather inside the dome. The smile behind the beard returns, crinkling the corners of his eyes. The old man lifts his hands, tips his head, and begins to laugh. His joy echoes down the long tunnel.

"It's been a long time," he whispers. "A very long time."

He paces around the bucket now full of water. A droplet falls from the ceiling and plunks inside. Water streams over the sides.

The old man slides his boots over the floor. By the time he reaches the other side, the shuffles fade and each step echoes with a careful heel-to-toe clap.

He stands straighter, exhaling.

*If we stay long enough, will his steps turn silent?*

"What's its name?" Oliver steps inside and points at the super sphere humming at the end of the lance.

"No name, my boy. This one didn't come from the North Pole."

"You invented it?"

"I built all of them."

He gestures to the oddball orbs on display but gazes lovingly at his greatest achievement levitating in the center of the room, created in the likeness of Flury. All of those plans in the garage, the countless drawings of spheres and domes and circuits, they all had to do with the super sphere.

*The snowthings were just practice.*

"The magic bag."

"Hmmphff, the magic bag, yes. But even the imagination has limits, my boy. I created this"—he points at the super sphere—"for Flury, an upgrade of sorts. When he didn't cooperate, I locked it up."

"And then he locked you out."

"He did."

"So what is it now?"

"An empty vessel." For the first time, the old man looks away from the super sphere. His eyes fall on Oliver. "What it needs is a soul."

"A soul?"

"Yes, a soul. Memories, if you will. Structure, personality, a framework of thought and judgment. The elven did it to all their abominables, as they called them. It gave their snowmen stability and intelligence. Without a soul, it's just a power source. But with one, it becomes more than you can imagine."

"How're you going to give it a soul?"

Grandfather doesn't answer. He paces a few steps, eyes back on the super sphere. Already his steps fall quieter.

"Flury knew what I wanted to do with the super sphere. You see, abominables like him see reality more clearly than mere mortals; they see through the human distraction of thoughts and delusion. Our imagination makes us a great species, innovative and powerful, but it's also our Achilles' heel, the source of our self-centered delusion. I am no exception, my boy, and when he saw what I'd become, he locked the dome and left me out in the cold to age."

"I thought Grandmother did that."

"They both saw through me." He stretched out his arms like a man about to lift tremendous weight. "I have suffered on this property a long time, my boy."

It's hard to imagine the super sphere levitating over that sharp point is empty and mindless because the sadness is still in the room, radiating from its shiny, etched surface, filling Oliver's chest. Had Oliver not been in there once before, he would've thought it was

Grandfather's misery. The suffering the old man spoke of hung like a scent, a vapor, a tainted haunt of despair sitting forever in the gut.

*Nothing good has happened since he returned.*

"Don't judge me, boy. You know the story, what I did to survive. There's no dishonor in my escape. I only wanted to be home, I deserved that much. I never intended for it to become this."

"You wanted to see Grandmother...your love."

"Mmm." He grunts, digging through his beard to find his chin. The light leaves his eyes. "If they had let me go, none of this ever would've happened. The elven are at fault."

His gaze turns faraway, as if the past plays out on the surface of the glittering super sphere spinning above the rod's tip. Grandfather appears distraught. When trapped in the North Pole, his love for Grandmother was his only reason for living. Did that dream die when he returned? Was the dream better than reality?

*My love.*

"How'd you do it?" Oliver says. "How'd you get home?"

"It doesn't matter. The journals were for you to know why I did it. History is distorted too often, intended or not. I wanted someone to know the truth."

He stands upright.

The hunch between the old man's shoulders has vanished. The popping of his vertabrae resounds. Just being in the presence of the super sphere has straightened his back. Oliver can feel it, too. He feels stronger.

"Your grandmother hid the journals from you. She didn't want you to know what I was, only what I have become. I was not always this, my boy. There is a reason for who I am today."

"Is there a another one?"

"You know enough."

"Why didn't you give me the last journal?"

"I'm not evil, Oliver. I just want to live."

"You're already living."

"I died long ago, my boy."

The old man exhales.

The joy has receded beneath an onslaught of bitter memories. He didn't die, but something happened when he returned. He thought happiness was waiting for him.

*What happened?*

A drop of water lands in the bucket.

Another drip hangs from a bundle of conduit snaking into a hole. Somewhere above them, the river is leaking.

Something shimmers around the super sphere.

Tiny droplets are orbiting like electrons in slow motion. Grandfather didn't seem to notice. He was looking right at it, the luminescence reflecting in his eyes that don't seem as deep set as they once were, but not seeing what's in front of him.

He's been living in his thoughts far too long.

*Our imagination makes us a great species, but it's also our Achilles' heel.*

"Your grandmother has a good heart, my boy." He digs deep into his beard. Digs deeper into the memories. "Better than mine, I suppose. But, in the end, we're both flawed."

Ker-plunk.

Another drop.

The mist shimmers around the super sphere; a faint rainbow appears like a solar belt. The miniscule droplets orbit around it as if the super sphere is a planet, which in a way, it is. Those miniature spheres Grandfather dropped on the floor used wrapping paper and tissues, the snowthings attract slush, sticks and debris. Flury's sphere pulls snow around it to form a body.

An abominable attracts snow to make a body.

*What about water?*

Oliver steps toward the bucket. "What are you going to do with the super sphere?"

He nods. The hidden smile returns. "Start by feeding it memories."

"What memories?"

"Mine, of course."

"How?"

He grunts and stretches. Tendons flex along his neck. If Grandfather is going to put his memories into it...

"You want to become an abominable."

Grandfather is mesmerized again. It's three times the size of Flury's sphere. Imagine what it could do.

That's why Flury refused.

That's why he locked Grandfather out.

*Too much power.*

Oliver flexes his gloved hand. He can feel the subtle tug of the wooden orb wanting to come back to him, to feed him strength. To call for Flury. Oliver catchs the next drop in his bare hand. It makes hardly a sound. Grandfather looks at the ceiling, unsurprised by the leak.

As if he's known all along.

"Those aren't sinkholes in the forest," Oliver says. "You've been trying to break inside, using the snowthings to tunnel to the dome."

"You can leave now, Oliver."

"But Flury stopped you, didn't he? That's what the battle in the trees is every night. Your snowthings are trying to crack through the ceiling, to let you in, but Flury stops them."

"I mean you no harm, my boy. You are still my grandson, but you must return to the house. Tell the family they must leave and not return. Your grandmother will have to stay, naturally. But she'll expect that."

"Are you going to make the elven pay for saving your life?"

"It's complicated, my boy. When you've lived as long as I have, you learn that nothing is ever straightforward."

"You should've died long ago. You're human. You're not supposed to live this long."

"Enough, Oliver." His hand clenches around the orb. Oliver feels the small hairs on his arms rise. "Return before I change my mind."

"Are you going to hurt the elven?"

"No more than they hurt me."

"I don't understand."

"Of course not."

"They saved you."

He nods absently. His hand relaxes, and the electrified air vanishes. He stares at the super sphere. The rainbow is vivid.

The wrinkles have vanished from the old man's eyes.

"I don't understand why you want to hurt them. You returned home to your love, you made grandmother live long like you; what else do you want? If you use the super sphere for revenge, you're going to prove the elven right, that humans don't deserve this much power. We don't deserve peace."

"Flury gave *you* the key to the dome"—Grandfather holds up the wooden orb—"in hopes that you'd change my mind, I know this. He knew that one day I would find a way back here. He knew I couldn't be stopped. I'm afraid, Oliver, that I've made up my mind. I did so a hundred years ago."

As the old man becomes younger, the sadness in the room becomes more potent. It feels heavier, more constricting. Grandfather thought Flury chose Oliver to convince him to do the right thing, but he was beyond changing. But maybe Flury chose him for another reason.

To feel the despair haunting his grandfather.

To experience the sadness of the empty super sphere.

Not to change his mind...*but to stop him.*

"I can't let you hurt anyone, Grandfather."

"My boy," he says, "I don't want to hurt you."

The old man focuses on Oliver, notices the heel of the young man's boot on the lip of the bucket, water sloshing over the edge.

He looks back at the rainbow-wrapped super sphere that's begun to rotate within the coalescing bands of water droplets. He understands what's about to happen and squeezes the wooden orb.

The atmosphere bristles, the air tightens around Oliver's forehead. The light dims in his periphery.

He kicks out.

Falls back.

Water splashes up his pant leg. The plastic bucket clonks on the concrete. Water spreads across the floor.

Then comes together.

A funnel rises, spinning toward the glowing super sphere.

The rainbow fractures.

Bands of light disperse off the walls as the water spout enters the gravitational pull of the super sphere.

Faster, it spins.

Grandfather is shouting.

Oliver's foot slips in the water. He rolls onto his side to crawl away, but something tugs his leg. He begins to slide toward the center.

"No! No! No!" Grandfather runs around the center post, unaffected by the force dragging Oliver across the wet concrete. The closer he gets to the center, the faster he's pulled. The super sphere wobbles on the rod's tip, a watery veil undulating over its surface. The floor quickly dries as every last drop is drawn into its gravitational field.

Oliver claws at the floor, peeling his fingernails back.

The smaller orbs pop from the wall pockets like artillery.

Grandfather's fingers brush against Oliver's outstretched hand as he's slurped into an electric white light.

And touches the super sphere.

Then perfect silence.

# 31

---

His body goes limp.

The boundaries that define Oliver—his flesh, his bones—flow like sand. Forms blur in unpredictable directions. Sounds are warped, unintelligible, punctuated by the watery impact of hardened cannonballs firing through him.

Colors smear across curved walls.

Round and round, round and round.

Hornets chase his watery tail.

*I'm flying.*

Time and space slow. Oliver begins to make sense of the hazy landscape with three-hundred-and-sixty-degree vision, seeing in all directions simultaneously. The hornets are not insects but a mass of orbs giving chase—the oddball spheres that were displayed in the wall pockets—nipping at Oliver's watery body. His grandfather is below, hands raised. A garbled sound roars from his open mouth.

There's an empty bucket on the floor and a body.

*My body.*

He's inside the sphere. He touched it. Humans are never supposed to touch a sphere...

*It just needs a soul.*

A wave of panic ripples through him. The watery mass quivers, and the orbs gain on him. It doesn't seem possible. His fleshly body has become a foreign object, a crumpled container, a discarded vehicle. He's inside the super sphere, a passenger flying through space.

*How is this possible?*

Grandfather, clenching the wood orb in his metal glove, aims his predatory spheres at Oliver. Each time one plunges into him, it takes a bite of water.

And Oliver slows down, becomes less.

*They'll take me apart like parasites.*

Each pass around the dome brings him closer to the old man's outstretched arm, closer to his grasp. More water. He needs more water.

The ceiling is still dripping.

With a thought, Oliver turns toward the leak. He focuses his attention, concentrates on the weakest point in the ceiling, and drives all his mass forward.

*Crack!*

He doesn't feel the impact. The super sphere rebounds.

Oliver's panaramic vision is jilted. A steady stream leaks from the conduit, splattering the floor. The parasitic spheres swarm him before he can circle the room, nipping away the watery body swirling around the super sphere. With each bite they take more water from him.

They feed on him, a frenzy in the air, sipping away the water that gave the super sphere a body, that allowed it to absorb Oliver. The room begins to dim. He's becoming less and less, going to sleep, going away.

Until he's barely floating above the floor.

*I'll never see Molly again. Never feel her hand in mine.*

The room's sadness floods inside him. The pain of loss, the fear of death. The orbs feast on the watery remains. The super sphere clinks on the concrete.

Begins to roll.

"You don't belong in there, my boy." The super sphere wedges against a boot. "Get back to your body."

Grandfather's callused palms grasp the super sphere. Oliver feels them against the etched surface, feels the weight of the old man's thoughts begin to pour inside.

His eyes pale.

*He's coming inside.*

Oliver feels the dense form of his own flesh against the floor, the steady thump of his heart pulses. His elbows burn where the skin is scuffed away.

*He's coming to give the super sphere a soul.*

Grandfather had planned, all along, to feed his memories into the super sphere. He wants to be inside it. He wants to become an abominable. He pushes Oliver out, throws him back into his limp body, where his chest rises and falls.

*I can't let him.*

The old man's grizzled body is on the floor.

The super sphere quivers beneath his old boot. The swarm of oddball orbs fall on the super sphere, throwing the water they stole from it back into the larger sphere's orbit, returning life to it now that their master is in control.

Oliver throws his hand out.

His fingernails scratch the concrete, crawl to the old man's pant leg, creep over his boot until he lays his palm on the super sphere's shimmering surface. Once again, the charge rips through him.

This time his memories—his awareness, his identity—remains in his body.

Oliver holds on, but his grasp is slipping. He can't get back inside. The etched lines slide under his fingertips. Grandfather is trying to keep him out. Oliver's hand goes numb. Then his arm. He closes his eyes and lets the super sphere absorb him once again.

Into the darkness he goes.

Into a bodiless space inside the super sphere that seems endless and welcome.

This time, he's not alone.

Grandfather struggles to push him back out, to put him in his body. *You don't belong here!* the old man shouts.

Oliver clings to the inner space, holding it with his thoughts, grasping with his presence. But Grandfather is too strong, too big. He feels the cold edge of the super sphere, the etched lines pressing into his awareness, the warmth of his hand lying limp on the metallic surface.

He begins to leak back into his skin—

The door is blown off its hinges.

It spins through the room, whooshes over Oliver's fleshly body, and snaps the levitating spire in half. A snowstorm fills the room. Oliver, clinging to the inner space of the super sphere, watches his fleshly body lift in the updraft and safety of powerful arms.

*Flury!*

The snowman pulls Oliver's fleshly body to his chest and crashes into the leaking ceiling like a wrecking ball. Water erodes the ceiling as the river above them finds a way inside. The swarm of orbs fall on Flury, nipping away his snowy body like flying piranha. They dart around the lab, the orbs gnawing at his arms and legs. Flury bounces off the floor, the ceiling and a workbench, soaring toward the exit.

The snowthings arrive.

Their slushy bodies ooze through the broken doorway.

They don't resume their grotesque forms that stood next to the windmill. They remain a neverending stream of gray slush that fills the room, surrounding Flury and plugging the leaking ceiling.

The slush streams toward the super sphere and enters the gravitational field.

Oliver grows.

But he's no longer just Oliver. His thoughts mingle with Grandfather's memories. Their minds, still separate, merge at the edges. They're becoming one.

*Oliver-Grandfather.*

Together, they're becoming an abominable.

And the gray slush surrounds them, gives them strength. As they fill the room, the cold torrent of partially melted snow cages Flury.

The snowman eludes the super sphere's gravitational pull, cradling Oliver's limp and empty body in his arms.

Rage fills Oliver.

It pours into his being from the outside of his consciousness, radiating from Grandfather's awareness. It contaminates Oliver's mind as if they were one and the same. It fills him with seething anger, bitter vengeance. The urge to strike, to destroy, to fight the burning pain. He's consumed with the urge to crush Flury, to slurp him up like the streaming snowthings that have given themselves to the super sphere's vortex.

The amorphous gray slush spreads around the dome's perimeter. The empty space shrinks. The rage grows hotter. Flury will be digested in the pit of Grandfather's rage. The snowman risked his life; he came here to save Oliver. Flury doesn't know that his body is an empty husk.

*I'll never walk again. Never kiss again. Never feel.*

He'll be trapped in the super sphere forever. And ever.

*Feed that,* Grandfather's thoughts ring. *Give your sadness to the anger; let it burn the ashes of grief.*

The gelatinous slurry snatches Flury's leg. The snowman eludes the grasp by reforming his malleable body, but Oliver's flaccid body hinders his ability to elude the closing predator.

Grandfather's laughter echoes within the inner space. He's toying with the snowman, making him pay for locking him out of the dome all these years, for making him age in the cold wilderness.

It's just the beginning of the old man's trail of revenge.

Oliver relies on the memory of what it felt like to close his eyes and take a deep breath. He calms his thoughts. Outside his circle of awareness, Grandfather continues laughing.

Oliver concentrates.

He forms a thought, a single action. He protects it, hides it. He nurtures it with all his being, gives it purpose. He doesn't think about anything else, doesn't contemplate the consequences, what it will do to his own fleshly body. Oliver simply gives the thought all his strength. All his love.

Because he can't let Grandfather do this.

Because he won't give in to the fury.

When all of his intention fills this thought, he lets it go. It travels throughout the super sphere and into the gray body, quivering throughout the cold slurry. The slushy body that envelopes the super sphere is Oliver's body, too.

And he tells it what to do.

Grandfather hears it, but it's too late.

The thought directs the slush to part near the ceiling and expose the hole. Water begins dumping inside. The grip on Flury loosens. With Oliver's fleshly body safely tucked against his snowy chest, Flury bolts toward the ceiling and buries his fist in the gushing hole.

The floodgate opens.

Earth and water crash down.

## 32

U tter darkness.

No pain, no pressure. Just utter darkness.

Oliver moves with thoughts through the stillness. Despite the crushing earth that lay all around, it's not until he remembers his body is gone that panic sets in.

*What am I if I have no body?*

The super sphere is his body now, but he's not the only one inside it. Other thoughts are out there in the darkness. Grandfather's thoughts have wrapped around him, pushed him aside, enclosed him in a tiny corner of the sphere. Oliver can't feel the smothering weight of the soil, but he can taste the bitter thoughts that imprison him.

*The anger. The rage.*

It trickles like an elixir, feeds the vengeance he's nurtured for a hundred years. And now that he's in the sphere, it infects everything. Grandfather's mind flexes and roars.

The fury is out.

*What is he avenging?*

Beyond the echoes of Grandfather's thoughts, somewhere outside the confines of the super sphere, water trickles. A thousand rivulets are wicking through the soil. The super sphere is packed deep underground. Buried somewhere near is the angry swarm of orbs. Some-where there are the dead orbs that once made up the snowthings.

Flury, too.

*I'm dead.*

His body has been crushed beneath a million tons of soil. Yet he feels no different in the inner space of the super sphere than he did in his flesh. How long will he survive inside it?

*Forever.*

Panic and fear ripple through the inner mind space.

If he could run, he would race away. If he could dig, he would climb out of this grave. But he's trapped.

The water continues to trickle toward the super sphere.

Oliver feels the strange weird of low blood sugar. Impossible, since he has no body. Hyperventilating, maybe? He's not breathing. He's pretending to breathe. It brings him comfort, breeds familiarity. He counts ten breaths and starts over.

Again and again.

When his thoughts cease to race, he reaches out like he did before, attempts to connect with the super sphere, to feel it like it is his body. If the trickling water continues to gravitate toward it, maybe he could climb. Maybe he could bring his fleshly body to the surface and breathe life into it.

*Flury, too.*

Grandfather has taken precautions. Oliver feels through the dark, his thoughts reaching out like appendages, but Grandfather's essence is everywhere, creating walls that contain Oliver, imprison him, keep him from interfering again.

Walls of pain and suffering.

*He wants the world to feel his pain. He wants to be understood. Wants the world to hear him.*

The earth moves.

A subtle quake rumbles through the dark. It feels like the soil is settling around them, packing tighter against the super sphere. It happens again.

This time the super sphere moves.

*We're rising.*

It's small jumps at first, but each successive attempt lightens the world around them. The trickling water is in the super sphere's gravitational field. Grandfather is building another body. He'll climb out of the earth. He'll find revenge.

Oliver spins through the dark. Grandfather's memories disorient him like a house of mirrors.

*I can't stop him.*

The rage is too great, the fury too potent. The old man has stoked this furnace for a century; it's too hot. Oliver can't possibly beat him.

So he begins digging through the old man's memories.

The most recent ones are saturated with loneliness. It's the years he spent on the property with only his snowthings and his thoughts. At night, he roamed the property, sending the snowthings digging through the earth to crack through the dome.

Flury always there to stop them.

When Oliver and his mom arrived, Grandfather knew his opportunity had come. He swept the entry road with the snowthings, had them dust the trails from the snow in the morning, and arranged for the footlocker to be found. Grandmother was helpless to stop him.

The world trembles.

The super sphere is rising faster. The surface is near. A cold sensation leaks through his thoughts. Darkness turns gray.

Then light.

*Snow.*

Water and fog are poor substitutes. The super sphere was built for snow, to gather it, to pack it. To be it. The water, having served its purpose, falls from the super sphere as the snow begins to swirl.

The world comes into focus.

The three-hundred-and-sixty-degree vision is restored. Images appear in the pale moonlight. Trees are toppled, and the river diverted. A whirlpool eddies below the fallen tree that served as Oliver's footbridge to the hobbit house. The stone chimney has toppled.

The sound of a locomotive begins to wail.

Oliver looks to the sky, expecting to see military jets, but the sound is all around. Snow is sliding across the ground and out of the trees.

Limbs snap, and tree trunks sway.

The howling continues.

A torso. Legs. Arms.

*He's building a body.*

Oliver dives back into Grandfather's memories. He tunnels beneath the hardened thoughts of recent past, digs deeper into his life. The memories are calcified and brittle. It takes great effort to push past the years of lonely bitterness. Back in time, he goes.

The birth of Mom and Aunt Rhonnie.

Late nights in the lab.

Building the house.

As the world outside the sphere continues to quake, Oliver digs past burning memories of hate and anger and finds the softer underlying memories.

*Pain and sorrow.*

He had escaped the North Pole. He travelled with a companion back home to find the woman he'd survived to see, the woman that kept him alive through all the isolation in the North Pole. He yearned to see the woman whose photo was tucked into the locket, the woman he wrote to in his journals. His most dearest was waiting for him at the end of this long and impossible journey.

The woman that kept him alive.

*My love.*

He arrived to find an abandoned house. The furniture and belongings were covered in dust and rat droppings. Spider webs filled the corners. His heart broke cold. He thundered through the house, opened doors, cried her name. Fear had never gripped Malcolm Toye like it did that day. And when he found her, he fell on his knees.

She was in the backyard.

Malcolm Toye collapsed on the soft ground. A crudely assembled cross was askew in a mound of earth. Letters were scrawled into the wood.

*Here lies Gayle Toye. Died of a broken heart.*

Scarlet fever had claimed her life, he later discovered. It did not matter. His sorrow was unquenchable. His rage, endless.

He would never see his love again.

And he blamed the elven.

Had they not saved him, he would be united with his love in death. Had they released him, he would have returned sooner. They were to blame for his pain and suffering.

*All of it.*

Grandfather, the monstrous snowman, thunders through the forest. He doesn't bother pushing trees out of the way; he walks through them. The trunks crack like fireworks. They reach the open field. Beyond is the windmill.

And the house.

Rage radiates through the air like waves of heat. The snow is inhaled from the field, swirling into Grandfather's body. The legs become thicker, the arms stronger. The chest swells.

Grandfather roars.

The windows on the house shatter.

Oliver's awareness is ringing. He tries to find a place for Grandfather's memories as they merge into his awareness. The sadness, the agony, is torture. But a question continues to rise.

*If the woman he loved died, then who is Grandmother?*

There are three vibrating houses that finally come together as Oliver's focus returns. Snow swirls in the distance. A small storm has gathered at the back steps of the house. Someone is coming for them.

*Flury! He made it out!*

Oliver can't see through the shattered windows. There's no candlelight, no movement. No way to tell if anyone has stayed.

He hopes not.

Flury barrels across the field. Grandfather lifts his arms, casting moonlit shadows, and claps at the pesky snowman. Flury eludes the crushing blow and crushes Grandfather's knee.

The world tips.

Before Flury can deliver another strike, Grandfather rebuilds the leg and swats him. Flury tumbles across the field, his shiny orb temporarily dislodging from his chest. The snowman returns from the trees for another charge. The hopeless battle resumes.

Something moves at the house.

Someone descends the back steps. The movement is slow and careful. Her hands are folded over her stomach.

*Grandmother.*

Her path is clear.

*No. No, no, no, no, no!*

Grandfather doesn't notice the old woman. He catches Flury in his right hand and squeezes, but the snowman's orb slips between his fingers. Grandfather stomps the orb, and the earth rumbles like an approaching storm. He picks up his foot, expecting to see the pest flattened.

Flury's orb jettisons away.

Grandfather, fueled by hate, anger and revenge, begins to inhale again. This time it's not the snow he's drawing upon. Flury, still a naked orb with no snow to build his body, begins to slow before escaping into the trees.

*Grandfather's going to absorb him.*

Oliver turns his thoughts away and, once again, drives into Grandfather's memories. The deeper he goes, the softer they become. The emotions become like magma, warm and sticky.

Dense.

Oliver sinks deeper, letting the underlying emotions, the foundation of Grandfather's hatred, saturate his awareness and begins lifting it out of the depths. The memories have been buried so deep, packed away so that he would forget the pain.

Oliver brings it out of his subconscious for Grandfather to see.

*Sadness, powerlessness. Aloneness.*

There's so much of it.

It gushes to the surface like a tapped well, spewing through the hardened layers of hatred and bitterness. Sadness flows into the outer banks of Grandfather's mind.

The snowy titan hesitates.

Grandfather's thoughts turn toward Oliver. He feels the

unearthed grief, the unresolved sorrow he buried all those years ago. For a moment, he seems curious to find so much, to discover that these memories have been the fuel driving the hatred, that his fear of being swallowed by his sadness drove him into anger.

And then he sees Grandmother.

The rage returns.

Oliver is scalded by an influx of vengeful thoughts. All the blame is focused on the old woman. Grandfather bats Flury deep into the forest and takes a giant step.

The ground trembles.

Grandmother falls to her knees.

Grandfather towers over the feeble old woman. Images of hate flit through Oliver's vision. Grandfather seeks to quench the ancient itch of revenge.

Oliver turns deeper into the old man's memories. The thoughts become hot. They boil like tar. There's one last wellspring of emotion he hasn't reached, a gold mine that's been feeding the hatred all these years, baking it into a hardened crust on which the old man has feasted until it was all he knew.

The old man lifts his colossal arms.

Grandmother gets to her feet.

With snow dusting her coat, she stares up. Her expression is a foreign one; a look that's never appeared in Oliver's presence. It's open and compassionate. Fearless.

*Loving.*

Flury emerges from the trees, but it's too late. The giant fists come arching down. The wind whistles. Grandfather howls.

And then Oliver reaches the bottom of his hidden feelings.

He finds the thoughts underlying Grandfather's mind, the pit of his emotions—the unresolved depth of his being. It is the foundation that supports everything he's become, a pool of resources buried deeply and soundly. Oliver feels it explode from hiding, feels it fill Grandfather's mind.

*Fear.*

Underneath all the hate is fear.

Perhaps if he'd reached it a second or two earlier, it would've made a difference. The lethal arms soften and slow, but they can't be stopped. The momentum carries them to the ground.

Grandmother disappears beneath their crushing weight.

A plume of snow swallows the sky.

Everything rings white.

## 33

S now falls.

The engorged snowflakes flutter to the earth until the world is white.

The sound of Oliver's footsteps is soft and muffled. Mesmerized by winter's hypnotic dance, he's mildly surprised to discover he has hands and legs. His fleshly body is back.

*Am I still in the super sphere?*

The trees are gone.

The landscape is flat and white, the air choked with snow.

He starts in the direction that feels like home, but nothing ever materializes, no matter where or how far he goes. Despite the isolation, he's filled with peace. No panic or fear, no tension or worry. Just a peaceful world, wherever he is.

Even the distant rumble of thunder doesn't shake him.

A darkened blot forms on the horizon. *The house?* When it grows larger, wobbling as it nears, he's certain it's not the house. The person is as short as she is wide. A long braid of hair is slung over her shoulder. What he thought were snowshoes look more like wide boots.

*Those aren't boots...they're her bare feet!*

She waddles close enough to see her blue-green eyes, the snow squelching under each footstep. She's not even half his height.

"Who are you?" Oliver asks.

Her brow protrudes in concentration, staring through him.

"What's happening?" he asks. "Where am I?"

"You are still inside."

"The super sphere? But...how did my body get here?"

"Your thoughts have crystallized." Her fingers are short and fat. "Thoughts can be quite convincing."

He's seen her before. She's in one of the pictures along the stairwell, between the second and third floor. She was on the end of the pier, who he thought was a child the first time. She's the elven. Those are her clothes in the attic.

*Something else is familiar.*

"Are you my imagination?" he asks.

"I'm afraid not."

She pauses again, letting him explore the strange sense of familiarity. It's the way she's looking at him. The way the wrinkles bunch around her lips. Her eyes are blue, but green around the pupils. No one has eyes like that, except...

"Grandmother?"

She blinks heavily. Nods once.

"I...I don't understand."

"Of course not. No one would."

He thinks maybe his thoughts have made her appear shrunken, that she's a delusion. But just because your delusion tells you this is real doesn't make it so.

"Why do you look like that?"

"This is my true nature. The North Pole was my home." She opens her arms.

"You're elven? I...I don't..."

"Like I said, no one would understand. Sometimes, I don't know how I got here, but life is such. What you see around you is my home. Thousands of years ago, I was born an elven. Of course, you've read the journals, you know about the elven."

"But how could you be one?"

"I met a human long ago, a man in great pain. I sought to help him, but my compassion was misguided and brought us here today."

"But you're...or were...I thought you were human?"

"I transformed into human once it was clear I could not remain elven."

"The hobbit house."

A tiny house built into the earth, something that would resemble the ice caverns in the North Pole. That was built for her.

"It was not an easy process," she says. "Nor pleasant, but I could not go home, not after betraying my people. I was destined to live among humans. It was better that I become one. But here, inside the super sphere, you see me as I was born. You see my true nature. Inside here, our true intentions are exposed, our true nature embraced. Here, there is nowhere to hide."

Another round of thunder.

Grandmother looks up. Snowflakes melt on her cheeks.

"You accomplished something I failed to do for a hundred years," she says. "You showed your grandfather his true nature, helped him see past the bitterness and anger. You put him in touch with the sorrow and hurt beneath it all."

"He's still here?"

She smiles.

It's an expression Oliver doesn't associate with Grandmother, but one so infectious that he smiles, too.

"Of course he's here. His body is dead. So is mine."

There's no way she could survive the impact of that final blow. Grandfather's fists fell like military tanks.

"I'm sorry," he says.

"It was time for my body to rest. But you saved me."

"Me?"

"Yes, you. Your grandfather doubted his actions at the last moment, and that's what allowed the super sphere to absorb my awareness before my body passed. Elven never really die, you know that. We simply pass into the abominables when our bodies expire.

We live in the inner world of our snowmen. As you can see, there's very little difference inside here."

Oliver wouldn't have known this was a dream. *Maybe the dream is outside the super sphere.*

"You, on the other hand," she says, "shouldn't be here."

"Too late for that." Panic clenches his heart and tears blur his vision. His body is in a deep grave.

"Your grandfather thought it was too late for him. His intentions, though, were misguided. I thought I could help him, save him from his thoughts and beliefs, but we can't live in the present when we're stuck in the past. And you can't help someone from themselves, no matter how much you love them.

"Your grandfather figured out a great many things, inventions that I thought would contribute to humanity. But when he created the super sphere"—she waves her arms—"I realized he was stuck on revenge. We were trapped on the property. The windmill, I'm sure you've noticed, always turns. As long as it does, none of us could leave. Not even Flury. Our lives had become stagnant. Your grandfather became angrier. Until you arrived.

"It took a beginner's mind, our grandson, to see with new eyes to resolve our beliefs. You freed us."

Grandmother slides forward and takes his hand.

"You did this. You saved us."

"I didn't do anything."

"You taught an old lady how to live and an old man how to love. You did everything."

Oliver grasps his grandmother's small hands. A smile broadens her cherub cheeks. Her grip is firm and warm. She doesn't say it, but he feels it.

*Thank you.*

Thunder pounds the heavens. This time the world quakes, the snow shudders.

"Ah," Grandmother says. "It looks like Flury has found us."

"What's happening?"

"The super sphere was buried in a mountain of snow when your grandfather collapsed. Flury has been searching for it. I believe he's close. He'll take you back."

"Back? Back where?"

"To your body, of course. You don't belong here."

"I don't have one. I'm..." He can't say it out loud. The word chokes him. *Dead.*

"Nonsense. Flury wouldn't let you die. Too many love you."

"I...I don't understand."

Wind comes out of nowhere.

The ground tips.

Oliver loses his balance. The snowflakes shriek past his ears, stinging his cheeks. He shields his eyes. Nausea curdles his stomach, and he begins to shiver. Electric shocks tremble beneath his skin.

His body feels like the jaws of a steel trap.

The storm swirls around him. The snow obscures her fading form. She's blurry.

Pain lances his sides.

Voices warble around him, some panicked and loud, others soothing. One voice is clear. It comes from the form fading in the sweeping snow.

Grandmother releases his hand. "Goodbye, Olivah."

He doubles over, falls backwards. The snow is hard like a wood floor. The weird feeling is back. It fills him, weighs him down, makes the world fuzzy and blurry and swirly.

His blood sugar is low.

## 34

"Where's his kit?" That's Mom's voice. She'd seen diabetic shock and knows what to do. She always remained calm, tested his blood, brought his sugar back up. She knows what to do.

*Why isn't she doing it?*

"He's dying!" That's Aunt Rhonnie.

"Look in his bedroom, Molly," Mom says.

"Are you joking?" Aunt Rhonnie shouts. "He's unconscious; he's barely breathing! He doesn't need an orange slice, for crying out loud. Give him one of those shots!"

"Stop it! Just stop it! Panic isn't helping. Just calm down." Mom repeats her request to Molly, but now her voice shakes. "We have to find out if his blood sugar is high or low. Do the wrong thing and we kill him."

"He's dying, sister."

"Rhonnie! Just shut it!"

Panic is in order. Oliver can barely feel his body. It's like he's received a transfusion of maple syrup. He can't move, not even his eyelids. So heavy, so tired. The wood floor is on his back, but the room is freezing.

Molly comes back. "I...I can't find it."

"Did you look in his book bag?"

There's an argument. Mom demands everyone start looking for it.

*The bathroom. The diabetic kit bag is in the bathroom, on the floor.*

The front door slams. "It's no good," Henry says, out of breath. "Trees are all over the entry road. There's no way we're getting out. We're trapped."

Aunt Rhonnie shrieks. "We're all going to die!"

"Did you get to the main road?" Mom asks.

"No," Henry says.

"I told you to get out there and see if you get a phone signal!"

"It doesn't matter. An ambulance can't make it to the house."

"We can carry him out," Mom says. "Or a helicopter can fly in. Go back out there and call 911, damn it!"

"Pour orange juice in his mouth."

"Rhonnie, shut up! He's unconscious; we need help now!"

Henry doesn't go. He didn't even try the first time because it's still dark and the forest is making strange sounds. And they just saw a snow titan crush their grandmother. No way in hell he's climbing over trees in the dark.

"Pick him up," Mom says. "Let's pick him up. We can't waste time; we'll call 911 when we get to the road. Come on, let's go."

Oliver focuses all his strength on his eyelids. They flutter open.

"Oh, my God, my God. He's awake," Aunt Rhonnie says. "Get the orange juice."

"Oliver? Honey?" Mom's hand is hot on his forehead. "Can you hear me?"

He moans.

"Sweetie, we're all here. Your blood sugar is off, all right? We're going to get you to a hospital, so just relax. Do you know where your kit is?"

*Bathroom.* He concentrates on the word. It sits on his tongue and moves to his lips. Mom lowers her ear—

Fffzzzzzzzzzzzt.

His body stiffens. The seizure is mild but lasts almost a minute.

Molly is squeezing his hand when he returns. "It's all right," she's whispering. "It'll be all right."

She sounds brave, but her voice is cracking.

"Get over here, everyone! Pick him up!"

"It won't do any good," Henry says. "Trees are everywhere. I couldn't climb through them, let alone carry him. It's just...impossible."

"We're carrying him out now, so get over here!" Mom throws Oliver's arm over her shoulder. "Now let's go. Helen, open the doors and keep looking for his kit. It's a little black bag with a zipper. Go back to his bedroom, then the bathroom. Now!"

Seizure number two makes number one look like a shiver.

Oliver had grabbed electrical lines on a dare in chemistry lab once. This was like that, only the electricity started in his brain.

About 10,000 volts worth.

He planks, shaking like a bell struck with a hammer. He floats somewhere near the ceiling. His body is bouncing on the floor.

The drab wallpaper flickers.

A fuzzy halo surrounds their heads.

Then he's back in his body, his eyes dry and burning. The voices around him slowly come up to speed.

Something is snapping.

The curtains around the picture window flap in the sudden wind. Jagged edges of glass are stuck in the pane like broken teeth.

A dark form fills the open window.

"Oliver?" Mom says. "Oliver? Listen to me, honey. We're going to give you some juice. Do you know where your kit is? Honey, please?"

Her hand is on his forehead.

Molly strokes his arm, holds his hand.

"Is it upstairs?" she asks. "Nod if you think it's—"

Aunt Rhonnie screams. There are words in it, but they're primitive. Helen returns and shrieks. Both back away from the window.

"It's back!" Helen manages to say. "It's back, it's back, it's back!"

They scuttle to the back of the dark room. Henry, too. A shadow grows in the open window. A large gray hand grabs the pane.

Flury barely fits through the opening.

"No! No, no, no! Get away!" Mom jumps up. "Get back out there! You can't have him. Get away!"

The snowman is too large to stand inside the room. Instead, he crawls toward Oliver. His eyes are darker in the dim room. Mom kicks his arm, punches his head. Molly stands over Oliver and chops at his arm. Snow sprays.

Flury ignores them.

Gently, he parts them with both arms. His frozen hands are cold but soft, sliding under Oliver. Like before, he holds Oliver to his chest like a child. Mom's grief is filled with rage as she chips away at his snow-molded forearms.

Molly hits him with a chair.

Snow spatters.

"Please," Mom begs. "Please don't take him."

Flury lifts him out of the house.

The wind howls around his hulking body, but Oliver's protected in his arms. Mom is at the window. Molly is climbing out to give chase. Oliver tries to lift his hand, to put his finger to his lips and tell them it will be all right. He knows where Flury is taking him. They can't get him to the hospital. The roads are blocked; the weather is bad.

But then the windmill squeals.

Trees lay all around it, but the windmill is still upright.

It's still churning.

*Still working.*

"No." His voice scratches his throat. "You can't...you can't..."

Oliver attempts to squirm from Flury's embrace. He's too weak, the snowman too strong. Oliver can't get the words out.

*You can't leave the property!*

The world is smudged with Flury's speed.

Oliver's eyes fill with tears. The frozen air steals his breath. He hunkers in the snowman's grip as the world speeds by. When the tears clear, Oliver can see pinpoints of light from distant towns. Treetops streak below.

*Flying.*

*We're flying over the property.*

The unbreathable wind is vicious, scouring his cheeks, numbing his face. Flury covers Oliver's head to protect him. In that pocket between his arms and chest, Oliver breathes easier.

They soar in perfect silence.

And peace fills him.

*No.* He knows the snowman can hear his thoughts. *I can't let you.*

The top of Oliver's head is numb. The arms aren't covering it anymore, not like they were minutes before. He holds his breath and turns his head. Through the streaming tears, the tiny lights are bigger. They're gaining on them. They must be off the property by now.

Oliver's stomach drops as they fall from the sky.

He clutches at the snowy arms. They're smaller and softer. Wetter.

Flury's footsteps thud on the ground.

Oliver breathes into his shoulder to keep the icy air from choking him. But it's not the wind that's grown more violent. He's more exposed because Flury's arms are thinner.

*He's shrinking.*

The highway is dark. The headlights distant.

Flury's footsteps grow heavy.

The wind begins to die. Lights no longer streak past them. Oliver scratches at the snowman's chest. The icy snow flutters away and doesn't return. A bright light burns inside his chest. Oliver can now see the orb pulsing, fighting the windmill's deteriorating effect.

With each step, it burns dimmer.

Pulses fainter.

When they reach the road outside the hospital, Flury is the size of an ordinary man. Oliver's legs dangle at his side. Like he'd done over a hundred years ago with his grandfather, Flury holds Oliver like a child.

It's no longer the wind filling Oliver's eyes with tears.

The snowman trots into the bright lights. By the time he reaches the emergency room entrance, he appears like a snow-crusted child carrying a teenage boy.

The doors slide open.

Oliver's weight heaves forward. He falls gently to the polished floor and slides across a pile of melted snow. He stops at the foot of an empty desk.

Nurses rush out.

"No, no, no," he mutters.

Several people hover. A woman gives urgent commands. "Who brought him in here?" she shouts.

Just before they lift him, Oliver opens his eyes. The ceiling lights are bright. He turns his head just as they begin wheeling him away.

He sees the weighted orb in a pile of slush.

The ornate etchings of Flury's heart glisten beneath the fluorescent lighting.

The metal surface is dull.

## 35

The delicate patterns of frost stretch over the window, their crystalline structures intersecting. Intertwining. Outside, the Christmas lights glow around the hospital courtyard, lending green and red halos to the frosty pane.

Oliver leans off the bed.

The floor is hard and cold on his feet. A draft sweeps into the back of the loosely tied gown as he brushes his fingers across the window. It's smooth and frigid, but his hand is warm.

He stares into his palm.

There are no lines besides the naturally occurring wrinkles. No tingling up his arm. He's warm because he's been in bed for days, not because the wooden orb is calling. That's somewhere on the property, buried beneath the river.

A lump rises in his throat.

Diabetic shock is a serious condition, but when he arrived at the hospital they diagnosed him with more than that: hypothermia, nutrient imbalance, exhaustion...all the signs of a drowning victim.

Each day he awoke in the hospital, a lump would rise from his stomach and rest in his throat. Oliver would lie in bed, staring at the ceiling tiles, trying to make it go away, trying to forget how he got here. But each day, he felt heavier. His stomach was filled with a weight about the size of the metal orb that's resting on the nightstand.

*Flury.*

Oliver picks it up with both hands. It's the size of a softball with the weight of a bowling ball. The nurse said he brought it with him. They thought it was a Christmas ornament.

He couldn't explain how he got there. When his mom and Molly arrived an hour later, having climbed out to the road and called for help, they couldn't explain it, either. Oliver woke the next morning with the metal orb at his side.

The sharp lines, once brilliant with light, are dark and recessed. The metal surface is foggy. If he could open the hospital window, he'd toss it in the snow and wait for his hero to pull the snow off the ground and stand in the courtyard. But the window won't open.

And his hero is gone.

The door opens. "I see your underwear," Molly says.

Oliver doesn't bother closing the back of his gown. He clutches the orb on his lap. Molly sits next to him, her weight sinking into the bed. Her hair hangs past her shoulders. No ponytails today. No makeup or jewelry.

"Where's Mom?" he asks.

"At the funeral parlor. Visitation is tomorrow. You wouldn't believe the response from all the charities your grandmother supported. For a recluse, she's real popular."

"No one knows what happened to her?"

"Coroner says she had a heart attack."

Grandmother's body was found in the backyard. After Flury took Oliver away, they found her in the backyard, hands folded over her stomach. Her complexion was pallid, eyes closed. It was as if she were sleeping between the house and garage.

Peace at last.

Flury had retrieved her after he returned Oliver to his body while Mom was desperately searching for the diabetic kit. Her body was unharmed by Grandfather's devastating blow. Maybe he didn't crush her after all, just invited her into the super sphere.

The lump rises into Oliver's throat, and, once again, he tries to swallow it down.

Molly goes to the helium balloons tied to a vase of flowers. Cards are propped on a table. "Ms. Megan wanted to come see you, but we told her you were getting out tomorrow."

She reads the cards, then tells him about Aunt Rhonnie asking about the will. Henry and Helen have told people what really happened, but no one believes them.

*Because it's crazy.*

Oliver traces the lines on the orb. The edges are crisp.

Molly puts the cards back and sits with him. They stare through the frosted glass. Somewhere out there, Christmas carols are sung.

He feels so heavy.

Nearly dying takes a lot out of you. It could also be the medication or the exhaustion, but he's slept for days, and his blood sugar is back to normal. And he's not tired. It's a heaviness that penetrates his gut, hovers in his throat. Every time he looks at the orb, it adds another pinch of sand to the weight.

Molly takes his hand. He cradles the orb with his other hand.

The lump won't swallow back this time.

And the frosty etchings on the window get blurry.

"It's not your fault," she says.

"Yes, it is." The words shake at the edges.

Oliver looks away so she doesn't see his lower lip quiver. She squeezes his hand. He hangs on like she's the ledge of sanity. But his fingers are slipping as he sniffles.

"I told him not to do it." His voice is blurry. "He shouldn't have. He didn't deserve this, not after everything he did. He's not just this."

He squeezes the metal orb.

"He was someone. He was better than me."

He tries to wipe the tears, but more come. The lump in his throat opens, and his chest begins to quake. It's no use swallowing. The sobs start as hiccups. He holds his breath and squeezes his eyes shut, but a river is flowing.

Oliver has always felt this way.

He's always felt like he didn't matter, like he was a burden. That weight was always in his belly, because everyone was better than him. And he knows it's not true, but it doesn't stop it from being there. Doesn't stop him from feeling that way.

And now he holds a true friend on his lap. Because of Oliver.

He tries to sob quietly. He covers his face, bawls into his hand. He's not just crying for Flury. It's his mom, his dad, his grandmother.

His grandfather.

It all weighs on him.

Molly wraps her arms around him. He drops the orb and buries his face in her hair, weeping openly.

"He chose you to help your family," she whispers. "You know why? Because he saw your heart, Oliver. He saw it was good."

They could hear him in the hall, but he didn't care. He had to get this out, had to let go of the weight. When he finally pulls away, he covers his face to wipe his puffy eyes. The aftershocks rattle his lower lip.

The tears begin to dry.

"He left you a gift," Molly says.

Oliver looks at the orb sunk in the bed. Molly shakes her head. She lays her hand over his chest.

Flury touched their lives. He changed his heart, his life. And that gift would last forever.

That night he sleeps deeply.

He dreams of snow in every direction. The wind swirls, but his heart warms. When he wakes, the orb is still dull and heavy.

But it is warm.

# 36

**M**olly turns the radio off.

The roads are still wet. April showers have been consistent for two weeks, and May flowers are already filling the ditches.

She pulls off the main road and stops in front of the gate. Weeds crowd around the brick pillars. Oliver expects it to open automatically, but the black gate sits still.

They sit quietly.

Neither of them has been out to the property since Christmas. Oliver runs his hand through his hair. It's almost as long as Molly's. He gets out of the truck to open the gate.

Most of the trees are still standing. The ones that had fallen have been removed, their enormous trunks squarely cut. Mom had trouble finding an arborist to clear the road in February. The rumors of the haunted property were persistent.

This place was dark and mysterious when he had first arrived a year and a half ago. Now light filters through the trees, highlighting the undergrowth.

*No more secrets.*

The house looks like a survivor.

Most of the windows are boarded. The attic window is still intact, watching them park behind Mom's car. Molly turns off the truck, and, once again, they sit quietly. She follows his lead, letting him go at his own pace. He tried to come out in March.

He just wasn't ready.

Oliver waits for Molly at the bottom step, their fingers entwine as she reaches for him. They start up the steps, but he stops and listens.

"What is it?" she asks.

"Listen."

They pause. "I don't hear anything."

"I know."

"And I don't smell the weird," she says.

And then he gets it. It's not the smell.

*It's the sound.*

Birds are singing. Squirrels are crossing limbs. Nature is rampant.

The property is open to the world again.

Footprints are stamped in a thin layer of sawdust on the porch. The contractors say the house will be habitable by autumn. They don't understand how the place worked. It's wired for power but never had any delivered. The contractors that ask too many questions usually end up quitting.

The glass panes alongside the door are intact. Oliver pauses, half-expecting a gray-haired woman to appear in the decorative glass. But no one is waiting for them when he opens it.

The house smells like mold, sawdust and plaster. A few of the pictures are on the steps, leaning against the wall. Above them are bright squares where they'd previously hung. The place still looks haunted, it just doesn't feel it.

Aunt Rhonnie wanted nothing to do with it, although the money she inherited apparently wasn't haunted. Mom let her have the majority of the investments. She wanted the property.

So did Oliver.

The kitchen is empty. The refrigerator is open and bare, so is the pantry. The chalkboard is still hanging inside the door. One chore is listed.

*Rule #1: Finish your work.*

There was a time when Oliver thought he'd never come back. There would be too much sadness out here. Flury wasn't just an invention. He contained a soul. Maybe it was a collection of memories, a soup of past elven that existed as one, whatever it was...he was real.

*And now he's gone.*

The cabinet above the sink is open, and the tea set missing. He finds it in the dining room, the table set. An empty teacup sits in a saucer at the head of the table.

Gooseflesh rises up his back.

"Look at this." Molly carries one of the framed photos from the steps. "I was putting it back on the wall and noticed this."

It's the photo of the ship at port with people gathered at the bottom of the ramp. The men wore bowlers. There are no women carrying umbrellas in what appeared to be a cloudless day, but there is the little girl.

Oliver rubs the dust away.

A very overweight child. *Not a child. An elven.*

*Grandmother.*

She looked exactly like he'd last seen her, inside the super sphere. They had arrived by ship as paying customers. Surely there were questions, but nothing they couldn't answer. She was a dwarf, they probably said. And once they arrived on the property, no one probably saw her again.

At least not looking like that.

The journals said the elven could transform humans into elven, and the process could be reversed. How long did she live in the hobbit house before deciding to become human? And why did she become human?

Why? Because she loved him.

She loved Malcolm Toye.

OUT BACK, the garage doors are gone.

They were blown off their hinges when Flury escaped the dome's collapse, when he whisked Oliver's body into the front room before charging across the field to confront the rising snow titan that Grandfather had become.

Something clatters on the concrete floor.

"I'll be right back," Oliver says.

Oliver peers around the corner of the garage.

Mom is squatting to the right of the filing cabinets, piling items into a box.

"Hey."

"Oh!" She lets a rag fly. "You scared me."

"Expecting a snowman?"

"I didn't hear you pull up."

She pushes a strand of hair under her headband. There are no earrings to twist. She stopped wearing those shortly after Christmas.

Never said why.

"What are you doing?" Oliver asks.

"Cleaning up. I've been putting it off forever." She spies Molly at the windmill. "Glad you came out."

He helps her lift the box onto the workbench. There are stacks of folders, old tools and miscellaneous cans. There are also mouse droppings on the shelves. *Nature's back.*

Oliver glances under the bench. The footlocker is missing.

He was never quite sure if Grandfather had been the one responsible for letting him have that. A part of him wonders if Grandmother put it there. Maybe she wanted him to find the wooden orb but Grandfather put the journals in it. She was genuinely shocked when she found them in his backpack.

The car is still there, but the shine is gone. Rust spots have already appeared on the bumper. The interior is water stained. When the dome collapsed, the car must've automatically found its way back. It hasn't moved since. Without a key, it would remain an ornament.

Mom is staring out the window, the glass missing.

"You all right?" Oliver asks.

She nods. "I've been avoiding the garage because I thought it would be too hard to remember my father. It was the only time I really spent time with him, watching him tinker with his toys while I played on the floor. But I keep looking at the house, expecting Mother to come out the back door. It's weird, but I miss her. And I never thought I'd ever say that."

He never told her about Grandmother's true elven nature.

Molly's the only one that knows what happened after he left the house with Grandfather. When Mom asks about it, he says he doesn't remember. It wouldn't change anything if he told her, but it seems like the right thing.

She was her mother. That's all that matters.

"The other day I stood on the bottom step of the staircase for half an hour. You believe that?" Mom's eyes turn glassy. "I just, uh, did it for her, I guess. I don't know."

"She loved us. In her weird way."

He cringes. He shouldn't have said "weird." She valued duty over feeling. She had to. He had a feeling there weren't many good feelings after she left home. Her home.

*The North Pole.*

"You want these?" She slides a stack of leather-bound journals across the bench.

"Where'd you find them?"

"Mother's room."

He opens the one on top. They're the ones she found in his backpack. He rubs the cover and slides them back.

He already knows the story.

THE WINDMILL IS STILL STANDING, but the blades locked in place.

"Do you want to walk out?" Molly asks.

"Your dad will be mad."

"I won't tell him if you don't."

Molly's dad wasn't happy with all the mystery after the event. She wasn't allowed to spend much time with Oliver, but Mom mended that fence when she went over to talk with him.

"They're good for each other," she insisted.

Many of the trees lay around the field.

They hike across the field and enter the forest where only a few trees have fallen. Oliver raises his phone and touches the screen. He only gets one bar of service. The compass, however, points north and doesn't shift. And neither do the trees.

Not anymore.

Halfway to the river, they come across a patch of fallen trees. In the middle, a pair of kissing trees still stands. Limp and faded, the bracelets still hang from the limbs.

They reach the river swollen with spring melt. Several new bridges have been created by fallen trees. They stay away from the river's edge, but when the path gets cluttered, Oliver suggests they stop.

"Maybe we shouldn't go any farther," he says.

"What?"

He's thinking of all the holes the snowthings drilled down to the lab. He can't remember where they are.

"I'll be right back," he says.

"Where are you going?"

"I just have to check on something."

Oliver climbs through a tangle of limbs and navigates to a cluster of fallen tree trunks. The crossing over the water is safer than the original tree. Molly promises to wait, but he's not even to the other side and she's already following.

She forgot she promised.

They hike up the slope where the trees appear unaffected. The ground is slippery, and several times they slide on their butts. Their clothes are caked with mud when they approach the bend in the river. The felled trees diverted the water in a new direction. The water twists into the newly formed pool. Somewhere beneath the swirling water are the remnants of the lab. Treetops rise above the water surface as if they simply sank in place.

"Look!" Molly points at the exposed roots of a fallen tree. The slope has eroded around a window.

*The hobbit house.*

The ground above is still intact.

Even a few of the chimney stones are still in place. They have to climb higher to safely reach it. Oliver uses exposed roots to slide down to the window. The river is only a few feet beneath him. He rubs the filth off the glass. A soft glow emanates from inside. There's no smoke from the chimney stones.

Gravel cascades on his head.

Molly is climbing toward the upturned roots of the great tree that served as the original bridge. Before he can say anything, she slides against it.

She's too close to the river.

"Oliver," she shouts. "I see it."

He crawls back to a safe spot and slowly slides down to meet her. A small hole is evident. Molly holds her phone inside it and illuminates the cavern leading back to the door. He opens his mouth to make her promise that she'll—

"I won't lie this time," she says. "You go first."

Oliver drops in.

The earthen cave is humid and stuffy.

The back of the cavern had collapsed, destroying the secret entrance to the lab. The rest must have been reinforced to remain open.

They shine both of their phones on the L-shaped root. The door, however, is jammed. The ground had shifted, wedging it into place. He uses both hands to pry it open just enough. Molly slides in sideways.

"Oh, my god," she exclaims.

Oliver sticks his head inside. The super sphere is in the center of the room. A soft glow pulses from the intricate etchings.

"Don't touch it!" he says.

Molly has her hand out. The super sphere is smaller than he remembers. In his memories, it's the size of the house. In reality, it's about knee-high.

He told her a hundred times how he'd been sucked into its inner space. Even now, this close, his stomach begins to twist in knots. But the dim glow suggests something is missing. He can feel the magnetic tug when he reaches for it, but it's weak and distant.

"This is it?" Molly asks. "That's what pulled you in?"

"Yeah. That's it."

His knees weaken. That's why he came out here. He had a feeling he'd find it.

*Grandmother and Grandfather are still in there.*

He tried to explain what it was like to exist without a body. He was pure awareness, just thoughts and emotions. There were no boundaries that defined him, no body to limit him.

But he still felt human.

And despite being interwoven with Grandfather, he still felt like an individual.

He could only assume Grandmother was right: *Grandfather had resolved his past.* If he hadn't, the river is right next to them. It wouldn't take much for the super sphere to become a watery titan.

"How'd it get in here?"

"I don't know."

The floor is water stained.

Maybe they did use the river, but only to move to higher ground, to hide inside the hobbit house until Oliver could find it. He should cover the super sphere so that no one does. They could hide the entrance and bury the window. It could exist here until he knew what to do with it.

Actually, Oliver knew what he wanted to do with it.

But at the moment, that seemed impossible.

*It needs to be home.*

"Oliver." Molly had wandered around the super sphere. "Come here."

She's standing in front of the fireplace. The hearth is open and clean. She's staring inside where something is propped against the wall.

The cover is leather.

*The seventh journal.*

# 37

J anuary 15, 1885
*Time, my love.*

*I have nothing but time.*

*I have not written in this journal for over a year because, quite honestly, I never expected to see you again. It became quite clear that the elven—despite my anguish, my tears and rage—were going to keep me forever. But if all goes well, my words will soon touch your ears, my lips will brush your lips, and I will feel your breath upon mine.*

*Home, my love. I am coming home.*

*I have lived almost two years beneath the ice, and today I stand on the deck of a ship crossing into the Pacific Ocean, the salt spray dashing over the bow and the sun warm on the boards. Water! So much water!*

*Now that we are safely en route, perhaps seven days from home, I am relaxing into the wonderful boredom. I care not to sleep because dreams have tempted my hopes for too long. I prefer to watch the stars at night, the sun rise in the morning and glisten on the green waves. I want to taste every second of this journey.*

*This impossible journey.*

*I have taken pen to paper, to finish this journal, because it was all that kept me alive in those early days, for when I did so it brought me closer to you. Even now, I can feel you at the end of my journey, a journey not possible if not for the only elven that believed in me.*

*Ginny.*

*She stands, right now, at the front of the ship. Her unusual size and shape has made her the target of the crew's ridicule. I am quite a sight, as well, my love. I carry fat like a polar bear and a beard like a beast! But my feet, unlike Ginny's, are normal. But she seems to care not. Never in her life has she seen so much water uncapped by ice.*

*She is my savior. My hope.*

*When my pleas fell on the elven's deaf ears, she listened. Even when Claus, a human among the elven, agreed to keep me an unwilling citizen of the colony—a prisoner!—she listened.*

*She's not like the others.*

*When they celebrated, she was morose. When they sang, she was quiet. Untouched by a smile, she worked hard to support the colony, but not because she loved them. It is a very strong sense of duty that drives her.*

*And that is what led her to us.*

*Little did I know, she had been watching me. She approached me last August. I was on the ice, pushing Flury's limits as I did every day. It kept my mind occupied with dreams that, one day, he would get past their arbitrary border and fly me home.*

*Reality, though, was suffocating that dream.*

*It was that day she met me at the extent of Flury's range. I waited for the stout little elven to approach, wondering if someone had caught on to my intentions. We stared at each other for quite some time.*

*"You believe in love," she said. "I want to believe, too."*

*That was the beginning of our friendship.*

*We would meet on the ice at the perimeter of Flury's range and plan our escape. My desperation was not enough to bring me home. It required her raw determination, her dedication, her sense of duty of what she believed was right and just.*

*She learned the shipping routes of humans (elven know everything humans do). She knew when the solar flares would be greatest to interfere with the elven's ability to track us. On the shortest day of the year, we met on the ice.*

*We left on Christmas.*

*Flury obliged to take us to his farthest reaches. When he could go no more, Ginny pulled a glove from her pocket. Like a metal ball to a magnet, she extracted the orb from his chest, his body collapsed in a heap of snow.*

*I must say, it was quite disconcerting.*

*For a time, he seemed to be my only friend. To watch the heart drawn from him like a bullet brought tears to my eyes. He had saved me from death, and now he brings me to you. I cannot thank him enough. She assures me, though, that when we arrive at home, when snow is on the ground, we can bring him back.*

*You will love him.*

*You will love Ginny and Flury. Together, we'll become a family. A strange one, to say the least, but one that will remain bonded by eccentricities.*

*Time, my love.*

*It is all that separates us now.*

*For now, I will spend it watching the sun track the sky. I will spend it counting the stars as I draw closer. And when dreams and reality become one, when I stand upon the threshold where I left you before this journey, I will fall into your arms.*

*And I will weep.*


WEEP, he did.

The following pages contain sketches of a ship, the ocean and a short, round elven near a thick mast. And countless drawings of a beautiful woman, Gayle Toye. His wife.

His love.

There are no more entries. Malcolm Toye had probably arrived home. There would be no reason to write.

Oliver closes the book.

Molly covers her mouth. Silently, tears track her cheeks. They remain in the hollow den as the light of the day diminishes, the weight of sadness filling the room. Behind them, trapped inside the super sphere, a man and an elven still exist because of love.

It's dark by the time they leave the subtle glow, crawling out of the mud and crossing the water. At the tree where the bracelets will remain forever locked, Oliver takes Molly's hand.

"I know what we have to do."

# 20 YEARS LATER

---

## 38

L arge maps bury the oak desk.

Notes are scribbled in the margins. Fresh ink—blue, red, and black—track various lines around the world, all leading to the white mass inside the Arctic Circle.

An X marks the North Pole.

Oliver pulls a stack of rolled maps off a keyboard, clicking through a website with one hand, a phone pressed against his ear with the other. When he gets an answering machine, the third one in ten minutes, he dials the number on the screen and waits at the window while it rings.

The second-floor bedroom, the one Mom used to sleep in, had been converted to an office ten years earlier. The frosted window faces the open field where the snow-covered windmill remains standing. The missing blades are the result of a severe thunderstorm. Beyond the wide open field, heavy construction equipment sits at the edge of the trees.

A wide path leads to the buried hobbit house.

A herd tramples down the steps, followed by children screaming.

"Hello?" someone says on the phone.

"Manuel?" Oliver trots across the room to close the door.

"Manuel, it's Oliver Toye! I'm so sorry to call you on Christmas Day. How...how are you?"

Pause. "Fine, Mr. Toye. How can I help you?"

"Yes, I won't keep you. I've been going through the itinerary concerning the helicopter pickup. I'm afraid we've run into a bit of a delay on our end."

Manuel patiently listens to the explanation. He's become accustomed to changes in Oliver Toye's schedule.

"There's only so much I can do," he answers.

"I'll pay extra. Money's not a problem."

"Money can only do so much, Mr. Toye."

"I understand. I'm only talking two days, Manuel. I can email the change order this afternoon. It's the last one, I promise."

Manuel sighs. He heard that promise last year, and the year before that. And the year before that. Seven years this trip had been in the works. Seven times it had been cancelled. Oliver paid for every failed attempt.

That's the only reason Manuel picked up the phone.

Oliver searches through the papers and finds a set of designs to answer Manuel's questions. The children's screams are now outside the house. Five of them between the ages of five and ten are sufficiently bundled for winter, racing past the defunct windmill for the snow-covered field.

"Yes, yes," Oliver says. "Everything's the same; the extraction's just a little behind, that's all. No, the design is exactly the same."

Molly enters the office, wearing an apron with frilly edges. *Smile Café* is printed in block letters along with her logo design for the coffee shop when they bought it from Ms. Megan. Her pixie haircut is dyed red and green on the tips. She slides a coffee cup across the plan, lipstick staining the rim.

He lifts it, mouthing the words, *Thank you.*

*Stop working,* she mouths back.

He responds with a nod. Molly goes to the door and holds mistletoe over her head.

"I can send those right now." Oliver jogs over, kissing her passionately. "No, no, no..."

Molly giggles with his lower lip between her teeth.

"I promise, nothing's changed. It's the family time capsule. It's already been approved for transportation. We just had a few last minute delays."

Getting to the North Pole these days isn't difficult. You can ski up there, fly up there, or walk up there and spend as much time doing it as you want. Expedition companies did it all the time.

Dropping a box off at the North Pole, however, was a different story.

Flury's metal orb could fit in a backpack. He could drop that in the snow when they reached the top of the world.

The super sphere was a bit more difficult.

The transport company wanted to know what was in it. How could he explain what it was, and that no one could touch it? How could he ensure that once it was up there, it wouldn't present a danger to future adventurers?

It took seven years to design a box to contain the super sphere with a lock only elven could open. And in the event that elven didn't really exist, that his grandfather was indeed psychotic—although the evidence suggested otherwise—or the elven didn't find it, the box would melt its way through the polar ice cap and sink to the bottom of the ocean.

Oliver and Molly would ski up to the North Pole. A helicopter would carry the box—a time capsule dedicated to the family of Malcolm Toye—and pick up the expedition.

It was risky.

But it was the right thing to do. The elven would know what to do with it. And Grandmother deserved to be home.

*Flury, too.*

"Great, great," Oliver says. "I'll get that over to you, pronto. Thanks for being so helpful, Manuel. This means so much to us, really. I know...yes, I know you know. Have...yes, have a Merry Christmas, and sorry to call. All right, bye."

"Everything good?" Molly asks.

"Still on for March."

She plants another kiss on his lips, wiping the lipstick left behind. They watch the snow start to flutter down from a gray sky. The children squeal with delight somewhere near the trees.

"Give me a few minutes," he says. "I'll be right down."

Molly leaves him to finish. When the documentation is finished and sent, he turns the computer off. Someone is crying full steam when he gets to the steps. Madeline took a snowball to the face. By the time Oliver gets to the kitchen, she's already back outside for more action, coming inside just long enough to tell on Ben.

Mom is bent over the stove. Her hair, now white, is too short to pull back in a bun. Headbands are no longer necessary. Helen and Molly, both wearing aprons, are at the sink. He gets the update: Aunt Rhonnie is running late for Christmas dinner (they plan for that). Henry won't make it. They plan for that, too.

Oliver volunteers to set the table.

"Can you check the living room, hon?" Molly asks. "I think something broke."

"What was it?"

"Something fell."

Their first child was born ten years ago. The last one, five years ago. Oliver had grown accustomed to collateral damage.

The living room is littered with stacks of opened gifts and errant bits of wrapping paper. The Christmas tree is to the left of the spacious bay window—the one Flury had climbed through to scoop Oliver up twenty years earlier. The snow has become thick. The children are racing toward the house, stumbling around the windmill as they lob snowballs at each other.

Nothing appears broken.

Oliver pushes boxes around to make sure a shattered ornament isn't hiding. He finds a plastic cup on the floor. Then another. When he's done scrambling through the Christmas carnage, there's five cups in all.

They're all empty.

Not a drop of juice or soda or flavored water is on the floor. The floor had its fair share of stains. Maybe a Christmas miracle had occurred.

The back door crashes open.

Helen and Oliver's mom stop the herd from pounding through the mudroom before shedding winter gear and stomping off the snow. Their laughter is contagious.

Oliver starts for the kitchen, but the Christmas tree catches his eye. There's a bare branch near the top. In most cases, something like that would go unnoticed.

Not on the Toye tree.

That branch is a place of honor, a branch inhabited by a special ornament that stays locked in a safe place all other times of the year. It's displayed for the family to recognize when they tell the story of elven and snowmen.

A wire hook dangles from it.

"Mom, Mom, Mom," Ben rattles. "You should've seen it. We were crushing the girls with, like, these big snowballs because, like, Cameron and Nicholas were on the sides and, and, and..."

Molly ushers Ben back to the mudroom. The kids stomp their boots, laughing and talking over each other.

"And then the snowball man took their side..."

Oliver wanders to the doorway. Molly doesn't hear them; she's busy keeping the snow out of the kitchen. He listens to the girls explain how the snowball man fought the boys, and then they all jumped on the snowball man's back.

"Snowball man?" Molly asks.

The children storm through the kitchen. Mom is passing out steaming cups of hot chocolate that they take to the dinner table. Oliver holds onto the doorframe. Mistletoe is taped above his head. Molly comes over to collect a kiss, but her gaze shifts over his shoulder.

Her mouth falls open.

Oliver turns.

The branch is still empty. The orb...the metal orb...the special metal orb called Flury...is still missing.

He goes to the picture window. Molly by his side.

In the field, far beyond the windmill, a figure emerges from a swirl of snow to stand near the trees. His body is thick and solid. Oliver feels a tingle in his arm, the heat in his palm.

The warmth in his chest.

They watch the figure made of snow pause before disappearing into a white cloud, swirling into the trees. The snowflakes settle to the ground like glittering diamonds, the sun catching the gleaming surface of a large metal object.

"Do you believe?" Oliver whispers.

Molly answers, "I believe."

# HUMBUG: THE UNWINDING OF EBENEZER SCROOGE (BOOK 4)

*Get the Claus Universe at:*
BERTAUSKI.COM/CLAUS

**Humbug: The Unwinding of Ebenezer Scrooge (Book 4)**

## CHAPTER 1

Ebenezer Scrooge watched the rain bead on the mahogany lid. *A nice coat of wax*, he thought. *Well done. Fitting.*

The rails were platinum, the inside lined with maroon velvet and a luxurious five-star mattress. No expense spared. Eb would've preferred something more reasonable—Jacob Marley wasn't going to see it, after all—but his dead friend's estate paid for the final resting place, so why sweat the details?

*Waste of money, that's why.*

The attendees were crowded beneath the tent, hugging each other for warmth and comfort. Rain pooled on the sagging canvas roof, dripping over the edge.

Outside the tent, a flock of black umbrellas protected the attendees gathered beneath the gray sky. They wiped their cheeks with tissues, holding each other close. Eb had shed one tear that morning. Considering he hadn't shed one since he was in diapers, a single tear was quite an episode.

If you asked him.

"We gather here today..." the preacher began.

The attendees wore black suits, black dresses. They wore pearls and furs, shiny shoes and sparkling earrings. Black veils and black hats. Eb wore a shiny tracksuit with two white stripes down the sleeves and legs and a round pair of spectacles that slid down the oily slope of his nose.

Very few in attendance were family because Jacob Marley had none. Except Eb. And he wasn't family, really. Not by blood, anyway.

These people were members of the Southern California community, representatives of charities that had received Jacob's goodwill; they were business associates and politicians.

Jim Thompson, CEO of Medicine Today, his unnatural tan defiant beneath the pallor of a wet umbrella. Marianne Clark, editor of *Wired Brain*, looking stylishly gaunt with a touch of gray in her bangs, heels spiking the soft earth. John Pendergrass, director of Body and Technology Research, with his age-appropriate wife touching the corners of her mascara-rich eyes.

They were all there.

They mourned the loss of a man that was "taken from his earthy vehicle too soon," the preacher preached. The crowd agreed and praised the Lord.

They were phonies.

They stole glances in his direction. He didn't praise the Lord out loud, oh heavens no. They looked at him because they were curious, judgmental. None of them consoled *him* for the loss of Jacob, his brother. Well, *like* his brother, the media corrected, often.

They were curious and unsympathetic because of the unusual figure that stood among them. It stood six feet tall, its skinwrap dull gray. Its trench coat, black and unusual for an android, was cinched at the waist. A top hat covered its head, quite silly. But that wasn't the worst part. The worst part was the face.

It wasn't the requisite eye holes and bump of a nose; there was no slot for a mouth where someone might insert a coin. That was last year's model. Eb had the most current servant droid, one that looked almost human.

He'd invented the droid, after all. Well, it was mostly Jacob. Eb helped.

Eb was at the funeral, but not in California. He was in Colorado.

It was absolutely unacceptable, in any culture or social status, to bring a servant droid *to* the burial. Eb didn't bring it, he sent the droid in his stead.

The newsfeeds were going to have a fit. They were going to skewer his callousness and question the poor decision-making, but he had his reasons. Not that anyone would understand. He had mourned that morning, shed that tear. They didn't see that.

In an attempt to appease the inevitable gossip, the dull gray droid projected Eb's features on its face rather than its own, as if Eb was standing at the foot of the casket, a tanned, square-jawed man. Unshaven. Grief-stricken.

Eb was neither unshaven nor grief-stricken. He didn't have a square jaw. If he did, it was hidden beneath multiple chins and a blotchy complexion. While the servant droid endured the rainy, cold season, Eb stood quite still in the dry, toasty projection room as the events unfolded around him as if he were actually there. Only dry. And warm.

He wasn't just there in spirit. He was there in every sense of the word. Just not in the flesh. The newsfeeds could debate all they wanted whether flesh or presence was more important at a funeral.

It was presence.

Eb raised his hands and rubbed his cheeks. The droid, connected to his actions through the sync suit, echoed his movements, patting away tear-streaked cheeks. Eb squeezed his eyes shut and practiced crying. It came so easily that morning, but lasted less than a minute.

Now his sobs were dry and rehearsed, thick with sarcasm. He couldn't remember the last time he cried.

Maybe he forgot how.

Crying was for little kids and weak-minded individuals. Eb was neither. It didn't matter that his attempts were disingenuous. His projected expression would be altered. The attendees would see a sincere expression of grief on the servant droid's face, where tears rolled as plump as rain, where he wiped them away and blew his nose in a white, embroidered handkerchief.

Sandy Kaufman, CFO of St. Mary's Children's Hospital, was outdoing him with the wailing. Eb brought up the volume of his grief, including sniffling and sudden, "Why, Lord? Why, why, why?"

It only drew more stares.

*How do they do it? I'm dying to sit down and they keep standing and standing and the preacher keeps preaching. How many times do we have to praise him? Jacob Marley was my brother, but come on, people. Just because he's going in the ground doesn't qualify him for sainthood. He lived quite an unselfish life, okay. Honestly, it was remarkable. But you don't rise to the top of the technology world without splitting a few lips.*

Jacob wasn't shrewd, but he could be ruthless. Only Eb saw that side of him. But Eb saw a lot of things other people didn't see.

When the service ended, some of the attendees shook the droid's hand. Eb reached out. The pressure was simulated inside his glove as they embraced. They were offering condolences to a dull gray droid with his face projected at them. And it wasn't really *his* face.

*Hilarious.*

A door opened twenty feet to Eb's right. The edges of the doorway curved along the domed projection wall, a squarish space carved from the dreary scene. A dull gray droid—an exact duplicate of the one shaking hands with the preacher now—walked into the room. This androgynoid wore a tracksuit similar to Eb's, the sleeves pushed up to the elbows.

As far as Eb was concerned, all droids were mindless servants that followed their programming. Tell them what to do and they did it because they were idiots. Jacob had begged to differ, arguing they had a personality that closely mimicked human behavior. They were still morons, simple as that.

*Dum-dums.*

"Auto," Eb muttered.

Disconnected from Eb's sync suit, the mourning droid continued to run the grieving program, freeing Eb to walk around the projection room.

"The news," Eb said. "Give it to me good."

"I don't feel good about this, sir."

"First of all, you don't feel. Second, that wasn't the question. So go, now. Give it to me."

"This was not Jacob's wish, sir."

Eb clawed the air, tendons stretching. "Did you or did you not do what I asked? And let me remind you the wrong answer gets you a one-way trip down the tumbler."

"But—"

"Zip." Eb snapped his fingers at him.

He really didn't want to recycle him. Servant droids were insanely expensive. Eb had more money than half the world, but there was no need to be frivolous. *Unless someone deserves it.*

"Yes?" Eb said. "Or no?"

"Yes, sir."

"You're sure?"

"I am, sir." The droid cocked his head to the side. "I am here to help you."

"I won't turn on the feeds and hear Jacob Marley willed his ownership to the Boy Scouts of Antarctica, will I?"

"No, sir."

"Complete and total and one hundred percent of Avocado, Incorporated, now rests in the name of Ebenezer Lennox Scrooge?"

The droid paused. "Yes, sir."

"What? Why'd you just pause?"

"I didn't use your middle name, sir."

"Why would you do that?"

"Because you don't use your middle name, sir."

Maybe a ride down the tumbler was in order. But then he'd have the same conversation with the same droid personality in a different body. There were seven of them, a hive mind sort of personality that would one day cause all of his hair to fall out.

"Never mind." Eb propped his elbow on his protruding gut and tapped his spongy chin like he was hammering a finishing nail into place. "Jacob wouldn't use my middle name, either. The lawyers will make it right."

A smile dug into the droid's flexible cheeks.

Eb tapped his jelly chin, never once reaching above the space where a dimple might reside. He rarely touched his face without washing. But in a rare lapse of judgment, he removed his round glasses and rubbed his eyes.

"Are you crying, sir?"

"No."

But he was, sort of.

Joy gushed from his stomach, a geyser of warm emotions that had reached his face, almost leaking from his eyes. *Almost.* Avocado, Inc., was his now. He couldn't remember crying twice in one day.

To be fair, he couldn't remember much about his childhood.

A line of grieving attendees was still waiting to shake the droid's hand, a few standing at the coffin with their heads bowed in hopes this unfortunate event wouldn't change their altruistic relationship with Avocado, Inc., once owned by Jacob Marley and Ebenezer Scrooge but now owned by Eb and Eb only.

A crocodile smile crept over his face.

He twisted the obsidian ring on his right hand, something that could be mistaken for a wedding band. An identical ring was on his left hand. He swiped his hands like a magician.

The funeral scene winked out.

The dome-shaped projection room went to sleep, the generic walls arching overhead. These were the moments Eb felt like a cooked goose beneath a serving dome.

"Avocado!" he shouted. "Come on down!"

The curved wall shimmered. A giant avocado appeared; a thick stem curved at the top, the word *avocado*—all lowercase letters in off-white—situated in the Buddha belly of the leathery fruit.

Colorful furniture appeared, original designs that conformed to every position the body could imagine. Jacob had insisted the kooky chairs and couches be arranged in an open office environment, a feng shui thingy that promoted progress by failure, thinking outside of the box. Eb was only interested in the progress part. The rest of it was stupid.

And failure was the wrong direction.

"Where is everyone?" Eb said.

"Many are attending Jacob's funeral, sir."

"Not all of them."

"It's also Christmas Eve, sir."

Eb glanced at his wrist, pretending to see a watch. "It's not even lunch!"

"The holiday has begun, sir."

"Bah!" Eb couldn't think of a word to express his contempt for such excessive year-end celebration. What could capture the guttural disgust he felt when employees—people he was paying, for crying out loud—flaunted excess in his face?

"Bah, unacceptable!" *That's not it.* "Call them back. They're paid to work till five o'clock."

"Many have left town, sir."

"They have laptops, right? It's kind of what we do; have them log in and work. Text them or message them or call the police, I don't care. I want every minute accounted for. You think I'm an ATM machine?"

"That's redundant, sir."

"What?"

"ATM machine is like saying automated teller machine *machine,* sir."

"You think this is a joke? That it's funny?"

Eb snapped his fingers and pointed in the droid's face. He walked the perimeter of the room, the spongy floor oozing between his toes. *Tap, tap, tap* on his chin. He passed projections of pumpkin orange loungers and seaweed green coffee stations and eggplant purple treadmill desks. Empty, all of them.

The avocado logo dimly lit the far wall.

"We're not an art studio," Eb muttered.

"Jacob felt this environment fostered innovation, sir."

"I'll tell you what it fostered—Peter Pan syndrome. There's a child-sitting room over there if you don't have a babysitter. Over there is a coffee bar for lattes and smoothies. And there!" Eb pointed at the back room. "Ping-Pong. I mean, come on! Is this a joke?"

There were times when the projection room wasn't big enough to contain his rants. The illusion of space seemed endless. He often forgot he wasn't actually in the Avocado plant and banged his head on the curved wall. But that was the point—to be there without actually being there. To believe he was outside when he was inside. It was all the beauty of living life in the safety of his home.

He adjusted his round spectacles.

"I want it out," he said. "All of it."

"Sir?"

"This ridiculous furniture! Burn it, drop it off a bridge, I don't care. Get it out!"

"But, sir, this work environment has proven effective. Avocado was ranked Fortune 500's number one innovative technology company."

"We can be better."

"What is better than number one, sir?"

"Number one A, just do it. All of this touch-feely weirdness is embarrassing. I look at it and just want to unzip my skin. Don't even sell it, just throw it out. Wait, scratch that. Put it on eBay, all of it. Use reserve pricing."

"I suggest we run your requests through predictive modeling, sir. These sweeping changes will greatly affect morale. I would expect widespread defection of some top-shelf talent."

The droid stepped next to Eb. The musculature writhed in his calves and flexed across his shoulders. His tracksuit was unzipped between the shapely pecs. Tension rippled his forehead as he cocked his head, a bird searching for a worm.

"Gone, Dum-dum. All of it."

"And replaced with what, sir?"

"Good old-fashioned desks in straight lines, not one of them crooked. I don't want to hear about freethinking. We run this company like a watch from now on. This is a business now. We do it my way."

"Why would you make their environment so unpleasant, sir?"

"It's all about the message."

Confusion wrinkled the droid's nose. "The message, sir?"

"Get in line."

The droid cocked his head, expecting more.

"That's it, get in line. Gets to the point, doesn't it? And that is the point. You know, it's time to rethink the slogan. I see it now, the avocado logo with a label stamped across the midsection. *Avocado... Get In Line.*" He swiped an open hand across an imaginary banner.

"Jacob would be disappointed, sir."

"Jacob is dead. Rest his soul, he was a good man, a great man." Eb sniffed. It was a little easier admitting to Jacob's altruistic greatness now that he was no more. It still stung, just a little. "He was my brother and I loved him. He also turned over all his shares to me. How nice of him."

"I did that, sir. Not Jacob."

"What? I'm sorry, I couldn't understand... aren't you supposed to erase that bit of information?"

The droid frowned. Moments later, a slight downturn of his lips indicated he had erased that information from his database and all traces of it.

"Jacob Marley is indeed dead, sir," he muttered.

"As a doornail," Eb said. "Now bring on the hammer."

The droid's shoulders slumped, the lower lip out and pouting. Eb ignored the tantrum on his way to the open door. When the droid didn't follow, he turned.

"What now?" Eb said.

"The stockings, sir."

"What are you talking about?"

Eb knew very well what he meant; he saw them hanging from a cherry-red pipe above the company kitchenette, one for every employee with a name stitched along the white, fuzzy collar.

"The employees, sir. They will be disappointed when they return from holiday."

"Becaaaaause...?"

"They will be empty, sir."

"And there should beeeee...?"

"Candy in them, sir. Sometimes little toys for their children or memorabilia."

"Are you saying Santa won't visit if I take them down?" A delicious smile licked his lips.

"It was Jacob that filled these stockings, sir. Not Santa."

Eb narrowed his eyes. The droid's shoulders slumped further, a loud sigh passing more oxygen than lungs could possibly hold. He didn't need to breathe, obviously. The sigh was purely a display.

*Where did he learn such things?*

Eb left the door open. "Remove the stockings. And the tinsel and the garland and all those trees. Christmas is over at Avocado, Inc. It's dead, just like Jacob. Let hard work reign."

He pumped his fist.

*Bah!*

If only there was a better word.

## YOU DONATED TO A WORTHY CAUSE!

By purchasing this book, you have donated to the health and well being of children with diabetes since 10% of the profits is annually donated to Juvenile Diabetes Foundation.

# ABOUT THE AUTHOR

My grandpa never graduated high school. He retired from a steel mill in the mid-70s. He was uneducated, but a voracious reader. As a kid, I'd go through his bookshelves of musty paperback novels, pulling Piers Anthony and Isaac Asimov off the shelf and promising to bring them back. I was fascinated by robots that could think and act like people. What happened when they died?

Writing is sort of a thought experiment to explore human nature and possibilities. What makes us human? What is true nature?

I'm also a big fan of plot twists.

CPSIA information can be obtained
at www.ICGtesting.com
Printed in the USA
LVHW082145210922
728986LV00033B/1032